No Hiding for the Guilty

by

Vanessa Riley

<u>Books by Vanessa Riley</u>

Madeline's Protector

Swept Away, A Regency Fairy Tale

The Bargain, A Port Elizabeth Tale, Episodes I-IV

Unveiling Love, A London Suspense Tale

Unmasked Heart, A Regency Challenge of the Soul Series

No Hiding for the Guilty, Book 5, The Heart of a Hero Series

Sign up at <u>VanessaRiley.com</u> for contests, early releases, and more.

Cover art designed by The Midnight Muse and formatted by For The Muse Designs

ISBN-13: 978-1-943885-17-6

NO HIDING FOR THE GUILTY

WHAT IF SUPERHEROES were mortals who lived and loved during the Regency? The Heart of a Hero Series tells all...

The military leaders of the fraught Almeida Siege are dying, but not fast enough for a chef with a grudge to bear and axes to sharpen. Using her position as cook to the famed inventor, Lord Hartland, Isadel Armijo learns that one of the butchers responsible for slaughtering her family will sup at Hartland Abbey at month's end. The chef is determined to serve the guilty man his last meal, one with a cake possessing a controlled detonation so she can watch him die. Only one person can teach her how to whip eggs with black powder, Wellington's hulking explosives expert, Hugh Bannerman. Can she persuade the recluse to return to society to help avenge her family with a dessert to-die-for?

With his soul in torture for the lives his actions have decimated, the hulking Hugh Bannerman is convinced his sins have manifested into leprosy. As the surviving member of his family, how can he take his place in society knowing his uncontrollable anger increases the spots discoloring his skin and puts others at risk? No, he'll remain in hiding until the Almeida Killer finds him or the incorrigible chef Isadel causes too much trouble, concocting a deadlier course, one part hope, a sprinkle of crazy, and a maddening sauce of desire.

Can two very different people find the recipe to right the wrongs of the past or forever remain prisoners to guilt?

Sign up for my newsletter at www.vanessariley.com or www.christianregency.com. Notices of releases, contests, my Regency Lover's pack, and other goodies will be made available to you.

Dedication

I dedicate this book to my copy editor supreme, my mother, Louise, my loving hubby, Frank, and my daughter, Ellen. Their patience and support have meant the world to me.

I also dedicate this labor of love to my support team: Rhonda, Felicia, Erica and Amy.

Love to my mentor, Laurie Alice, for answering all my endless questions.

And I am grateful for my team of encouragers: Sandra, Michela, Felicia, Seressia, Piper, and Ms. Bev.

Chapter One: July 1813 Devonshire, England

The velvet fog engulfed Isadel Armijo, swallowing her whole like a lump of brown bread drowning in white soup. She flinched at a noise from behind. She pulled on the reins of her stolen horse and swiveled in the saddle to see if she was followed.

Nothing.

Nothing but night was behind her. And nothing would be for her if she didn't keep moving. Bundled up in Papa's old coat and breeches, she was still just a female alone, but one on the greatest adventure. One of honor. Well, that's what she told herself when she snuck away from Hartland Abbey.

She kicked her mount forward. The thick fog closed in. Isadel couldn't see, couldn't breathe, couldn't feel anything but heaviness as if she'd be dragged down at any moment. She swatted the air with her straw hat as she had from the boat deck the eve she emigrated from Spain. The half-done thing had been scooped up from a blocking tool of a neighbor's burnt out workshop. The lady spy had slapped it upon Isadel's head as they fled Badajoz.

If Isadel closed her eyes and thought hard of that night, she'd smell the soot that consumed her city. If there was a God, then he should let black powder smell the same. Then, this hat would be a crown ordaining her destiny.

A branch slapped her cheek. The horse must've veered left and into the woods. Fear swept through her. What if this wasn't the way to Bannerman, but to another of Lord Wellington's spies? None of them had the skills she needed. Bannerman was the one, the only one up to the task and the only one who hated her enemy as much as Isadel.

Clinging closer to the horse's neck, she had to trust the beast knew the way. Trust—the word made her raw nerves snap like uncooked fidelli noodles, but this past year, she learned that her employer, Lord Hartland, was friended by men of precision, those set to provide justice. Who else needed justice more than Isadel? Who else had lost as much?

Her mottled colored mount whinnied but kept moving forward into the thickets. The night had grown dark again. She could barely see and hoped this gelding could navigate its way like the boat captain that spy woman, Joanna Pearson, had bribed. The captain slipped through the low salty clouds of the Bay of Biscay as if he possessed an inner compass guiding him toward the North Star. Isadel understood, for her inner compass aimed solely at vengeance.

The animal lurched then started to the right again. She stilled her fingers on the smooth leather strap of its rein. Humming her mother's tune, the one that timed her whisking strokes to perfection, didn't distract the horse. It began moving faster down a steep incline. When they reached the bottom, the clouds parted. She could see again and witnessed moonlight kissing the white stones lining the trail. It was the first light she'd seen since leaving Lord Hartland's Abbey at sundown.

When the housekeeper discovered her missing, the old battle-ax would screech that "the half-breed" done run off. This time the old woman's fear of Isadel's kind being evil or a thief would be true.

Stomach souring, she slapped the reins between her palms. These hands were meant for making pastries, forming biscuits, for stirring delicate sauces, not unlocking doors and unfurling the stocks keeping a horse stabled. Yet, her fingertips had grown tired of wiping midnight tears. If she did nothing, her gift of pastries and breads would feed her enemy, the man who had destroyed her world. Moldona would come to the Abbey at month's end.

Deflating in her saddle like a cake that fell from too much checking, she threw her arms tighter around her mount's neck and clung to it as if it were her father. With a breath, gulping in the strong sweaty horse's lather, she sat up straight and dared her eyes to grow wet. A woman destined to kill shouldn't be weepy. That was a victim's plight, and she refused to wear that crown anymore. Her greatest wish must come true. She'd risked everything to make things right, her spotless reputation and her safe employment from a man who made sure his staff treated her fairly. The earl's disappointment in her character would kill her faster than the lashings he could demand to punish a horse thief. If he exercised his rights like the wealthy hacienda owners in Spain, he'd ask for a hanging.

Too late to turn back, not that she wanted to, she kept on, urging the horse saying, "To Bann-er-man, horse. To Bann-er-man."

Another hour of hard riding and the smell of the sea, fresh and salty, seemed stronger. Soon, she should be able to see Sandon Manor, the castle hiding the reclusive spy. Fingers vibrating, she swiped at her mouth dabbing at the fresh blood coming from the corner. She'd bit down with the last jostle of the horse. How horrid she must look, probably seeming more like a lost urchin than a cook. She couldn't wear her neat uniform and keep her seat, and who needed to fret about getting creases upon her starched apron while stealing away? Riding like a man, in men's breeches just looked easy. It wasn't. It was quite hard for someone with short legs. Papa would say she was barely enough stones in weight to fill a messenger's saddlebag.

Patting the horse, she gave him a moment to catch his breath. She needed to let her pulse slow and leaned back, gazing at the rocky incline ahead of her. The slope stretched high, sticking into the clouds headless as if it had been axed like a roasting chicken. Her stomach rumbled and all she could think of was how odd it was now to remember being hungry. Did they feed prisoners in English jails? Maybe they'd shoot first and ask questions later like the British soldiers had done at Badajoz.

Righteous anger welled inside her growling gut, but so did a little teaspoon of hope. With a click of her heels, she urged the gelding forward. If the horse had done its job, she'd see Sandon from the top. Then she'd know that she'd stolen the right horse, that she'd come to the right place. She'd have a chance to no longer live with hate. "Go to Bann-er-man."

Gravel flew on every side. Isadel became

breathless. The final push through the fog made her heart flip against her ribs and stay there. The pounding in her chest hurt so badly her ribs would surely poke through her coarse nankeen shirt. Papa's shirt. Bracing in the saddle, Isadel held on as her mount leapt above the clouds to the top, a flat plateau covering the hill.

Quiet surrounded her and she tugged at the strap, stopping the horse. The air smelled clean and sweet, like after the rain or a good cleaning. The salt, it burned her nostrils, only because she breathed so hard. Yet maybe it cleansed. If there was a heaven, this had to be it—quiet, pure, sweet—unseeing of the horrors below, untouched by the death of innocence—the scream of a sister, the unanswered begging prayer of Papa.

Clouds swirled for a moment, then opened and showed things—tree groves, the waters of the Bristol Channel. Joy leaped inside. They'd made it to the coast. Sandon had to be near. The tired part of her wanted to linger in this peace, but to stay in heaven was to deny the hell she'd lived. Morning meant discovery of her theft, no new mercies, no more chances. She steered the horse to the edge. The wind picked up again, spreading the fog, making it thin in spots. The gaps appeared like the insides of white Emmental cheese.

With wide eyes, she beheld the sight she'd seen from the boat smuggling her to these shores, the high turret of Sandon Manor. It was again alone in the night sky just as it had been nine months ago. With her finger, she traced the structure down to the rest of the castle, which lay shrouded by trees. The turret looked daunting, almost whispering, "don't reach for me," but Isadel had to. She stood in the stirrups and became deaf to the warning. She risked too much to turn back now. Bannerman had to see her. He had to help.

With a gulp, she hunkered down and pressed forward. The horse flew down the hill, galloping faster, sinking deeper into the steamy fog. They moved as one, splashing through mud puddles. She blocked low branches with her hand and ducked under tree limbs. The horse knew the path, slipping through openings that didn't seem to exist. It trotted, weaving and threading through the dense blanket of leaves. The horse stopped on the castle's rock-strewn drive.

Isadel sized up the worn door, the overgrowth of vines hugging the limestone brick. That sense of being alone, of not wanting to bear the company of others, closed in upon her, but she welcomed it and pushed it into her heart. Nothing alleviated her misery more than the isolation of not explaining, of not searching for ways to fit into this very English world. Emboldened, she jumped down and walked with her chin up to the door.

It took three knocks, three shifts in her stance, three stampings of her short boots, before the door opened. A grizzled man with a lantern and a balding head glared at her. "We've no use for beggars, boy."

Boy? She surely must look like one with her hair pulled up in her hat. Yet, being thought a man might serve her. "Sir." She coughed and deepened her hoarse voice. "I'm no beggar. I'm a cook...chef."

"Don't need one of those either."

A thief and want-to-be-murderer had no room for shame. Shoving all the pride she had left into her spine, she stood up straight, probably exposing her ankles from her father's old breeches. He wasn't that tall either. "I bring a message for your employer, Bann-er-man."

The man wriggled his hooked nose. "Jump on your horse and leave, cook-chef. Take it with you."

She curled her tongue and tried that long name again in what she hoped sounded clipped, very English. "I'm here for Mr. Bannerman." She kept her voice even making sure no hitch of feminine desperation could be heard. "It's a matter of death."

Brow furrowing with more crevices, the fellow pulled a knife from his pocket, waving it as if to intimidate her, but she'd skinned too many chickens for that. "So you're looking for him? You'll have to kill me to get to him."

Kill this man? He needed to know her private thoughts of murder had nothing to do with his master, well not really. She raised her hands and shook her head. "Not here for that."

"Then what, boy? Why did you come?"

Like Papa, she spread her feet apart and tried to seem rooted and certain. "Your master is safe from me. And he'll see me. I come from Lord Hartland." She let her gaze lift to the grand stairs behind the gatekeeper. "Is Bannerman in the tower? I can run up there and deliver the message."

Happy her tone sounded clear, she pushed inside, but the old fellow stepped in her path.

"I said no visitors."

She was too close to lose out now. Fumbling with Papa's coat, she produced the letter and fluttered it, exposing the earl's wax mark. "Tell the master that I have a letter from Hartland. He has to see this."

He held out his palm, but there was no way Isadel would give him the letter. She couldn't, not without an audience with the explosives expert. "I must only offer this to Bannerman."

After sixty beats of her heart, the man nodded his

thin pointy chin and waved her further inside. "You don't look like an assassin."

Assassin? Isadel wanted to be one, just not for Bannerman. "I'm a messenger, today."

"Scrawny you? Yes, that's what Hartland would send. No turret for you, boy. The drawing room. Easier for you to make your delivery then go."

So, Bannerman was up there. Did he enjoy the air, the hazy night sky, that feeling of being on top of the world?

Before her longing for peace drove her up those stairs, she focused on the old man and traipsed behind him. Trying hard not to stare at the holes in the wall or the torn tapestries, she focused on what to say to Bannerman. Yet, the melon-sized holes, the broken lath and plaster sent a tremor to her middle. What could have done it? Who would dare destroy the gilded trim, the papered orange walls? This place was nothing like the duke's beautiful Abbey.

The butler turned to her, and she dropped her gaze. She wasn't here to assess the housekeeping. This destruction was none of her business.

The fellow stopped at a door half-off its hinges. He pressed it open and waved her inside. "Wait in here. Make sure the brass doorknobs and books remain."

Without protest, Isadel nodded. What the old man thought of her meant nothing, just like the insults of her employer's staff. Talk was cheap, and it couldn't kill a soul that had already died from sorrow. Every hope she ever possessed went away with her father and sister's murder at the hands of British pigs. The only thing worth anything to Isadel was revenge.

The door shut behind her with a thud. How it

managed to stay upright was a wonder. The room was cold and grey. A fire seemed to be dying. Someone had left it to wither. Bannerman? He couldn't be in the turret and here, too. Maybe the rumors of him dying and becoming a ghost were true, but then why would Lord Hartland keep sending him notes?

She rubbed at her forehead. A hint of oak and tobacco hit her nose as she walked closer to the desk. The one time she made Bannerman tea, he had sat in Hartland's library with a pile of books about ancient medicine at his feet as he puffed on a pipe. Reading seemed to ease his restlessness.

Her skin prickled as she took another deep inhale and prepared to see the big hulk of a man again. The right words to get him to agree to return to the Abbey Estate and help her kill her enemy hadn't materialized.

Her stomach soured, rolling in her famished middle. She hadn't thought this part out enough. Pacing from the large patio door to a book-laden desk, she tried to number her arguments. She stopped and fingered an open tome upon the smooth maple writing surface. A recipe for skin lotion made with arsenic dotted the page. That's not very good. Papa had warned her and her sister about the horrible practices women used to lighten their skin.

With a shake of her head, she stepped back, then loosened a button of her bulky jacket and fanned her head with her hat. Her nerves had her heart racing again. She shoved the hat back on, scooping up a thick curl that had come loose. Her resolve of not caring what she looked like, or even that she favored a boy, began to slip. She would see the fastidious Bannerman again as a wrinkled frog.

Maybe like a genie or a handsome prince, he'd grant her wish. She didn't need a kiss to break a curse, but craved a black powder recipe, which would make beastly Moldona disappear.

The door behind her blew open, rattling pages from the rush of air. The shock of it hitting the wall made her duck as if avoiding gunshot or a cannon's fire. She bit her lip and spun. A huge man barreled toward her. "Bannerman?"

"Yes. It's good to know the name of the man who will kill you."

Dark gold, almost red hair covered his face like thick lion fur. The wavy locks that had been parted to perfection were gone, replaced by wild curls. He looked like a beast, a large, hulking beast.

She stepped toward the door, but he flung a poker in her direction. It whizzed past her head, missing her temple by an inch. With a thunk, it sunk into the wall. "I didn't say you could go."

A gasp left her, but then she caught his hazel eyes, the ones she'd spied at the Abbey Estate, the ones that lit in laughter to Lord Hartland's jests. Wellington's explosives expert stood in front of her. "Bannerman, sir, it is you."

He swiped at his mane. "How dare Hartland send someone for me again. I'm done."

Stomping toward his desk, he kicked an emerald chair, sending it sliding across the scarred mahogany floor. It stopped an inch from her boot, but she stood still and stared at him.

As if filled with remorse, he rubbed a gloved hand over his face then pivoted toward the hearth. "Boy, what favor does he want? Or does he send news? Has he found the Almeida Killer?"

More confused at the changes in the once well-groomed man she'd seen a few months ago than by his gibberish about Almeida, she pitched her head side to side. "I'm not sure if his note has more news of a two-year old bloodbath that savaged my Spanish lands. But, I know he wants you to return with me."

"No! Hart will not order me around. Nor will one of his foot soldiers."

His voice felt like thunder. His shaking fist would surely hit with a punch of lightning, still she held the note out to him.

"I swore to him I'd kill the next messenger who came to me." Bannerman flexed his gloved fingers. "I guess you're the lucky one he chose to die."

Death didn't scare Isadel any more than living with regrets. She folded her arms about her. "I've always been lucky like that."

"I'll give it to Hartland. He knew how much the former me liked a good joke. But a dead man has no room for laughter or more guilt. Return to Hart and tell him no."

She stamped her foot like a girl, but hardened her voice. "Do your worst, or return with me to Hartland Abbey. No middle ground."

He came near. She could smell the stench of metal coming from his arm or his hand—so like her father's apothecary shop. His arms flexed as he hovered. He was large, larger than she remembered, but as a good servant, she'd never been this near to him.

His scent, ferrous or sulfur, strangled. "No one gives me ultimatums."

If this was the end, part of her was glad of it. Straightening her spine, she held her breath and waited to be throttled, waited for darkness to overcome her when he choked the air from her throat betwixt his large hands. That had to be a better fate than going to prison or living with the knowledge she'd failed at her one chance to kill her enemy.

Hugh Bannerman raised his hands ready to punch the messenger through the wall as he'd done with everyone else who'd stood against him, but the boy merely did the task Hart had requested, just as Phipps, his man-of-all-work would do. Hugh took a breath and lowered his fists. He turned and let his frustration meet the desk. When he tapped it, the legs split and sent his piles of research spilling to the floor.

He flexed his palm, but the rapid action hadn't caused his hand to bleed again. Relieved, he pivoted but frowned to mask his concern and said, "So you are prepared to die, boy? Or is Hart prepared to let you die? Must be tough knowing how expendable your life is?"

The foolhardy messenger shrugged. "I sent myself. Didn't know there were extra benefits for coming."

Hugh almost laughed. The boy wasn't frightened, maybe he even had a death wish like himself. Hart was a better spy for he probably prepared the boy. Maybe even told the lad of Hugh's vow to never take another life. Never again would he willingly take an innocent spirit, even of his enemies. He'd be a man of principle like his brother.

"Hartland says the situation is dire."

"It's always dire. I have retired. I'll be merciful and give you one last chance to leave. Mercy is a good thing for an active spy to possess." Hugh rubbed his stubbly beard. The dry skin beneath itched worse with each treatment. "Pity, I'm retired. And volunteering is a dangerous business. Why did you elect yourself?"

The sorry fellow in baggy breeches that hit the floor bent his head. "I need... Lord Hartland needs you to return."

His voice sounded light and weak, maybe even feminine. "So, Hart's running out of men. You're barely breeched. What are you like seven?"

The slight fellow tossed the note on the floor at Hugh's boot. "Old enough, and I wanted to see the man he brags on, the one who killed hundreds, even people standing beside him with his detonations and nary a scratch happened to his person."

At least this boy had guts to utter such nonsense. Perhaps this gall is how he slipped past Phipps. "There's always a scratch. Some just can't be seen."

He turned and struck a stinking sulfurous match and lit candles on the mantle. Pivoting back, he pointed to the paper. "Why don't you pick that up, and we'll start this again?"

The messenger put a shaking hand to his hip. "With the threats or without?"

So, the fellow was nervous. Good. He thought about forcing him to scoop up the letter, but the runt would probably freeze like a scared rabbit or vomit all over himself like the last two grooms. Hugh relented, bent and picked up Hart's impressive parchment folded with perfect crisp line. "I'll have to keep my option to kill you open, you know. Especially since you're making me work."

A hint of cloves or maybe cinnamon wafted from the paper. Very odd for Hart. He started to open the letter then stopped. It would be no different than the last summons. Something was in crisis that needed his explosion making skills or maybe, just maybe he'd figured out the identity of the Almeida Killer and sent a warning. Hart was a good man, even to his gruff friends. "The world didn't end with my rejection of your master's last two requests. I'm sure it won't with this one."

Staring as if he could see through Hugh, the boy's eyes, a cross between henna and gold grew wider. "But you must return. There will be no hope for me if you don't."

Bannerman closed his gloved fingers about the paper. Had he left some bit of greying skin exposed? Maybe he hadn't been careful and the messenger saw his strange leprosy. "Did anyone ever tell you it was impolite to gawk?"

"You kicked a chair at me, sir. Perhaps that makes things even."

Stuffing his one hand behind his back, Hugh leaned against the hearth, and looked away from the young man and the shadows consuming the dim room. Sandon wasn't always like this. "Be gone. I don't make idle threats."

Waiting for the boy to wilt and blow away, Hugh let his gaze drift into the flames. In the smoke and flying ash, he saw the face of another young man, one with a quick wit who talked for days about what he would do with Sandon once their father relented and allowed him to manage it separate their stepmother's influence. Then Henry would wax on about the missionary trip he would take. Grandeur and respectability—that was the Bannerman family bond.

Both the living and the dead would hate how Hugh allowed the place to fester like the plague rotting his skin. He whipped his palm near the flames reaching for the missing poker, remembering too late that he'd sent it crashing into the wall. He pivoted and eased his arms to the side. "You're still here? You came to die?"

The fellow looked placid, too calm. "I have a death wish. That is why I am here."

The letter in Bannerman's fingers seemed less important. Curiosity about the messenger and his boldness took control. He had a kinship to the absurd, something he'd forsaken for too long, not since his brother. With a grunt, he dropped the letter to the scratched surface of his desk. "You didn't just come to drop off Lord Hartland's note? Out with it."

Pulling at his loose collar and baggy jacket, the fellow shifted his stance. "You are right. I came for me. Lord Hartland doesn't know that I am the one delivering this correspondence."

Hugh groaned loud and long. "Let me guess. You need revenge. I've injured someone in your family. A drunken row? Or better, I killed some traitor in your blood..." He paused for a second, his eyes for the first time taking notice of the footman's off colored skin, the thicker full lips. "Well, one of your bloodlines. A traitor who dares to be against Mother England. What are you, Spanish? From Almeida?"

When the boy shifted his stance, Hugh readied to pounce. The Almeida Killer had already killed three of his fellow commanders of that siege. Soon, the only living English soldiers remaining would be Hugh, Nev, Moldona, Cox and Wellesley. "Take care your next action. It could be your last."

The boy shuffled his lean fingers, ones surely too delicate to maim a living soul, over his mouth. He wiped off beads of sweat. Then he stopped and shoved his nervous palms to his backside. "I want revenge, but not against you. I need you to teach me how to make an explosion, one deadly controlled explosion. I only need to kill one man."

As if he had held his breath, the boy let it out in a huff then shrugged his shoulders.

Foolish mortal. If Hugh could find humor from the misguided fool, it might give ease to his nerves tonight allowing more time for the latest lesions on his hands to heal. "Killing someone sounds easy, very righteous in the planning, but things rarely work as intended. Consequences follow even when things don't work."

"This one has to work. I don't want others hurt, just Moldona."

The room seemed to close in upon Hugh. Luckily, his practice of subterfuge kept him upright. Moldona wasn't his rival anymore, just the man who'd stolen Betsy, the love of Hugh's life away. "So, you want to murder the Conqueror of Badajoz?"

"I'm from Badajoz. You hate him. Lord Hartland said you did." The messenger stepped closer. Desperation painted his long lean face. "I need your help."

"Everyone is from somewhere. That doesn't make you special. Go back to Hartland. Tell him no. I'm not returning."

"I can't go back." He bent and pulled a knife from his boot and tossed it at Hugh's foot. "Kill me as you said. I'm a horse thief. As Lord Hartland's friend, it is in your right."

The amusement drained away as he stared at the shiny blade. It wasn't the type you'd have to fend off a footpad, but something he'd seen in a kitchen. He picked it up. "Boy, do you know who I am? I don't kill like this."

"I know who you are. I came because of that. And I'd rather die here than a little everyday with my memories." The fellow spun and ran. His footfalls didn't sound as if he'd fled toward the house door but deeper into Sandon. The boy said he was a thief. What could he possibly steal from here?

"Bannerman!"

His man's yell told Hugh he'd soon find out.

Rushing out of the drawing room, he saw old Phipps running from the stairs. His face was blood red like when he discovered a new hole in the wall, or something else Hugh had broken.

"Lord Hartland's groom. He's in the turret. I think he's going to jump."

Suicide was a coward's death. His admiration for the messenger died.

Bannerman turned and put his fingers on the shaft of the family sword, Henry's sword, but pulled away as if he'd touched flames. He didn't think himself worthy to finger the prized possession only to scare off a coward. Instead, he'd use his fists and readied to smash sense into the fool. He pushed past Phipps and pounded to the stairs, taking them by twos. The old structure creaked, surely his weight would make them break and fall apart on his next fevered rant.

When he reached the turret, he found the boy sitting on the broken sill with legs dangling in the night air.

He truly would jump and that set Hugh's heart pumping like it did when he struck a match to a detonation cord. It would only be a few more seconds before the blast and the smell of death claimed the air. "Boy, it doesn't have to be this way.

You are living on your hate. You think it goes away when you die?"

The messenger didn't turn, but kept facing straight ahead pointed toward the sky. "The air does feel cold here. If the fog weren't so greedy, you could see for miles, maybe even eternity. The air feels cold like God's breath. If I squint, maybe I can see him stir the waters."

Pounding closer, Hugh came near enough that he could grab the lad or assist him in leaping. It was too soon to test his vow of never killing. One more footfall, a few more seconds, that's what Hugh needed to make a difference. "So, what's your name?"

"You didn't care before." The gravel in the boy's voice became less, but it held no tears. It sounded of raw anger. "Don't pretend now."

"Boy. I'm a spy. That is what we do, but this is crazy. And why stain my walls? Old Phipps and I will have to clean up your bones from the garden."

Still not turning, he let go of the sill with one hand and cupped his eyes. "That will be a hardship since cleaning is something you are not apt to do." He sighed. "Those soft clouds. The rush of the wind, so peaceful and endless... You think this is what freedom truly looks like?"

The wobbly window started to crack. It moaned like it would break. Hugh had kicked it in his last crazed fever. Well, he punished it and every spare wall in Sandon. Now close enough to grab the boy, Hugh could stop the suicide, but a man needed a chance to choose. Another day, he'd give into weakness again, for those demons of depression pressed late into the night, even at Hugh. He leaned over and grabbed the upper edge of the open window. "You have too much humor inside to jump. Come inside and convince me of why I should help you kill Moldona."

"You just don't want to clean." The boy leaned forward and kicked his boots like he was at the water's edge. "Tell me why it's best to see a tomorrow with no justice."

Above the peaceful wind noise, the fool's voice sounded as if it bore pain. The boy was too young for that. He didn't know the frustration of guessing how to tamp down his own strength or how to stop wearing upon his skin the guilt of every death he'd caused. No that was Hugh's special torment. "You don't know anything. You are young and alive. Everything seems tragic."

Hugh reached out and grasped his shoulder. "This ends now."

The boy's hat flew away as they struggled.

Hugh's fingers tore off the jacket and pieces of his shirt, revealing a corset and curves. He'd uncovered a lass. "What? You came to trick me?"

Raven hair spilled down her back as she turned. With her hands, she covered her chemise and tottered on the open sill. The wood gave way. She fell forward, but he caught an arm. "Woman."

He refused to let go as they both dangled out of the window.

Chapter Two: Windows or Closets of the Soul

Feet swinging in the air, Isadel tried to free herself of the brute latched onto her arm. "You fool, let me be. I wasn't ready to jump."

His arm tightened about her. "This is a funny way to show it. Stop fighting so I can save you."

The strength in his muscles would surely pull her apart, but she didn't want to be saved, not half-dressed. She fought him harder, punching at his thick forearm.

"You're not falling from my window, woman. Well, that's if the window holds us both."

Thoughts of death had pressed her. It wasn't her time, but maybe this was the nudge she needed. "I prefer a quick end, not dangling into infinity. Let me go."

"Boy, Woman. Stop squirming before you make me fall."

She wanted to punch him again, but she didn't want him to die. He wasn't the cause of her misery. Yet, the anger dangling in the top of her stomach wanted to drop, wanted to go somewhere else than stay trapped inside her limbs. "Why live without justice?"

"You'll not know if you give up now. Please come back into the window. Let me help you."

She couldn't wish her life over, but refused to plead for anything. "I ask nothing more of you, neither to die or to live."

Bannerman pulled her into his melon-sized arms and stared into her face. He glowered like a snarling bear then flung her to the floor.

With a bang, she hit the wood planks and rolled. Glimpses of dark oak boards and white ceiling alternated within her vision until she hit the wall.

When the world stopped and settled, the plaster won. She lay flat on her back staring up at the vaulted ceiling of the turret. It hovered above, snowy and foggy like clouds. Then the bear-like Bannerman with sinful hazy irises crowded her view. Dark creases lined his thinned eye sockets. Lack of sleep must be his companion, too. Maybe sickness visited as well.

Her heart quivered with guilt. She felt sorry for him and even worse for trying to make Moldona his problem. "You've been sick? Sorry."

With a shake of his head, he stood adjusting his torn stained sleeve as if he smoothed finery for the ballroom. "That's an empty word."

Ringing his hand, he kicked her jacket to her. "Cover up, woman, then tell me why you lied to get in here."

With her shirt and jacket torn clean off exposing her chemise, she should feel shame, but she didn't, only tired, and hungering for something to end on her terms. Tossing the shirt as if it had been cut up like a child's paper snowflake, she gathered up her father's coat and slid inside. "I stole a horse to come here. I can't go back without you. Then, I thought why go back. I'd only face a magistrate and Lord Hartland's disappointment in my character. I don't want to see his face twist like those on his staff."

As if her honest statement had befuddled him, he rubbed fingers through his hair, but stopped. His right hand bled, sprinkling crimson drops onto his rumpled gold locks. He stopped and rubbed a smear between his forefinger and a thumb. "Ruinous woman. Look what you've done."

Hoping to catch him distracted, Isadel jumped up and pivoted to the door. "I won't be a bother anymore."

Before she could cross the threshold, he'd grabbed her with his good hand. It slid to her wrist and latched on to her. His skin felt dry and paper thin. He spun her then grabbed her about the middle. "You'll not cause such an upset and crawl out of here."

She tried to break free, but he had her arm pinned. Shirt ripped to shreds, hat gone, she wanted to go. But maybe Bannerman would try to humble her as Moldona did her sister. No one would do that to Isadel, not without a fight. "You've made your point. You want none of me. I'll turn myself in. Let me go."

He scooped her up over his broad shoulder. "What? Now you're ready for jail? A minute has changed your mind? Another minute, and it will be changed back. Then you are bound to do something foolish that will cause me more injury. You can't be trusted."

That instinct to do as she pleased, to live by her own wits started pulsing in her veins. She thrashed and kicked but couldn't get free of his grip. "Let me go. I'll not be used up by you. I'm no flirt. Not asking for this. Let me go."

He jerked open the closet and tossed her inside. "You'll not be looking for another open window to jump from either."

The door slammed shut as she sprang up from the hard floor. She didn't hear the kiss of a metal lock, but even as she shook the handle like a mad woman, the door refused to budge. "Let me out of here."

His voice vibrated the door. "In due time."

She let go of the handle as if it were a red-hot spit that had been seasoned over the hearth. She clamped her mouth to keep the begging words from her tongue. Trapped like she'd been in Papa's root cellar, overhearing the killing of her family, she panicked, pushing and kicking at the door. "You can't keep me."

"Looks like I am, for now."

She shook the door until her fingers vibrated. It barely moved, and from the way it did, Isadel knew bulky Bannerman probably leaned against it. She peeked out the keyhole and only saw darkness, maybe green, the fabric of his waistcoat. Until he decided to move, she would stay in the closet. Too weak to counter his strength— too feeble to push on the sliding door of the root cellar and save Papa and Agueda— Isadel wished then as she did now to have taken the same bullet to her temple as her sister.

Sliding down the door, Isadel died inside all over again. Miss Pearson tossed her onto the boat to escape the carnage the British soldiers left. She said she was rescuing Isadel, but all she did was sentence her to a coward's death daily. Closing her eyes, she could still see the burning city. The spy Pearson said let the dead bury the dead. Badajoz, her beloved father and sister—all gone while she fled to the land of her people's slaughterer.

Gasping but trying to keep it inside, she craned her head against the door and tried to remember Papa's voice. She couldn't hear it anymore, but Mama's song still felt strong in her mind. To keep calm, she had hummed it when she learned Moldona would come to sup at Lord Hartland's Abbey. Isadel let the tune vibrate her lips and focused on what it felt like to dance in the air out the turret's window.

"You alive in there, woman?"

Debating whether to respond, she opened her eyes to the small closet and accepted she had nothing more to lose. "Yes."

"Good." He said. "Let's keep it that way."

Lord Hartland's friend sounded concerned. Even though he told her would not help, he acted as if he cared even risking falling. "You didn't have to toss me to the floor."

"You didn't have to try my patience. I still reserve the right to kill you."

His tone sounded more agitated than furious. Rough and grumpy, maybe he might have a heart that could be turned to help. Her sister would know how. Pretty Agueda could do anything.

With a sigh, she tucked her legs beneath her, then filled her lungs again, sniffing the cedar lining of her prison. "I suppose I'll wait for you to open this door. If you persist at this punishment for more than a day, return Lord Hartland's horse."

"More orders, woman?" His tone had sharpened. "I don't take orders from civilians. I give them."

"But since you're retired, you can't give them any more."

"I didn't retire from being a man, so I don't take

kindly to orders from a green girl."

"Then take suggestions. Dice up some onions and put it on your open wound. That should cleanse it and keep it from becoming gangrenous."

"Onions? I'm not food."

His voice sounded snappy as if she'd said something lunatic. She could match him. "You don't look like you'd taste good anyway. Get the onions. They will help."

He pounded on the door. "You think you are funny. You want me to be ridiculous."

She didn't want him to grow angrier, but Papa said cuts could be nasty business. Closing her eyes, she laid back against the door hoping to feel him move from it. "I'll say it again. Onions. You need onions on that wound."

He grumbled something she could not understand, but she did not care. She'd offered advice. Sooner or later, she'd be free of this closet. Hopefully it would be sooner so she could return to the Abbey Estate before Moldona's visit.

Scooping a piece of her torn shirt, he pushed it onto his glove which now held a good red stain. Hugh sat and scooted his back against the door. He should revel in the fact the sprite had quieted. What a mouth on that one. Her silly command to return Hart's horse or to put onions on his sore made him laugh. Rubbish.

Of course, Hart would get his horse back, not that he'd notice or mind. And onions were for eating. Hugh tapped his stomach. Eating had been something at which he was fond of, but the books said a bland diet of white foods would calm the eruptions and slow the progress of his leprosy. Onions were yellow. Ridiculous. "Phipps!"

No one showed at the door, which was unusual for the spry fellow. What if this woman didn't come alone? Was Phipps dealing with her companions— the guilty Almeida Killer or killers?

A foolhardy girl would be a great distraction to allow the fiends to strike. Hugh's blasted pulse ticked up. If Phipps faced danger by himself, he'd... Hugh didn't know what he'd do. Vowing to never take another life had become his creed, but injury to his most loyal man would surely test his resolve. "Phipps!"

"In a moment, sir. Just stowed the horse. It's one of Lord Hartland's."

His man's voice didn't sound distressed, only mildly annoyed. Very normal for Phipps.

Relief washed over Hugh, pushing out of his tired lungs. Nothing was working to make him better. Everything stole his energy. With the strength of an ox, he should be able to defeat anything, including this leprosy.

That's why he knew his condition had to be a curse, one earned from his sins, every faceless and known person he'd killed in battle, working for Wellesley or by accident. Killing for King, country, or happenstance with explosives was second nature and it made him an indispensable killer, but all good things had to end. This time Hugh would die.

Hugh stretched and knocked the door with his elbow. "You still alive in there?"

A tap came back, a weak feminine one. She hadn't killed herself in the dark. "Good. I don't want to clean in there either."

"I'm sure that's true."

"How can you have a sharp tongue and yet want to kill yourself? You should keep chattering and allow others to do the dirty work for you."

"No. No British butcher will kill me."

Her voice sounded loud, clear, and bitter. How much did she know about Hugh? And why hadn't the clear determination ringing in her words been there moments earlier on the sill? He patted the cloth over his wound. "Tell you what. I won't let any of them get to you. That would just leave me and at the moment, I'm undecided."

"Let me out, and then do it. I'm not afraid to die."

Well, that was obvious. Yet, for a suicidal miss, the girl seemed to possess the spunk of a warrior. Another contradiction. "You're not one of Wellesley's spies? If you are, you need better training. The first lesson is annoyance is a nuisance. You're the first to be killed."

"So annoy you more and my work will be done?"

He coughed to cover a laugh. Her boldness hit his dormant funny cord inside, but humor didn't push her to the window's edge literally. "Tell me why you want Moldona dead."

"He killed my family at Badajoz."

"You mean your family was killed under his taking of the city?"

"No, he killed them, but not before humbling my sister. That's what girls like us get."

Moldona? He was a skunk, but rape and murder? Hugh never should've helped him so Moldona could be in command at Almeida.

By default, this girl's burdens could be his fault. Hugh looked at his hands, the growing red stains. When would there ever be enough blood on his hands? Would they ever be clean?

What was left of Hugh's marrow was stubborn.

Unlike the boy...woman in the closet, he wouldn't stop trying to find a cure. He wouldn't stop wanting to live, though he didn't deserve to. Hugh stretched and knocked the door with his elbow. "I'm not coming for you yet. Need to get a handle on this wound you made me reopen."

She didn't respond even when he elbowed the door again.

A couple of minutes of this odd impasse stirred his impatient gut. His thinned skin itched from the odd silence. Not even the rhythm or hiss of air sweeping past the open window soothed him. He never liked quiet. The absence of noise meant his mind would wander. The noise of regrets—boom, boom, boom. Too many faces frozen with fear right before the detonation of one of his well-timed explosions. Nothing was worse than the past, the things he caused couldn't be changed and he needed to take care of this sore. With his skin so thin and leathery, it had to be cleansed or it would become gangrenous like the girl said. "Phipps! Bandages."

He waited for Hart's crazy messenger to shout, *'and onions'* again, but she stayed silent. That surely couldn't be good.

Poking at the reddened cloth, he stopped. The lotions and tonics did nothing for his leprosy but made his skin dry like desert sand. Lifting the cloth too soon would disturb the fresh clots. He could bleed out this time. "You really made this cut bad, woman."

"I told you how to make it good. Sliced onion. That's what Papa would suggest." Her voice became louder, clearer, maybe even prideful. "It was something he learned from Mama."

Thoughts of his stepmother flashed through his

mind. And it made him recoil. She always tried to mother him and his brother but not too many years separated them. "Was your mother a trained a physician?" He heard his snide tones and kept going. "Perhaps a graduate of the Academy of Science?"

"No. Just an enslaved woman who learned things to survive."

Didn't the girl look mulatto or Blackamoor? He closed his eyes and tried to remember but only saw piles of thick ebony hair. Focusing again on the window, the darkness and stars now showing, he wished his own fog would blow away. "So, what was your mother? African, Jamaican, American, other? Tell me what remote place would know more than English physicians or even the ancient Greeks. I am sure that none of these sources would suggest onions as a cure-all? Ridiculous. "

"Don't believe me. Ridicule me, but not something which could help."

The clear tones of her voice shook his confidence in dismissing her. What if she were correct? What if he scoffed at something that could bring restoration?

His man lumbered into the room. "Sir. Where's... You're bleeding."

Hugh dropped his hands to his side as if he'd been caught stealing secrets, but contemplating the girl's foolishness made him feel caught, naked, exposed to ridicule. "Go get more bandages."

Phipps didn't agree but charged at the window. He leaned over with his hand cupped to his eyes. "The boy? Were you not able to stop him?"

"I stopped him."

Pivoting, Phipps's lips scrunched into a frown. The creases around his mouth deepened with deep disapproval. "Sir, you threw him out the window?"

Didn't his man know him better? Twenty years of service should be an indication of his character, well more so his resolve. He had vowed never to kill again and that pledge extended to wayward boys and girls. "What do you think me capable of doing?"

Touching the broken trim and fingering a recently patched indention in the wall, Phipps looked as if he were dusting, not poking a thumb into Hugh's self-righteous statement. "You're capable of many things, Bannerman. I've seen the devil on your shoulder as much as an angel. You tell me who was with you in this room that looks vacant."

Punching through the floor to focus his anger wouldn't exactly help Hugh's cause. It might feel better, but he'd felt better a little too much, ramming huge holes in the plaster of Sandon. "I didn't kill anyone today. Nor did anyone get tossed or thrown from the window. The devil's still here."

A crease or two relaxed on his brow. Maybe even a sigh released. "If you are sitting on the boy, he's a goner. Where is he?"

"He is a she, and I tossed her into the closet."

The man's eyes went big, but he'd served too long to think Hugh offered a spy's misstatement. However, the lines on his forehead returned, and he nodded. "Well, he/ she...is alive in there? Mighty quiet. You sure they haven't..."

Hugh banged on the door. "Say something so Phipps, my man-of-all-work, will know you live."

"Get him onions for the wound," she said. Then again became quiet as a mouse.

"What?" Phipps's face scrunched up. "He...she must be kidding."

Hugh groaned. "Just bring me bandages. I need your assistance while I keep the door barred from our jester sent by Hart."

"And bring him sliced onions." His prisoner tapped on the door. "Onions. It will purify the wound and stop infection. The wound will heal better."

Now Phipps smiled wide. "Sir, do I heed the voice, your captive's voice?"

Onions? She did sound confident. Could she know something of it? The girl claimed to work for Hart and that fellow invented everything. Was Hugh desperate enough to try this? Yes. Yes, he was. He'd do anything for healing. He made a sawing motion in his wounded palm. "Bring me onions."

The stunned look on his man's face as he peered over his glasses said everything. "Bannerman, have you lost a lot of blood? Feeling dizzy?"

"Phipps, if you keep delaying, I will lose more."

His man dragged to the door. "Taking the word of a thief?"

Desperation must not look so good on someone so big, but that was the suit of clothes Hugh had been made to wear. What exactly did he have to lose by taking the word of a so-called horse thief? Someone who'd just attempted suicide. Yes. Hugh was truly desperate. He nodded. "Bring the onions."

With a shrug, his man clasped the broken trim of the threshold. "I'll be back as fast as I can. I'd recommend you keep your temper at bay. Can't keep the walls up and trap the messenger in the closet." Phipps left, fussing under his breath.

Hugh bent a knee, pulling it closer to lay his palm on. It had become heavier.

"Has this place been under attack?" Her tone was

lower. "It looks like war hit it."

He couldn't answer as he shifted his boots along the rough floorboards. Sandon, the home of his father and his father's father barely stood. It creaked in the wind from its poor conditions, the result of Hugh's neglect, his uncontrollable rage. Sandon would've fared better under his brother. Henry was a man given to drawing and inspiration. What marvels the world would have seen had he lived as he brought light to the missionary work he'd planned. Hugh's unthinking actions snuffed his brother's wick.

Hugh was not meant for estate management. The work of a soldier was to serve his country and kill the enemies. What does a man of war do when it's time to be at peace? Battling Napoleon wouldn't go on forever. "What is your name, girl? Hello in there. Do you have word of Almeida?"

The girl never answered, leaving Hugh to wonder if she were an enemy, for why else would she come to him now?

He banged on the door with his elbow. "You still alive in there?"

Isadel heard the slower beating on the door. His last words sounded drained, kind of choppy. Her hearing was very good and she could tell if a dish was done based on this hiss of the steam, the thumbing of a rolling boil. The huge man could be bleeding out. There was no coming back from that. She'd seen a blood letting go horribly wrong, and her papa wasn't able to save the woman. She pushed on the door. "Let me help."

Nothing. Bannerman gave her no answer.

Though she may have helped him injure himself,

he was a grown man making his own decisions. If he needed her, he'd ask.

Footsteps sounded. Someone came into the room. Maybe they'd help him. She relaxed against the door, folded her arms, and tried to pretend she did not care. But she was her father's daughter. She cared very much, particularly when he said he injured himself struggling with her.

Annoyed, she knocked again.

This time the door opened. She pressed on the crack and it opened fully. Blinking like a crazed person, she let her eyes adjust to the candlelight. Her gaze locked on the hulking man leaning against the wall.

His skin was pale on his cheeks, his eyes closed. "My man has brought the onions. Now what?"

The bits of her torn shirt wrapped about his fist had turned red. He was still bleeding.

She scooped up some of the bandages and bound his hand, making the loops tight. She put all her weight upon it. He fidgeted, and then looked at her. "You know what you are doing?"

"I guess you better hope so."

His gaze lingered and once she had the wrap secure, she took a second to secure her jacket button. Shirtless with her chemise showing, she didn't want to give him a show. She'd seen how the English pigs stared when they saw her not as a cook but as some mulatto mistress.

"So what is your name, girl?"

"Armijo, Isadel Armijo."

"You know medicine Miss or Mrs. Armijo from your mama?"

"It is Miss. And I picked up what I could from my parents. Papa was a physician. Better than your Academy of Science."

"What do we do now? There is the onion."

"It'll need to be chopped fine and applied to the wound once we get the bleeding to stop."

"Phipps wants no part of it. He's gone. You have to do it."

He took a brass stick from his boot, hit something like a button, and out popped a blade. He held it out to her. The gleam of it caught her eye but so did the burs to the cutting edge, the dings in the tang. Someone had been very mean to the knife. "Here."

When presented with a knife what does a chef do? Since there is no Moldona around to kill, she decided to dice up the onions. "I don't need this dull thing."

She batted down his hand forcing the dull knife away, and then grabbed the burlap bag of onions releasing the pale-yellow orbs to roll on the floor.

"So how are you going to cut them? Are you a hand-to-hand combat expert in addition to your medical degree?"

"You make jokes." She moved slowly to her boot and pulled out a leather sheath. Holding it horizontal so he wouldn't think she tried to attack him, she slowly pulled her sharp knife free. "I'll use this."

With his good hand, he reached out but stopped. "What do we have here?"

Her blade was short but smooth and held not a single nick, nor would one ever dare to be there. "It's what a chef would use, not the garbage you have."

"The garbage could slit a throat. Not sure if I like that yours is bigger than mine."

"Boy and toys. Is this foolish thought international?" Making her motion slower than a snail, she moved to the onion. "I need very fine slices. You've trusted me thus far. I haven't run, though I could've."

His eyes widened, but then he nodded and released her hand. "I suppose. You know a spy doesn't say what he or she can or cannot do. He acts."

"And ruin a good knife? You are insane."

Laughing, Bannerman sat back. "Then commence."

She peeled the tough skin of the onion away, then sliced into it creating paper-thin wafers. She dispatched the pale flesh showing the fine strokes her mother had taught her, strokes Isadel had perfected in the village Moldona destroyed. When she looked up, she found Bannerman's light eyes staring.

For a moment, a mere thirty seconds or so, she demurred and fought the urge to bunch up her jacket. Her appearance wasn't neat. No apron dressed her outfit, just a father's jacket and man's pantaloons, and her corset peeking over the lapel. "I'm a very sorry site. Seems my shirt has gone to another cause." She took a breath and raised her head. "Give me your palm and let me dress the wound.

The man shrugged then rolled up his sleeve. "I've..." He pushed out his arm exposing mottled grey skin. "Be careful. I have an illness."

There was no redness like scarlet fever. His skin was sallow but other than maybe a lack of sleep and fresh air, he looked big and healthy to her. She reached for his hand, but he blocked her and pulled back. "This is not a joke. My skin is cursed."

His voice didn't sound of thunder this time. It held a warble like a cornered animal led to the butchers. "Just tell me what to do."

"You are being silly. Let me do this."

She wanted to lift her knife to him for being too stubborn, but she was no one to talk. "Let me unwrap the wound to check it. Then, I'll let you do the rest."

He stuck his hand out. "Fine."

She took her time and unwound the bandages until she came to the bits of her father's ruined shirt. Stopping, she caught her breath, remembering the holes in Papa's chest, in his good going-to-pray-at-the-iglesia shirt. The English soldiers were ruthless. Moldona was ruthless.

"See, the site of me has you weepy. I told you to let me do it, woman."

He plucked off the rest of the cloth. "Now what?"

"*Es mejor remojar*... Soak it in the bucket." She cleared her throat. Remembering the past made her speech fast, very Spanish. She worked her jaw and said slowly. "Rinse it very good in the water."

There was a smirk on his face. "Don't know why you are hiding your native tongue."

"Better to be thought slow-witted than a traitor."

"You sure you're not a spy? One of Hartland's creations for Wellesley?"

When she looked at him as if he'd taken leave of his senses, he shrugged then struggled to get the last bits of the reddened cloths removed. Finally done, he barreled his fist into the bucket.

Water flew up from the bucket, splashing her, but she wouldn't complain, not with the grimace painting his face. The wound had to be deep. It couldn't have been caused by their tussle at the window. Maybe his curse was real and not just something said to scare her.

"You are struggling. Let me clean it." She leaned

in, but he jerked the bucket away. Water sloshed.

"I told you no. I am sick. I don't want you contaminated."

Though the wound needed scrubbing like how she'd remove silk from an ear of corn, she'd not press. Waiting another minute and watching him thrash and slosh, she could take no more. "Lift it out," she said and held a towel for him.

Like wrapping a crust around a tender beefsteak, she dried the badly scabbed hand. "This will sting."

"You mean it will sting more? You are cruel."

Lumping up the onion slivers, she pressed them deep into the flesh. "Babes. Why are men babes?"

His eyes watered. "I'm no babe, lass."

She wasn't sure if it was the rawness of the onions doing him in or the pain, but a feeling of satisfaction whipped through her. "I said it would sting."

After ten minutes of light whimpering, he pumped his fingers. "It feels a little better. You may not be a complete menace."

She sliced up another onion very close to him making sure he couldn't miss the odor. Surely distracted by trying not to tear up herself, she waggled up more of his sleeve. It was scarred and mottled. A healed lesion scabbed his elbow. His vanilla skin waged war with grey spots. He was sick.

He frowned as she lumped onions beyond the wound up his forearm. "Is this necessary?"

"Seems you are letting these wounds get the better of you. My father would suggest a plaster of aloe. He was very good at doctoring my town. He would've had you healed up in no time."

"This is no rash. It's leprous."

With a shake of her head, she dismissed the notion. "My father has healed people of worse.

Everyone came to our town to be cared for by him."

"What town was this?"

"Badajoz." The word charred her tongue filling her with renewed rage. "The killers led by Moldona murdered a man known for healing, a man many including you red coated men came to for help." She stashed the knife in the waistband of her pantaloons then slapped a bandage on his palm, winding and wrapping in the onion slivers onto his palm and wrist. Once she made sure it was good and tight, she dumped his hand and stood. "You know it is Badajoz. I told you before." She stood and looked to the door. "Why pretend to be dense?"

He changed from a lethargic red-eyed lump to a stallion galloping and blocking the door. "It's the spy's tenet number one, strive for underestimation. I hope you are not thinking of leaving."

"I should go back to Lord Hartland and face my punishment."

"As I told Phipps, you are mine to punish. I am a man of my word. That's tenet number two, keeping my word. Once I have the horse returned, Hartland is no longer injured, but you've barged in here and disturbed my peace. You even laced me with onions like a mutton. That alone is worth punishment."

He seemed dangerous again and she doubted he'd let her go.

"I promised Hartland to kill the next foot soldier he sent to retrieve me. Lucky, you." With his good hand, he wrapped a strand of her hair about it and yanked her chin up. "Since you are a chef and not a soldier, I suppose you think I will spare you?"

She barely reached his chest. He had to be six foot maybe six and a half foot, but she wouldn't let him know he frightened her. Though, at this moment, he did. She put her fingers on the shaft of her knife, pulled it out and handed it to him. "Do your worst or let me go."

He grabbed the knife and spun it so it rested close to her neck. "Are you more stupid or brave? Or do you think I'll be easy on you because you're a woman?"

His skill with the weapon showed. For though it rested on her skin, it barely pricked. Yet, she knew better than to thrash about. The shards of her knife would dice her to bits. She relaxed within his hold. "I won't beg for my life. I'll only ask again for what I came for. Teach me how to control black powder."

"You risked your position to come to a stranger —"

"You're not a stranger. I saw you at the Abbey Estate. "

Releasing her, he stepped backward. "You know nothing of me."

"I knew enough to find you. And I've heard the stories. I know you hate Moldona, too."

Bannerman's forehead crinkled as his eyes drifted. He was reaching for something, a notion or bits of images of seeing her in the background at the Abbey.

"You won't get close to him now. Hartland won't trust a horse thief."

"I found you. I can get to him. I just need the right weapon to do it. Will you teach me?"

"Moldona has many sins, but my hands are stained too."

"Then, out of my way. I'll go back and beg Hartland's forgiveness. Perhaps something will happen to give me a chance at revenge."

Again, he blocked her path. "You will not be leaving, especially as you have me smelling like a roast. I didn't think chefs left without dishing the final course."

The tilt in his brow, the smirk on his face, it hit her. He wanted something. She remembered standing near him with no shirt just a baggy jacket and corset. She bunched up her lapels. "Name the price for my freedom."

"In due time. I must assess your story and give you a shirt. I'm a little tired of you clutching that jacket like it is gold."

She felt her brows rise; maybe they flew from her face. "Your shirt will swallow me. I'll trip over the lacing. And nothing can replace my father's."

He nodded. "Follow me."

He led her down the dirty hall to a pristine door. No scratches, no dings, perfect and polished.

She braced as he opened the door. But unlike before, he pushed on it as if it were hallowed ground.

"I have a shirt for you."

As he shoved her inside, she gaped at how clean the room was, orderly and untouched by rubble. Butter colored walls, a pile of books on a nightstand, an unbroken burgundy chair, a perfectly situated emerald-green tapestry rug. This was another house, not Sandon.

Bannerman walked to the closet and pulled out a crisp shirt, one too small for him and shoved it in her hands. "Change into this. In addition to being your warden, I am a gentleman. When you're dressed, come out. Don't touch anything."

"Why? Is the owner coming back?"

"Not this side of glory, girly. Be quick."

He pushed out of her way and slammed the door.

She pulled off her father's coat and slipped on the shirt. It was fine silk and though a little big, she liked it. Looking in the gilded mirror, she spied a connecting door. Wondering if it led to escape, she stared at but didn't move toward it. With her luck, Bannerman might expect that and she would lose the little rapport she'd built. Her sister Agueda wouldn't run, not when there was a man to soften and ply to her cause.

Isadel wasn't a coward, not in that sense of running. She feared other things, like disappointing Papa and not being strong. After wiping her eye, she scooped on her jacket then headed to the door.

When she slipped out of the room, she found Bannerman waiting, staring at the room as if he were somewhere else.

She cleared her throat. "So now what, warden?"

"Nothing until my man comes back and your story is verified. How long do I marinate in onions?"

"Let it set for an hour then we'll wash the wound again in hot water."

"Chef, in an hour the water Phipps heated will be cold. My man won't return in time to get more heated. Seems your recipe is flawed. Not quite what your father would do."

Waving her knife, he offered the rebuke as if he knew the man. As if he knew the disapproval Papa would have at her plan for revenge.

Shaking her head, she folded her arms. "Thank you for the shirt. Now take me to the hovel you call a kitchen. If your man servant can heat water in there, then I can."

The humor in his eyes faded, hiding in the contemplative flakes of gold in his hazel irises. "If I take you to the kitchen, what promise do I have that you will not escape or find more ways to do harm?"

She took the knife from him before he could move and aimed for his heart. "If it was harm I sought, I'd find it. You might be big, but I'm fast."

A smirk the size of a plantain or banana filled his face as he pushed her hand down. "Well, put that knife away and come, chef. More rubble awaits."

He left her with the knife and turned his back upon her. Foolhardy man. Maybe he thought he could overpower her. "Is there some spy tenet about trusting strangers?"

He paused and scratched his beard. "There is one about meekness and allowing an opponent to believe they have the upper hand. It makes them comfortable and open to mistakes. Come along, chef, and play nice."

She stuffed the knife into her waistband again and followed. With a goal of learning Bannerman's secrets with black powder, she wouldn't let her mind wander to despair. Yes, she was small. But when focused, she shared the rage of a giant, at least the size of Bannerman. Maybe more so.

Chapter Three: No Good, Dirty Kitchen

Perhaps it was cruel setting the girl up in the hovel Phipps called not fit to stable animals, but where else would one keep a chef but in a kitchen? Hugh held the door open wide. "Welcome to the kitchen of Sandon Manor."

Miss Armijo stepped inside. Her mouth went slack as if she'd seen a ghost. Perhaps there were of a few burnt dinners of days past haunting the ceiling. "How can you be so cruel?"

"It's a beauté." He chuckled and pushed deeper into the room. "Like what you see?"

"There are no words for a travesty such as this. Dishes and broken pots stacked to the rafters. Why would you allow such? That room upstairs. It's nothing like this or the rest of the house."

"That was my brother's room."

She poked at a stack of plates. "Did he run from here screaming?"

With his good hand, he gripped the big table and bent over it. "No. Henry Bannerman never saw Sandon like this, but my brother is not coming back. He died in the park at the rear of the estate from one of my first explosions. Black powder is unpredictable. It's not something easily mastered, even for a chef."

Her cheeks trembled for a second, and she looked away as she began sorting through dishes. "Is there a bucket so that I can heat water?"

He scanned the mounds of dishes and saw one stashed under a bench. He reached down and tried to seize it with his hurt hand before stopping. That was unwise. He shifted to his other hand and picked it up. "Now what?"

"Go fill it with water."

Looking around, he wondered where to do so. This place was foreign. Though Hugh loved food, he hadn't truly spent time in its preparation.

"The scullery. A house this big must have a scullery with a cistern for water. The abbey had pumps to pull it inside."

Over the piles of ruined cloths and dirty pots, he looked around and saw a tiny room. Could that be it? He went inside and discovered double stone sinks and a faucet. He tucked his bucket underneath and twisted the lever. Cool water fell from the pipe filling his bucket. Feeling accomplished, he returned to the kitchen.

Miss Armijo had cleared a path. The stove blazed with a purgatory fire. She took the bucket from him and set it on the stove. "Good. This will take a half an hour or more to heat. It's hard to say."

"A scullery maid... Would she know how long it takes to heat water, but not a chef?"

"One might. But a chef never guesses at things like this." Poking at slots, Isadel looked to see where the wood or coals would be added. "Certainty is the best measure. This is my first time using this stove."

"Certainty is a luxury."

"I suppose it's not one of your spy tenets. Pity."

Yes, he was testing her. She was different from the people Elizabeth, his stepmother, had last employed to staff Sandon. Why would Hart have a mulatto chef from Spain? Weren't their enough in England? It didn't quite make sense. But the duke was into collecting eclectic things, why not people. "How did you come to work for the Duke of Hartland?"

She had her back to him as she gathered up pots and pans and towed them into the scullery. "Miss Pearson's doing. My papa, he helped the English forces in Almeida and they remembered. She tried to smuggle our family out but only I made it."

"Your father was in Almeida?"

The chef picked up a Wedgwood platter and wiped the gravy stained side. "Yes. He saved a great many people that day, but his doctoring was repaid by your people butchering him and everyone in Badajoz. Barely two years have passed. Are your memories so short?"

One look at her with her tightly curled fingers, the lines furrowing her temples foretold that her memories were long and fresh. What images in her head inflamed her soul? She swiped at her forehead then picked up a huge ladle. "Miss Pearson, she set me up in my position at Abbey Estate. You had my roasts on your last stay. Was it something to complain about?"

"I don't recall. It's been months since I was last at the Abbey."

She glanced at him and stared as if he spoke lies. "Short memory, aye?"

His brainbox had been quite sharp when it came to details, but that was before his illness, before every thought had been consumed with finding a cure or a way to atone for his guilt. He sat on the edge of the table and watched her. She floated about the kitchen poking here, peering there as if she were doing reconnaissance, but for what? Who was she spying for?

More pots clanged. "Last time you were at the Abbey, you had two servings. You cleaned your plate."

"If it's good, why stop before it's done? I was taught to clean my plate."

A small smile snuck onto her face, which hadn't before had one. "Well, that's one thing you'll clean. You looked healthier with a full meal in you."

Dumbstruck at the lift of her lips, he wondered how he or Phipps ever mistook the lass for a boy. Even with her hair spun into a knot on her head, she was sort of pretty and moved with grace. Not a boy's stance in the least, not with those hips.

"What are you staring at? You've never seen a chef in a kitchen."

"Honestly, no." He patted his big stomach. "But I know they exist. Phipps will verify your story or falsehood. You could confess now. I would be more merciful. Remember, that's a spy's tenet."

With an eye roll, she turned back again clearing dishes off the floor. "Why couldn't cleanliness be one? How could you let a place get like this?"

If her claim of being a chef was true then perhaps working in a disaster of a kitchen would be a good start for a punishment. He folded his arms, his mouth twitching with satisfaction with each clang of a falling pot. Yes. This was the start of a good punishment.

But if she was the Almeida Killer, why hadn't she tried to kill or maim him like the other victims?

According to Hartland and Pearson's reports, each victim, each one of the ground commanders of Almeida seemed to have been caught off guard. Staler, Parks, Roan—each with a throat slit in their beds. He sighed and flexed his fingers. Maybe a pretty tan face dressed as a woman or as a harlot—could that have distracted each?

He was distracted watching Armijo. Was she humming something?

The alleged chef came near, swinging the bucket. "The water's warm enough. Time to put a final dressing on the wound."

Her slight accent, the slight clipping of the dr—in dressing fell pleasing on his ear, even as her use of the word **final** made him question if he she played him for a fool. "Set it down. I can manage."

She sloshed the bucket, setting it on the cleared table surface. "I told you I would fix it for you. Sit on the bench, not the table where food is prepared."

He did as she commanded and slid onto the closer of two benches. "What a curious creature you are? I thought a horse thief would show more contrition or at least a softer tongue."

She grasped his hand without responding. When the jerky unwinding of the bandages could no longer keep him from uttering a wince, he yelped and pulled back his hand.

"Sorry," she said, but she didn't seem sorry with the slight smile that had appeared again. "Now for the last layer. Are you ready, Ban—Bannerman?"

That accent of hers came out again and it soured him that she was hiding it. "I'll do it." As fast as he could, he held his breath and undid the final wrap, then dunked his fist into the hot water hoping the heat would distract him from the searing feeling stinging his hand. "From what I can see, you are young and healthy. It's too much of a risk."

She pushed on his elbow to sink his hand lower in the bucket. "I said I would do it. My word is worth the risk."

"The same word you've given to Hartland...before or after you stole his horse?"

Drying her hands on her chocolate baggy jacket, she frowned. "The one said to my late father, those mean more than anything. He was a healer. He would help you."

"Promises to the dead don't mean so much when time passes."

Her burnished brown eyes lowered as she stretched a fresh bandage. "Your man has a supply of these cloths in the scullery. Are you given to bleeding a lot?"

He drove his fist into the cloth and mangled it twisting the smooth fabric until none of whatever plagued him could contaminate her. "That's none of your concern."

She knotted the cloth, tugging it tight and giving it just enough of a yank to remind him that she was no dove. "Well this kitchen is my concern now. It's unsanitary and can make you sicker. Leave me here and let me make this place neater."

"I can trust that you won't escape? Can you give me your word?"

"Yes. Now leave." She pivoted without asking to withdraw and tugged the bucket of onions and fouled water to the scullery.

Was she a servant, a chef, as she claimed, another in Hart's collection of misfits? His doubts had begun to mount again as did his worries of his lesion becoming septic. Could she have tricked him with the onions? Well, he'd know in a few hours if the fevers started. "I guess I trust you for now. You have given me your word. I'd hate to have to chase you down and kill you. We were starting to get along."

She didn't turn to face him but waved her hand. "Yes, yes. Now leave."

The woman either meant she would keep her word or she was confident in her trickery. He took a final look at her scooping up the horrible pans and towing them to the scullery before backing out and heading to his study.

Once inside, he went to his desk and rummaged in the pile of books until he found the notes Hart had sent weeks earlier. Each victim had been killed at close range with a knife. A knife. Maybe there was a league of killers and this little chef had been dispatched for him.

Was that how they were trained? Drop into the commander's lives, cause a ruckus, gain confidences and then, wham...strike? His heart pounded as he flexed his hand. Phipps brought the onions, so, they couldn't have been tainted. His man was loyal. He would never be in league with devils.

That feeling in his stomach, that something was afoot twisted his gut. Maybe Isadel Armijo and the like were trained by the best assassins, Napoleon's assassins. For how else could these intelligent men have allowed themselves to be killed so easily except by lowering their guards with an intriguing female? For a man like Hugh, being led astray by a woman was a fate worse than death. He pulled his stick knife from his pocket and started to sharpen it. He'd get the better of the chef before she struck.

* * *

Isadel stoked the fire in the hearth. She doubted there was enough water in the world that could be heated to clean all the horrible dishes. How could that man let it get to such a state? Didn't he know kitchens were where magic happened? Lumps of grain, gushy yolks spun in roaring waves of heat to make lusty crusty loaves, buttery biscuits, a heady caramel meringue.

She slapped the poker against the crimson bricks then dusted her hands against her coat. Isadel was careful not to get the sleeve of her borrowed shirt dirty. It was very fine, very soft with a weave she'd only seen created by Lord Hartland's master tailor. She smoothed the cuff as she ducked it inside her jacket. This place made no sense. Ruin was everywhere, but Bannerman kept his brother's shirt and one room clean and tidy.

Well, she held onto her clothes too, her father's. She had that in common with Bannerman. How could she have misheard his disdain for Moldona? In his discussions with Lord Hartland, why did it sound as if Bannerman hated Moldona? Maybe he did hate him, just not as much as her.

Picking up the poker, again she tapped the crossed wood in the hearth. A chunk broke free landing at the edge of the orange flames, hissing and spitting sparks. Anger boiling, roiling at the top of her stomach, she hit the log again splitting it. She'd risked everything to find Sandon for nothing. With what she'd done, how could she return to Abbey Estate? If she begged Lord Hartland, would he take her back?

He was good hearted, but he surely wouldn't let her around Moldona. She'd have to hope Moldona stumbled and broke his neck. The man should come to Sandon. There was definitely enough debris here to do the job.

Yet, that notion was no comfort.

She'd failed her sister, Agueda and Papa again. At least she acted this time, even if it was for naught.

A scream filled her stomach and roared all the way to her tongue, but she muffled it, stowing it in her breast with the rest of her rage.

With a shake of her head, she focused on the piles of dishes. Would Bannerman be grateful enough for her cleaning the hog pen that he'd relent? Could he be made to understand? She still had the sense he wanted something, and took comfort it wasn't in the way other men looked at her when her hair was out and dressed like a woman. She loved the safety of the kitchen. No one bothered her here. No man wanted anything from her but her biscuits.

The door swung open and she startled.

Bannerman pounded inside. "Just checking to see—"

"To see if I was still here?"

A grin swept across his face. "That and to make sure you hadn't been crushed by a mound of plates."

She took a pot from the stove. It hissed with steam as she dumped it into the bucket she'd chosen to soak the vessels with the hardest set stains. "As you can see, I haven't run, nor have I been trampled or quit."

He climbed up on the table she had just scrubbed clean and sat. "Tell me about Badajoz."

She rolled up the sleeve to Papa's coat that had fallen. She started working at an oily film that looked like gruel stuck on the bottom of a pot. "What was this, a poultice? It smells of tar, like something my father would make."

"I asked about Badajoz."

"Yes." The pot slipped from her fingers and slammed into the basin with a clang, kicking up suds. "Do you want to know what it smelled like before the English guns, before there was blood everywhere?"

"I heard Badajoz was bad. If it was like Almeida, then I know it was bad. I fought in Almeida. Moldona served there too."

"Did he kill other Spanish families at Almeida as he did in Badajoz?"

"No. No civilians—"

"Then it wasn't like Badajoz." Her fingers shook, and she balled them up as if that would hide how she felt. "Was there something else you wanted?"

"Moldona's name makes you angry. Any other names you take issue with upon hearing? There were other commanders of Almeida who also fought in Badajoz."

"Ban-Ba." She stopped, controlled the curl of her tongue that had started teasing the accent she tried hard to hide. "Bannerman could be one, even if he's not one of the Badajoz killers."

She put her back to his growing smile and took a second pot from the hearth. It hissed with steam as she dumped it into the basin. Somewhere between washing the third fork and straightening a bent spoon, she felt the heat of his stare. "What do you want?"

"Tell me of your father."

"You want to know about the man who helped you redcoats take care of your wounded at Almeida only to be cut down by the English no more than eighteen months later. Is that enough insight for you?"

Bannerman folded his arms, still seated on her clean table. "Do you cook spicy food?"

"Why, because I am a Spaniard? No fretting. I cook suitably for weak palates."

He put a hand to his scruffy beard. "I wondered if you seasoned your food with anger."

She straightened her shoulders. "Are you calling me, like you people say, an angry black-Blackamoor woman?"

"I wouldn't call any woman who can work a knife like you angry, at least not to your face, but I do wonder how many have come away unscathed. Have you ever killed a man, Miss Armijo?"

Lifting a pile of clean wet dishes, she put them down hard next to his hip. "Not this week. But keep sitting on my clean table and we'll see if the number holds."

He popped up and grabbed her wrist. "Have you killed a man?"

His eyes, his expression had drained of humor. The pressure he exerted on her wrist hurt. He could probably snap her in two if she made a false move.

"Have you, woman?"

"No, I have not. That is why I came to you."

Releasing her, he shoved his hands behind him. "I'm giving you some leeway, Miss Armijo, but do not forget you are my prisoner. And cleaning the kitchen will not pay your debt."

She held his gaze even as his voice became harsh as if he'd barked a command to a soldier. "I know you will not be easy."

"I'm not easy with many things, but why clean when you don't have to? I never said it would be your punishment."

Grasping his bandaged limb, she used it as a spit poker and pointed out the plentiful piles yet to clean. "The horrid condition of this kitchen and scullery cannot be unseen. It's a tragedy. You don't stand down, not when you can help."

He swiveled his neck from side to side as his finger clasped about hers. Maybe it never hit him how bad he'd let things get. Maybe he needed someone to bring attention to the tragedy.

Gently, she eased his palm to his side and went back to her stack of plates in the basin of the scullery. The Wedgwood platter that had been soaking would not relent and held onto its stubborn stains originating from weeks or months of neglect. With her chin up, she returned to the kitchen passing him to set another pot onto the stove. "You are a monster to keep a kitchen like this."

He marched over to her crowding the free space she'd made through the dishes. He was large, larger than when he trudged into his study, or when he'd flung her onto the floor. "Miss Armijo." He made his voice low, softer than before. "You come to me, knowing the weapons I excel at, maybe even hearing I murdered my brother, you call me a monster for a dirty kitchen? Seems this rubble is the least of my sins."

"Can't you be redeemed if you use your skills to right a wrong?"

Lifting his damp sleeve, he showed her his scabbed elbow. "My sins are on my skin."

At this she laughed, she laughed hard to keep from crying. "No, that's what you say about the descendants of Ham, all who look like me." She wiped at her face, pushing away some beads of perspiration that looked suspiciously like tears. "You might not be so pale or bleed so easily if you had a proper meal."

"Food solves all problems, woman?"

She stirred her pot of water as if it were soup. "There is life in it. The power to keep away death."

"Yes, and you want to take a proper meal and do in Moldona. Why not just poison him or slit his throat? I have a few friends that recently met an end that way. Seems effective. If you are Lord Hartland's cook, surely you'd have access to do it. With the chemicals he keeps, I have no doubt you'd have a wide selection from which to choose."

"It could end up in the wrong mouths. I want a controlled detonation like the ones you and Lord Hartland joked of, the ones he says that only you can do. I just want it to kill Moldona and harm no one else."

"Explosives rarely work like that. Why not use your knife work? If the onion is a small example of your prowess, I'd think you'd have a fair chance at Moldona."

She stared up at him and wondered if the smell of soapy water of an almost clean kitchen had forced his senses to leave. "And what if he overpowers me as you did?"

"He doesn't have my strength. He's weak in so many areas. You could have a chance especially if he's swilling Hart's port."

Bannerman moved closer, took a knife from the water, dangled it until its gleam caught the light. "I was at Almeida. I was one of the commanders. Moldona served under me. So perhaps I am responsible for him. He learned everything from me. You could say I am responsible for Almeida and Badajoz."

Was Bannerman trying to make himself the focus of her rage?

She grasped the knife's handle and took it from his finger. The hold was so slack; it was as if he wanted her to strike. But Isadel knew what biding her time, biting her tongue meant. The past year in an English kitchen schooled her well. "Lord Hartland has said Wellington's special reserve did what had to be done. Did that include the murder of innocents?"

"Killers are in the ranks, to be sure. I am or was one. And innocence or the perception of it is another spy tenet. Innocence is in the eye of the beholder. I know some of my deeds now require penance."

She swallowed the lump in her throat, the hard knot that seemed to grow and choke all the air away from her lungs. Bannerman baited her and it was working. Looking down she found her fingers clenched about the knife, but it was Moldona who needed to die.

She dropped the knife in the water as if it had been heated red-hot in the hearth. "Is that what you are doing, hiding in this wreck of a place? Is this your penance? The evil you've done must be great."

His wide eyes squinted as he shrugged. "Guilt can grow thick like iron chains." He turned and walked back to the table and almost sat on the surface when he popped up. "You seem determined to clean this kitchen. Once you give up, stay in here until I return. I'd rather not put you in irons or toss you back in the closet."

"You don't trust that I will stay? You think I will run before your man can verify my story?"

"It's a fair reservation. You come dressed as a male, when clearly, you're not. What other falsehoods are you capable of?"

"No falsehoods. But maybe a few secrets and knowledge of herbs that could heal your lesions quite nicely." She pushed up her sleeve to dip deeper into the basin.

His eyes widened like saucers. "The white spots on your arm. The discoloration, what is it from?"

That voice of his, which had been low and steady, cracked a little. "What are those?"

She squinted at him and dunked her hand into the water. He looked like a blend of a naughty boy and a wide-eyed lamb.

"What's this discoloration on your arm? How did you fix it? Your father?"

"Remember, you don't believe me. You have to wait for your man to come back." She stepped close to him flinging droplets from her hands. Some fell on his scuffed boots. "You can't look at me and see truth. Can you?"

Reaching around her, he stirred the water with his good hand. "You know who I am. I don't have the same luxury, but maybe you know something about freckles. There are tiny ones on your nose."

His fingers had become sopping wet. He flexed and flicked water on her flared nostrils. "But I will know about you soon. You could take this one last chance to confess."

His tone sounded richer, almost playful. That couldn't be good.

Starting to fidget under his gaze, she walked back to the scullery. "The mottled markings were worse once, but Papa, he made it better. He treated many afflicted at Almeida. Even more in Badajoz and other places he travelled."

"I'm not one for games. We'll see if your story matches."

"And what if it does? Will you change my punishment?"

"I don't like liars. I'd hate to put you in that category so soon. In my acquaintance, females usually lie later." He pounded to the door. "Yell out when you are finished."

"No need to yell. I won't be done until morning. I don't half do things, especially in the kitchen."

He nodded. "Then I will be back, but if you tire, come get me from the study. No escaping."

"You could chain me like a dog to the meat spindle, if you are so concerned. If there is a roast in the larder, you'd get two benefits, a clean kitchen and dinner."

His brow raised, shifting his countenance to a scowl. "You're not a spit dog, but a wily woman. I could sit on that table and watch, if you'll change your mind about cleaning."

She tried to stop herself but couldn't and slapped a palm onto her hip. "I will be here in this kitchen. Take my word. I say what I say. It is what it is."

As if he enjoyed pushing her, his smirk returned. "You're just saying that to keep me from sitting on the table again. My man should be back in the morning. If your story is true, it will bode well for you." He put a finger to his chin, trying no doubt to look contemplative. "You did overhear at Abbey Estate that I was good at finding people?"

"Is that another spy's tenet?"

"It's a Bannerman Tenet."

He marched out the door with his shoulders straight and stiff as if his warning delivered a crushing blow, but she had no intentions of leaving. The knowledge she wanted was here, held by a man who almost seemed desperate to keep her. She sighed and looked around. There was still three quarters of a cluttered room to clean, and piles of dishes to stow. Hard work never scared her, but a giant of a man whose mood changed from moment to moment, who'd admitted to killing his own brother—that made her stomach knot.

Chapter Four: Blessings from the Abbey

"Bannerman. Sir, awake."

Something pushed on Hugh's shoulder and he reared up and swung his fists. It wasn't until he finished blinking like a crazy man that he saw his man ducking behind his cluttered desk.

"Whoa, Bannerman. On your side. Your war batman, your man-of-all-work at peacetime. My father's father served the Bannerman family."

He lowered his hands. "Sorry, Phipps. You don't have to recite our history. I have my wits now. I thought... Well, you're not the Almeida Killer."

Phipps rose, his face a mass of grim lines. "I thought maybe you were—"

"Dead? No. Not done in by my leprosy or the alleged chef."

"You told me to leave you, but if the bleeding left you weak, the wench might have gotten the best of you."

Hugh stretched his arm and tested his bandaged hand, wiggling his fingers. "Nonsense. It takes a great deal to do me in. And the alleged Miss Armijo and I have come to an understanding for now. Did you confirm her story from Hartland? What have you learned?"

"It's bad." Phipps said as he wiped beads of moisture from his brow. "The news from Hartland's Abbey is bad."

Hugh punched his desk. The hit crumbled two of its legs flopping the thing onto its side, his research spilling again to the floor. A dust cloud ushered forth, choking the air, reminding him of the thunder, the belch of sand and smoke, followed by the quiet of a well-done explosion. "I hate liars. Just when I thought could trust—"

Frowning so hard his lips would fall off; Phipps shook his head. "Will you stop destroying things and listen? Hartland told me the Almeida Killer is on the move. We knew the fiend and his allies have killed Staler, Parks, and Roan. Now, Sampson has been found dead."

"Same method?"

With his index finger, Phipps traced a line on his neck. "Yes. Cox thinks he's been shadowed. Only you, Moldona, Nev, Handle, Cox, and Wellesley are left. It must be a network of killers to have this reach or to be this effective. Hartland's convinced of this. He wants you to come to the abbey for your protection. He says it's best with your condition."

Though grateful, Hugh ignored the charity of his friend. He wanted death on his terms and surely had no taste to be catered to like an invalid. "Henry wouldn't send me there. With his very Anglican humor, he would be in search of nine other leapers, so the ten of us could wait outside Jerusalem Tavern for healing."

"That is good punny, puritanical, perfect pitch.

Henry would be proud."

Would his brother be? Hugh bent and lifted his desk and kicked a few books underneath to prop it up. "While Moldona and I are expendable, Cox and Wellesley are not."

Phipps helped as he always did, picking up a few more papers. "What about Nev?"

With his pinkie, Hugh smoothed the wrinkle out of the top piece. "Never liked him. He's on his own."

"Bannerman, be serious. The killer could be on his way. Hartland has sent for Moldona. He and his wife are heading to the abbey after they're done with a bit of traveling."

Betsy was coming? Betsy and Moldona were heading to Hart's, even more of a reason not to go. Hugh smoothed his collar as if he where readying to see his old love. The last time was a year after Almeida. Her mourning for her brother who had died during the siege was still very thick. Yet, there were moments when she crumbled in his arms and took his kisses. They were engaged for a week before she sent him the note. Moldona swooped in and won her.

Fist tightening, he went to the window and looked out at Sandon's wild park. "Hart will keep them safe, but this killer must be caught."

"Mrs. Moldona, the former Miss St. Claire were regulars out at Sandon Manor, her and her brother Charles. God rest his soul."

"Charles St. Claire was a good young man. I miss those times. Henry was still with us. That was before I killed..."

"Your stepmother was a great host. She sent a letter for you via the abbey." Phipps handed him a lilac colored envelope, which smelled like the woman's gaudy perfume. "I guess she like everyone else believes Sandon Manor is abandoned."

"It is, Phipps. Nothing but ghosts and the best man-of-all-work reside here." Hugh shook himself, ridding his head of the stewing that Betsy or his stepmother, Elizabeth stirred. He took the letter. "I wonder what father's mistress wants."

"Your father married her, Bannerman. And she's gone on to marry an earl. She's Lady Rhodes now."

"Another old man." Flicking open the seal, he scanned the letter, "Another request for me to come visit and an early plea for a yuletide stay with her and Rhodes."

"That's six months in advance, Bannerman. A little hard to say you didn't know."

What was she trying to prove? He crumbled up the paper. "Why visit her? She'll parade a few marital candidates in her mission to marry me off or she'll try to get me to take a mistress to liven up Sandon as she put it. Some stepmothers only knit."

Phipps shrugged. "She does care about you. Perhaps, it is best if we head to her in London or even to the abbey. It's fortified and best to withstand an attack, not this bramble, a hovel set in isolation."

"You think Sandon is too worse for wear?"

Phipps didn't answer but moved to the window, pulled the curtain from covering the wall and exposed a cannon ball sized hole, one made with Hugh's fist after receiving the report of the second commander's death. "Sandon has seen better days." Hugh pivoted and with as much dignity as possible went back to his desk. "What did Lord Hartland say about the girl? Is she a chef on the run?"

"Yes. Isadel Armijo worked at the abbey for Hartland as his chef."

Hart's chef? She told the truth? "You are saying

that Miss Armijo's story is accurate, well the part about being his cook? In that, she did not lie?"

Phipps nodded. "The man himself verified her story. He also said you can keep her a while with his blessings if you send him a few of her meat pies. He adores her flaky crusts."

Since Hartland was a married man with nothing but eyes for his duchess, Hugh wouldn't take flaky crust as anything but flaky crust. "Did he say how he came by her?"

"Seems her father was a local physician who knew how to do good field medicine, a cross of what we'd call a physician and a doctor. Armijo journeyed from Badajoz to Almeida to help with the wounded. He saved quite a few of our men. Wellesley himself remembered his good works and sent Joanna Pearson to get his family out of Badajoz. Unfortunately, you heard how in the aftermath of the siege, our troops went wild. The physician and his eldest daughter were killed. Only the chef made it out."

Hugh wiped at his mouth struggling to reconcile what he'd heard. Miss Armijo hadn't lied. She had lost her family, and Hart wanted her meat pies. "So, she wasn't lying about working at Abbey Estate or being a chef. Did he say who killed her father?"

"He didn't know or mention it, but he said she is a very good cook. Lord Hartland agreed that you should dole out punishment then return her to the Abbey."

If she hadn't lied about working for Hart or that her father was a physician, did that also mean she told the truth about Moldona being her family's murderer? Did her father possess cures for skin conditions? Hope for the first time in a year built in Hugh's chest. He paced back and forth before stopping in front of his broken desk. "So, Hartland doesn't mind insurrection? Must be some mighty good pies."

"He was glad she was able to deliver his message. Hartland wants you aware of the danger. The Almeida Killer is coming for you. It is only a matter of time."

"We still have to be found, Phipps. An abandoned Sandon is still the best course."

"I suppose so, but it doesn't stop me from yearning for what it was or what it could be again with a little work, a little hope."

His man wasn't just talking about patching holes in limestone. Hugh didn't have any hope left in his chest. Too many sins. Too many memories.

"Where is your prisoner, Bannerman?"

"That is a good question." He pivoted and craned his ear toward the hall. "I left her in the kitchen."

"The kitchen... That kitchen? Alone? She could be in danger in that nightmare or perhaps she left as you slept, and I won't get a pie. Or she returned to the tower—"

Hugh held out his hand to stop the list of concerns, each of which had already started to fill his brainbox. "I fixed the tower room and made it cozy and safe for her when she quit. Then I waited outside the kitchen for her to yield."

"Did she?"

"The girl banged a few pots and uttered some Spanish words that surely had to translate to the devil come take him and the dirty kitchen, but she never surrendered." He sighed at his failed plan. "I think we should go locate our prisoner."

He stretched and lightly pumped his hand before clasping the doorknob. His palm was sore, but it felt better than it had in a long time. All the tomes from his father's and the best herbs that he could import from China—none had a remedy. Could Isadel, the chef from Badajoz, have one? Could she create one of her father's elixirs to patch him up, too?

"Sir, how did you two past the time whilst I was away?"

They pounded down the hall heading to the kitchen. Hugh braced as he tried to quell his building suspicions for the house was too quiet. "Last night, she proved she doesn't frighten easily. Wasn't cowed in the least by the dirty dishes, but that was hours ago." She couldn't have fled. There was something about her—independent, determined, stubborn—something that should have made her stay.

Phipps bound ahead and ripped open the door as if it were the lid of a treasure chest.

They walk inside. Hugh blinked over and over, but nothing could prepare him for the sight.

A spotless gleaming kitchen stood around him.

Moving to the nearest wall, Phipps touched it. "The dead salmon color has been resurrected. I can see it again without stain or blight."

"Funny, Phipps." But his man was right, and Hugh stood breathing in the fragrant, fresh, clean-smelling air as if all the oxygen had been baptized in citrus and pine.

For a moment, he was transported to years earlier when Sandon teemed with life, the hopes of doting parents for their two sons, one to inherit the lands, the other to serve in the military. Then everything changed, diphtheria, death, a father's mistress, and more deaths. Hugh blinked again and marched to the scullery. "Miss Armijo, are you here?"

After searching the rest of the gleaming kitchen, the spotless table, the polished metal of the spittle, he found the chef curled in a ball near the fire.

"Bannerman, did you help her with this?"

Hugh's shoulders rose of their own volition. "No. I don't know how she did it either."

Phipps looked from side to side, touching this or that and then examined his clean fingers. "Can we keep her?"

"She's not a puppy or the neighbor's sow that wandered onto the property." Hugh bent near her ear. "Miss Armijo, wake up."

Her chestnut brown eyes opened. "What? Where? Oh, Bann-er-man's horrid kitchen." Her formerly slight accent had become thick, a wonderful blend of Jamaican island flair and Spanish notes, at least that's how he heard it in his head.

Her eyes opened wider and she pulled a knife from beneath her. "What is it?"

The blade gleamed like the rest of the kitchen. Rather than batting it away, Hugh raised his arms to seem defenseless. "You came to me from Hartland. Don't you remember?"

She stared at him as if she could read his mind. That wouldn't be good if she could, too much desperation and disbelief stirred in his skull.

"Miss Armijo," Phipps said as he came closer. "We don't mean to harm you. Lord Hartland's not mad at you."

She didn't move or lower her knife. Surely, she remembered everything. She said his name...but she didn't trust him. "You're worse than me, Miss." He put his hand on hers and drove the point of the knife to his neck. "Waving a weapon is useless if you don't intend to use it."

Her fingers slacked until it was just his strength holding up the blade. Her eyes had settled on him, no longer roaming from side to side. "You awaken with a smiling man just about on top of you, you see what you do."

Handing the knife to Phipps, Hugh stood up straight. "Shall we try this again? Morning, Miss Armijo."

"I...I must've fallen asleep." This time, her tone was clipped, normal, almost English sounding.

The change soured him almost stealing the joy he had at beholding her work. He lowered his good hand to her. "Phipps has confirmed your story with Hartland."

She took his hand and arose. The woman was small, but her grip had substance, maybe even strength. She must be marvelous at kneading bread into submission.

"May I return to the Abbey? Or will my employer send me away to prison?"

Hugh put his palms on the table about to hop onto it, but remembered her warning and leaned against it. "Hartland said I am to choose your punishment, and you will return to the Abbey Estate when I say you can. If you want to make it back by Moldona's visit you'll have to be a good prisoner, a very good one."

Her face blanked. Her eyes, perhaps blended pools of chestnut coloring and secrets, lowered. "What must I do?"

He searched her tight countenance, her healthy bronzed skin. How different they were, each from different worlds, his English, hers Spanish, but they shared something in common, distrust.

Did it permeate her innards as much as his? Did she always wait for everyone to prove how weak or fallible they were? "I haven't decided. What, Miss Armijo, do you think your punishment should be?"

Isadel crossed her arms and prepared for Bannerman's latest trick. She couldn't figure him out and that frightened her much more than his breaking things, his hurling her into a closet, or his no good, disgusting kitchen. Noting the stares of each man, she moved a little closer to the older man holding her knife. She'd have better odds taking on his strength than Bannerman's. "I don't know. Maybe it should be measuring out your black powder. I'm good at measuring things."

His glare became crinkles about the eyes. Then he laughed. "You are bold and singular in your thinking. Are you sure Hartland did not try to make you a spy?"

He made jokes and that was better than him ogling her, not that he had. She just had this sense, stronger than yesterday that he wanted something from her. Whatever was in his head, it made her want to find the skillet and prepare for battle. She forced her fingers to unclench. "No."

The butler came near and swiped a finger along the bench. "Everything is clean, even the larder and scullery. Miss Armijo, I see you don't miss a thing."

Yes, she did. That was why her family died. If she'd seen the soldiers coming, she could have made Agueda hide. They wouldn't have seen her loveliness as an invitation. Isadel tried to stop fisting her hands, but anger boiled over inside. "I don't know what will satisfy either of you in terms of punishment, and I don't care to think upon it, not without proper sleep. Show me to a cell or the servants' quarters. Dole out the terms later."

Folding his arms about his big chest, Bannerman laughed again, harder as if he'd held it in for years. "You've done well here, Armijo. Even Phipps agrees, but as I said, cleaning the kitchen was not your punishment."

"It should have been." The older fellow said under his breath as he poked at the stacks of clean dishes.

"Phipps, my man-of-all-work and loose lips, we must think on this very carefully." He tossed the man a look that chilled, before returning his countenance her direction. "Miss Armijo, though I know you are quite capable to navigate poor conditions, I have a place for you. It might need dusting." He waved his hand, motioning as if wanting her to follow as he left the kitchen.

It wasn't like she had a choice, so she pulled her father's jacket closer about her and charged behind the large man.

Her stomach rumbled as they went into the long hall. She pushed at her middle to hold in the noise as she followed him all the way to the tower.

He half bowed and pushed open the door. "You've been in here. I think you liked the view."

"Why are you testing me?"

His countenance sobered. "I don't like surprises. You've proven that I can trust you in the kitchen, but what about here in the tower where you almost jumped?"

"If you are worried, put me elsewhere."

He rubbed his neck. "Say you're not suicidal, then I can let you stay in here. I hear cleaning can take the life from you."

"How would you know about cleaning?"

That sly-smile-not-quite-smirk appeared, and she found her lips curving up too. Oh, she must be tired.

He waved her to the cot. "It's comfortable. When I can't sleep... I find it good for my back. You can see the stars on a clear night, even hear the waves. That is if you last that long."

He wiped a hand over his face as if that could erase the poet's lilt in his voice as he talked of the peace of the turret. "You will be comfortable. It's the best room at Sandon that's not Henry's."

"Then where do you actually sleep?"

"I don't, not so much."

A gasp, maybe some sympathetic air left her lips, but it made him frown. He turned and headed to the door without mention of her punishment or when she'd return to the Abbey.

She rushed to him and clasped his mighty arm. "Wait."

Beneath her fingers, his thick tendons tightened. She drew her fingers away and looked to the ground. She had forgotten her place. A prisoner couldn't touch the lord of the manor.

"Yes, Armijo."

"Sorry. But you were leaving without telling me how long my sentence in the tower would be?"

"Nor have I decided what would be appropriate. I have free rein on this matter from Hartland. I must think upon it carefully."

That wasn't an answer. She had no hope of returning in time to do something to Moldona. She fidgeted with Papa's coat. "You could let my punishment be service in the kitchen."

"Now that it's clean... doesn't seem much like a punishment. But you will make us dinner."

She looked up and caught his gaze, intense,

studying her. She slid her hands into her pockets as if that would hide her from his scrutiny. "Are you forcing me to cook, Bannerman?"

"Do you want to eat?"

Her stomach rumbled louder this time. The traitorous insides. Since Bannerman was giving her freedom in the place she felt most comfortable, she bucked up. "Have fresh vegetables and meats in the kitchen by four, then I will cook."

"I'm glad you volunteered." He lumbered across the threshold. "I thought you'd see it my way. Cooking doesn't suit as your punishment either, but it's a good way to pay for your lodging and board. I'll have some hot water sent up for you. There are stains on your new shirt."

He'd noticed? She nodded as she fingered the greasy spot on the cuff of the shirt he'd given her. "And soap and a rag, too. Keep that kitchen clean, rubble free or no one eats."

He dipped his chin. "Yes, chef." His face held a small smile as he closed the door.

Alone, she pulled off Papa's coat. It too had spots. A hot damp cloth could do wonders upon it to blot out the dirt and who knew what she'd encountered in Bannerman's kitchen. That was hours in her life she'd never get back, but since she'd almost jumped from the window that stood six paces from her, she didn't have a right to complain about time.

Pounding to the glass, she touched the frame. A lock, a large iron rusty thing had been braided through loops keeping it closed. No breeze or smell could come through a locked window. She touched it and felt the cold metal. It hadn't been there before. A chill set in her fingertips. Bannerman did this while she cleaned.

It had been his plan to keep her even before his

man returned and verified her story.

The door opened. She spun to see Phipps entering carrying a bucket and some towels. "Miss —"

Isadel's lips curled into a deeper frown. "Knocking would be good. Even if this is my prison."

"Sorry. It's been a long time since there have been guests." Phipps lowered the bucket and the towels, but in his hand was a small cloth. He walked to her and handed it to her. "Sandon wasn't always so gloomy. There were once many guests. His stepmother, Lady Rhodes, the parties she would thr —"

She balled the cloth in her palm. "Where they treated to iron locks on the windows?"

Phipps frowned and swallowed his smile. "Not that I can remember." He rubbed his neck as he scooted to the door. "Bannerman's very cautious. He wouldn't want you to get in trouble, like before."

"Let him know that I will serve out my sentence whenever he thinks of it. No more need of locks or spies."

"I'll tell him. Thank you for helping Bannerman with his hand. He can be quite stubborn when it comes to things. Stubborn and caution can be self-defeating."

Was he just talking about Bannerman? She could sense the warning was meant for her, too. Yes. She'd been irrational and hurting when Bannerman refused to help, when she thought she'd be hung for stealing a horse. "Let him also know that the desperation in me departed when I chose to keep a man from bleeding to death."

With a nod, Phipps plodded to the door. "I'll knock as long as you are here, Miss Armijo.

Hopefully, your stay will get easier."

The door closed and Isadel's heavy eyes burned a little. Nothing got easier, not without with her family and knowing their killer still possessed freedom. She slid off her coat and started sponging the grease stain on her sleeve. The heated water and scrubbing like she'd done all night made the spot go away.

Why couldn't hurts be the same, a little scrubbing with tears and then all gone? Staring out the locked window, the barrier to the blue morning sky made her sad. Those days were the best ones after a foggy night in Badajoz. The hillsides came alive with wild flowers, and father's laughter as sisters danced in the fresh scented air.

Pulling Papa's coat about her like a blanket, Isadel sank upon the cot. Her heart was too heavy for standing. She wished the wool still smelled of Papa and his elixirs. It felt good to snuggle up against him in one of his bear hugs.

They shouldn't be memories, unavenged memories. Yet, what could she do now as a prisoner to a recluse in a tower of rubble? She'd come to get him to teach her how to make controlled explosions. Maybe he'd let her borrow a cup of black powder like sugar.

Not knowing where he kept such weapons, she lay back half-laughing, half-crying. He put a lock on the window because he did not trust Isadel to sleep in the tower without throwing herself from it. He'd never trust her with black powder. Scooping up some and trying to use it without instruction would be like attempting to make a cake with no recipe.

Not knowing how to control the powder, she'd never risk innocents even if Moldona would die. She wasn't like those evil men who killed everyone in Badajoz even after they'd won the battle and defeated Napoleon's forces.

Resigned, she closed her eyes and returned to continuing her nightmare, a man in regimentals noticed her sister, Agueda. He grabbed her long straight hair and towed her out of hiding. Papa tried to free her, tried to stop them until the ruby men stole his last breath, then took Agueda's too.

From a crack in the flooring, the shine of a sword's blade flashed light into Isadel's eyes, flooding her hiding spot in the root cellar. She heard their clear tones, their increasing laughter as they abused and killed Agueda. She remembered the way one said Moldona and his clear response as they left the slaughter. The family was a few hours away from escape with the aid of an English spy. A couple hours of hiding separated her family from freedom and darkness. If only Agueda hadn't been noticed.

But Bannerman, another proclaimed spy, noticed Isadel. She yanked on her curls, untwisting them about her fingers and stared at the rusty lock on the sill. Perhaps there was a way to sway her prison guard yet. For everything started with a notice and a pretend smile that hid anger.

Chapter Five: Sleeping Suspicions

Ten minutes past four. Bannerman paced at the bottom of the stairs waiting for his chef prisoner. His mind had been turning all day, weighing the possibilities. Could Miss Armijo be the answer to a silent prayer, one he'd been afraid to mouth?

He plodded down the hall all the way to his study and back, stewing. The chef worked for Hartland. She had eavesdropped, spied upon his guests, and stole his horse. Yet, Hart would take her back into his household. The inconsistencies were maddening.

Hugh slow punched a wall with his good hand, cracking the dull bisque plaster. Phipps would be mad when he returned from the village or had he lost count of Hugh's attempt at anger management. He studied his hand, the plaster dust filling the indentions about his knuckle. Nothing covered up the want of hope, the need for a cure-all, the hunger for salvation.

If Wellesley sent Joanna Pearson to save the Armijo family, then the odds where high that her father was owed a debt, that he had used his skills to provide medicine and aid to the King's forces.

"Sir, what are you doing?"

Phipps stood at the foot of the stairs. His hair was combed and smoothed. It looked as if he wore a clean livery.

As he plodded toward the steps, Hugh brushed off his fingers on his tattered green waistcoat, and dangled Henry's gold watch from his pocket before pulling on a kid glove. "Who are you trying to impress?"

With a smile that gave too much away, Phipps dimpled. "No one, but if Lord Hartland's description of Miss Armijo's skills are correct then we are in for a treat."

"Your head is turned by the promise of a meal?"

Brow rising as if he inspected the troops, Phipps circled Hugh then stopped. "Yours must be too. Master Henry's fancy watch and is that a fresh shirt?"

Hugh didn't want to admit it, but it was. Something about the way the chef was concerned about cleanliness made him concerned. "Yes. I suppose we both have expectations."

"Speaking of such, you should send Lady Rhodes a response. Your stepmother still has an expectation to be part of your life. She thinks of you as family."

"Yes, the grown son she never birthed. I am in no mood for needling. And she would if she came to Sandon."

"I think she would look at you as a project and help you restore the place. It could be as it once was."

Never could Sandon be grand and peaceful like it was when Henry Bannerman walked the grounds. Anger at himself for letting Sandon comes to ruins set his hungry gut rolling. "Why are we acting silly over a hoyden who might just be an average cook or taking credit for dishes of another?"

Wanting to force his hands into his pocket, Hugh caught his bandaged hand on Henry's watch and flailed around like a fool until he became free.

Phipps chuckled and then stopped. "Hard to look debonair in bandages. You seem more agitated than usual." He clutched the banner as if to hold up his old legs. "What has happened?"

"Nothing."

"Another death, Bannerman?"

Hugh ran a hand through his own rumpled locks. "I imagine someone, somewhere has but not here, not another commander. Our fugitive chef has not come down. I wonder what could be keeping her. That is all."

"Well, you worked her hard enough to kill her. You don't think she's run off?"

His man talked nonsense, but maybe it wasn't nonsense. Though he'd locked the window, maybe it wasn't a good idea to stash Armijo in the tower, the same room from which she'd tried to jump. Cold sweat beaded at the back of his neck, but he counted it as fever from his illness not fretting. Hugh pumped his hand, open and closed. "She's a young healthy woman. Hard work in the kitchen hasn't done her in. If anything, it's her hatred for Moldona that will injure her."

"What does your old friend have to do with Miss Armijo? She's not one of his mistresses? Oh, his poor wife, Betsy St. Claire. She chose poorly. She should've chosen y—"

Phipps had finally looked up from shining a brass button on his deep blue coat. The shift in his man's expression, a tensed jaw, a line existed where a mouth that had run on too long said everything. "Sorry, Bannerman."

Hugh's famous temper stirred. From the foolish running on to his impatience with the chef, Hugh was only a few fevered words away from exploding. "No, she's not one of Moldona's mistresses, but she has a grievance with him over Badajoz."

"Badajoz, the bloodbath? That was a shameful happenstance."

How much happenstance was there in slaughter? Maybe the same amount of bad luck that led young soldiers to leave a barrel of black powder in the open to combust and kill six hundred at Almeida including Betsy's poor brother. In the midst of the fierce battle, six hundred died from a careless explosion. The anguish in her voice when Hugh spoke with her months later was unfathomable. Could Miss Armijo suffer the same pain with the loss of her family?

Engulfed in questions and remorse, Hugh lowered his gaze to the torn carpet. "Our side won in Badajoz, but the commanders lost control. It was reported that the regiments committed atrocities to civilians including killing Miss Armijo's father and sister."

"Is that true, Bannerman? Poor girl."

"Truth should be an easy thing, but it's twisted by the beholder's self-interest. Miss Armijo believes Moldona is guilty. She came here hoping I'd teach her how to exact her revenge. I refused and now we are waiting for her to cook dinner."

His man's eyes grew so wide it seemed as if they would pop. "That is the height of irony. You refused to help kill a man who has caused you nothing but embarrassment and loss."

If Phipps only knew the depths of the man's

treachery, he'd wonder how Hugh could leave him living. Trying to live differently felt weak to Hugh. How had Henry chosen a peace-filled life in world filled with war? He shook his head. "Moldona is Betsy's husband. For that fact alone, he will remain alive. She's lost too much."

Tapping the railing of the stairs gave Hugh something to focus upon instead of counting the seconds until the chef appeared. "Did Armijo complain of the room?"

"Only of the lock."

"Well, she'll have to prove she hasn't the inclination to jum...jump. Phipps, check out side." Hugh leapt up the first step, then another, until his tree trunk legs moved faster than a flying cannon ball. "The girl was clever and had a head start. Make sure no horse is missing. She is a horse thief."

The sound of his own heavy footfall, half-stomping, half board creaking stirred up more flames in his hungry gut. The wench had made a fool of him, when he'd begun to place hope in her.

He jumped the final set of stairs; happy he hadn't fallen through the weak floors. He marched to the tower door, ripped it open, and then froze.

The chef wasn't gone, but standing half naked before him, just a mere shift separating her from the chilly air. She fell backwards fumbling her way into the shirt that billowed like window curtains.

"What!" Her voice screeched. "Can't you knock?"

He pivoted as best a gentleman could but being all man, one made for reconnaissance, an iron map painted in his head. A mental image of her loveliness, the generous curves the thin cotton couldn't obscure would stay with him longer than it should. "Sorry."

How he or Phipps thought the chef was a man

was ludicrous. Madness really.

"You are still in here, Bannerman. I'm not dressed. This is not proper."

She was right. But that didn't make him move.

"Go on!"

With a few blinks, his proper brain returned and he dragged himself out of the door. He closed it and put his whole weight upon the battered wood frame. "I didn't mean...I thought..." He wiped at his face marveling at the perspiration beading his now flooded brow.

Hugh wasn't a schoolboy and hadn't always lived the life of a monk as he did now. And he definitely wasn't the novice who became flustered because Betsy walked beside him. He cleared his throat. "You're late for dinner. The kitchen remains as you prescribed."

"You saw nothing?" Her voice vibrated through the wood panel, stroking the base of his skull.

Hugh saw too much and would remember or imagine more. "I'll knock as long as you stay here. I apologize."

The sounds of her moving about, pulling on boots echoed. "Why were you in such a rush? Are you that hungry?"

He didn't want to seem a fool, but acting like one did not help. He closed his eyes and just blurted out the truth. "I thought you had left. My anger doesn't let me think sometimes."

"Mine does. It makes my brainbox focus constantly on revenge. I have no rest from these thoughts."

He laid his head fully against the door. No one alive understood how it felt to be trapped in anger or regret. Only his brother did and Hugh's showing off to impress Betsy with his controlled detonations took Henry away. "Some anger just isn't meant to leave. I'd like to say time makes things better, but it doesn't. It just makes you older with more responsibilities and more things to lose."

"Then, it is good that I am young with nothing to keep me from wanting Moldona dead."

Her tone was so flat; it made him wonder to what lengths would she go to watch Moldona die.

The door opened and Hugh fell backward. He caught the frame and stayed upright. Popping up and pivoting, he stared at her.

Her hair was up in a bun and the baggy jacket and breeches swallowed her whole as before. Somehow that didn't seem fair. "Well, chef," he said, "the kitchen is waiting for you. I'd like to understand for myself how great your talents are. Hartland is willing to take you back after betraying his confidence."

"I guess you'll have to taste and see what is good."

Before he followed, Hugh watched her float down the stairs engulfed in course fabric. Sharp-tongue, direct, and yet demure, the chef wasn't like Betsy or the memories of her. With the image of the young woman's dark curly locks dripping to her waist, shadowing her shift, sticking like perfume, Hugh had that sinking feeling he'd unleashed some new type of explosive. He paced to catch Isadel as fast as he could.

Isadel stirred the pot watching the gravy of the beef steaks come together. Wishing and humming, Mama's song allowed the onions to develop the perfect translucent glow and kept her head from exploding. The tune of flying to heaven and finding the grace of the day, that had to calm her blood and keep Isadel from dying from embarrassment when she faced Bannerman again.

Wishing she was Agueda who knew no shame, Isadel beat her spoon again in the thickening sauce. The savory goodness would contrast the richness of the buttery crusts of her meaty pies. She pushed up her sleeve and pivoted to the big plank topped table. She'd already set two places, one for Phipps and one for Bannerman. In a small cast iron dish, she'd take a few morsels back to the tower to eat and hide.

Looking down from her woolgathering, she saw a lump beginning to form. She hummed and stirred, tipping her pan over the flame until she made the liquid shimmer satin. Bannerman and her beet-red cheeks would not defeat her gravy. Here she was thinking she could gain Bannerman's sympathy and soften him up as Agueda did with all men, but now she couldn't even look at the hulking man.

Though he hadn't done or said anything untoward, the thought of being ogled like a beef steak for a hungry man left her feeling small and used up. She'd forever hide in Papa's jacket just to feel big. Yes, big enough to serve justice.

Footsteps sounded outside the kitchen door. The rhythm of the footfalls was impatient. "Chef, how long will you keep me and Phipps waiting?"

She wanted to yell out to Bannerman that she did hurry, but all she could do was hum. It was that or run back to the tower and burn her gravy.

Finally, it was ready. Taking great care, she poured the gravy into the thick porcelain gravy bowl. After setting it on the table, she lifted the pies that she'd left to warm on the hearth, ten in all, and put one on each plate. The rest she pushed onto a Wedgewood platter. With a final tweak, she positioned a water glass in front of the bone white plate. Having cleaned and put away every dish, she found it easy to set the makeshift table for the two men. For a moment, pride filled her lungs. Bannerman and his manservant would eat well tonight.

Feeling satisfied at her presentation of the meaty treat, she clanged a spoon on her pot. "Dinner is served."

The words hadn't fully left her lips when the door slammed open and the two men barreled into the kitchen, almost shoving each other in haste. Phipps jumped to a spot and liberally poured browned gravy over his pie, but Bannerman stood to the side.

He leaned over the table and tapped his fingers. "Why are we eating in the kitchen, chef?"

"Oh, you have a dining room? I must've missed it in the filth. Be assured food is much better and safer in a room that is not set for collapse."

His smile thinned as if he gritted his teeth. "This manor is very durable, I assure you. But perhaps you are right, we should see about fixing it up a little."

Phipps's fork fell to his plate with a heavy bang. "What? Yes, let's fix the place up."

Forcing her tone to lower and sweeten, she focused on her pot of gravy, not on Bannerman whose gaze had her cheeks burning. "Eat up. Put your dirty dishes in the scullery when you are done. Good evening."

"You are not joining us? Aren't you hungry?"

"Kitchen staff doesn't dine with the master. I'll be in the tower."

He kicked the bench out blocking her path. "I

insist."

She looked down, focusing on the scratched-up wood. "I'd rather not."

"You are my guest and my prisoner for now. Both categories supersede kitchen help."

"This is not normal." She'd rolled up her sleeves again to show him her Blackamoor forearms, but he'd already received an eyeful upstairs. "I've worked with the Abbey's large staff. I know my place."

"Are you more comfortable living in a place of low expectations?"

She stepped around the bench and picked up her dish. "It's better to be underestimated, safer that way."

"Living confined will make you look to breaking free. You'll do crazed things like steal a horse and ride hours to see a cursed man."

"It... It wasn't prudent. Gentlemen, excuse me."

"Do you seriously think you can kill a man? You can't even hold my gaze. You're a—"

"Woman?" she asked no longer able resist his baiting. "The weaker sex? 'Twas Eve that cost Adam a rib and mortality. Who's the weaker one, the giver of the apple or the one who eats?"

Phipps stuffed more pie in his mouth. "Could you make apple pie, too? I could get apples."

Bannerman grabbed her elbow. "Look, I insist you stay and eat with us. All your meals will be in our company. That is part of your punishment. It will also tell me you haven't poisoned me and Phipps."

His man raised his head so fast Isadel thought for sure he had left his teeth in the pie. "Well, here is to a delicious last meal." He dipped the last bits of his crust into the gravy and kept eating.

"Will you aid my digestion and my suspicions and eat with us?"

She jerked her arm free. "A more fitting punishment, Mr. Bannerman, would be to clean the dining room. It could be done within a day or two and then return me to Abbey Estate. Phipps, your master is standing in the way of setting a fair punishment. Why do you think that is?"

The butler wiped his mouth of crumbs. "Maybe a bit of sense has finally hit him."

"I'm right here you know. You don't have to speak of me as if I'm absent."

"Why are you stringing my punishment? I'm not a kite." She put her pot down, and forced her fingers not to clutch her jacket. "Tell me what it is that you want, so I can do it, then leave for the Abbey."

"Bannerman," Phipps said, "The Abbey sounds like a sanctified request, so be careful how you respond."

The huge man cast a look that silenced Phipps's chuckles. "As part of your punishment, you will tell me your father's recipe for skin conditions. You said he had one. Give it to me and if I think of nothing else and you happen to cause me no more worry, I'll send you back in time to face Moldona."

Phipps squinted as he shook his head, but his mouth was full, maybe too full to respond.

Isadel tried to block the man-of-all-work's antics and focus on Bannerman and his offer. "You go from fretting about me poisoning pies to trying to purloin my papa's potion. Incredible."

The big man smirked a little. "You have a way of phrasing things, Miss Armijo, but that doesn't answer my question."

"You believe me now that I could know it. Even

though my papa was trusted by your Wellesley, you must be at a loss to believe a woman...a weak woman."

"Hartland says your father was a great physician. I am inclined to believe him."

"Because of another man, your light eyes have been opened. I thought they worked well earlier in the tower even without any intervention." She covered her mouth and fled toward the closest hiding place, the scullery, and closed the door.

"Go after her, Bannerman. An upset chef might stop cooking." Phipps's voice was loud, but so where the boot footfalls that followed.

The ground shook as a pounding sensation rattled the door. "Open up, Miss Armijo."

"I've thrown myself in here, Bannerman. Nothing left for you to do." She stood back and watched the door shake.

The hinges and panels lifted and he set the poor broken frame down with a thud. "I didn't feel like shouting through the door," Bannerman said. He stepped closer, crossing the pebbled floor of the scullery. "Now, can we try this again in a civilized manner?"

"Civilized? You just ripped off the door, you big lion." Wanting to hide in Papa's coat, she folded her arms about her shoulders as tightly as she could. Why can't I go?"

"Miss Armijo, I have requested you eat with us. It's a simple order. You can return to your room afterward."

"I mean back to the Abbey." Lowering her tone, she started again. "I have to work twice as hard to be deemed acceptable. I can handle that at the Abbey. I don't want to do that here with you looking at me as if I were still half-naked."

"I told you I was wrong for not knocking, and I saw nothing I hadn't seen before."

She dropped her head. "How can I ever hold your gaze?"

With his gloved hand, he lifted her chin, the motion soft and gentle. "You were mostly covered up except for some mighty strong arms. Yes, you do have to prove yourself. Hartland is a trusted friend and he vouches for you, but I must still get to know you. Miss Armijo, you know what it means to trust, do you not? And I must prove myself to you too. You're not alone in this. We are both trying to find our way."

So close to him, she sensed his power and the strength of his desperation. A man so big surely couldn't voice it, but his gaze said the words, please help me. No power on earth could make her pivot from his wide hazel eyes. "I know what trust costs." Taking a step back, she scooted her palms up Papa's billowy sleeve wanting it to be a shield to Bannerman's sweet talk. Nothing plied her heart more than his sad eyes. "Is there no other way to punish me other than to take the secrets of a dead man? If Moldona hadn't killed him, Papa would be here helping you."

Bannerman crowded her again. "I want to trust his daughter, Isadel Armijo, who diced me up with onions to cleanse a wound as her father would. You could've left me bleeding or fixed it so my wound would fester." He ripped up his sleeve and showed the scarring on his arm. "I could expose more damaged flesh to you if you want see a similar amount of exposure." He jiggled the thick leather belt at his waist. "It would be no problem."

"Stop. This is a scullery." She slapped at his hands, knocking them from his buckle. "Unless I am washing you off with lye to be stowed away, don't."

His smirk was pure evil. "You're looking at me again and you touched me. At least my being ridiculous can give you some comfort."

"You're too big to ignore."

"Miss Armijo, you know what I have. The leprosy is killing me. I deserve to die, but no good can come from me for my last days if I'm covered in sores, with paper thin skin."

It wasn't fair to barter with a man's life not remembering Papa's voice, whispering, haga lo que es correcto, a toda costa, paloma mía, do what is right, at all costs, my dove. She nodded her head. "Retrieve aloe stalks and Gynocardia seeds."

He rubbed his skull as if she said a joke. "Not Gynocardia seeds." His big chest deflated as if it had sprung a heavy leak. "One of my books talks of Gynocardia seeds. The East India traders call it, Chaulmoogra. It does not work. Your father was wrong."

Unafraid and angered, she shook her head. He'd basically called Papa a liar. She closed the gap between them and poked through his waistcoat drumming a big solid rib bone. "Your book is wrong. You English believe you are always right, that you can do no wrong. We both know that is untrue."

"I have tried those seeds. It does not work, Armijo. It is possible for a self-righteous chef to be wrong."

"Your people have labeled the wrong tree as *Chaulmoogra*. Ask the traders to bring you the true seeds of the *Kalaw tree*. Those seeds and those alone, have the oil I need to save you, but don't believe me. Keep to your books, your chaulmoogra, your English ways, and return me to the abbey. I'm going to the tower."

She tried to pass him, but Bannerman clasped her hand and drove it deeper into his chest. His heart pounded beneath her finger tips making hers race.

He dipped his chin and stole her gaze again. "When you want to kill a man, you go for his heart. A quick sharp jab with your knife will do it. Don't hesitate or delay with lies. I need no more false hope."

"I'm not lying. And why would I waste a good knife cutting through all that muscle?"

Deep-set crinkles appeared around his eyes that had lost their seriousness. He tucked her hand on the crook of his arm. "It's time for dinner, that is if Phipps has left some. I here it is very good."

When they arrived at the table, several pies remained.

"Phipps, get word to our London merchants. Have them import the Kalaw seeds as soon as possible. Tell them I'll pay double upon confirmation that these are the Kalaw and not Gynocardia or Chaulmoogra seeds."

When he sat, she shoved her hands in her pocket so he couldn't take it again and she wouldn't crave his power. He had the strength to right wrongs or even to admit them. He didn't have to come to her.

"Sit, chef, and get used to us. You will have to verify the seeds. You have to be our guest for a few weeks."

Clasping an inner seam in the wool jacket, she peered up at the ceiling. "Not as if I have a choice."

"No, you don't. You will have to make due with our arrangements at Sandon, which includes eating with Phipps and me. And the way Phipps is devouring your pies, you can be well trusted in the kitchen. You are no typical prisoner. You have the run of Sandon, for what it's worth."

"Am I free like the wind? No. There is a brass lock on my sill."

"That is for our mutual protection, you from jumping. Me from barging in thinking you leaped. If I had remembered and not thought you too clever, I would not have barged in upon you."

She couldn't complain of his logic though she wanted to. "I should count my circumstances lucky."

Phipps coughed as if he were interrupting something. "I think we're lucky. This food is magical. Bannerman, eat."

Her warden reached and grabbed one of the pastries from his plate and popped it into his mouth.

She wasn't exactly holding her breath, but she exhaled when a smile exploded on his face. No one could beat her pastry crusts.

"Very good, Miss Armijo," he said when his face recovered. "I should've known. Hartland is exact. You are a wonder."

"Thank you." Hoping his contentment would cause amnesia, she picked up her bucket and aimed for the door.

"I don't want to force you, Armijo, but if you voluntarily comply, I'll show you some things about black powder during your stay. It won't be enough to give your murderous dreams hope, but it should show you that I'm trying to trust you."

The breath caught in her lungs. She stopped and stared at him. She saw no tricks or pity in his hazel eyes. "You are serious?"

"But, Bannerman," Phipps said between bites.

"You said you'd never touch the stuff again."

"I will show her the basics. Miss Armijo, I want you to understand the danger and power of the powder. You need to understand both. Now, sit and eat." He waved his hand toward the skewed bench. "Compliance may help me arrive upon the final tasks to complete your punishment sooner, give or take the timing to identify the seeds. Who knows? It may simply be eating with two men who may have forgotten table manners." He chuckled and pulled another pie to his plate. "Sit, Armijo. Taste. Your handiwork is good, very good."

His voice had a lilt that bordered on charming. That notion seemed a little frightening, but she'd acquiesce for a chance at learning how to use black powder. She pivoted and crossed back to the table. When she sat on the bench he'd kicked out, he hooked the edge with his foot, lifted it and her, setting the bench back in line with the table.

Though Phipps had almost cleaned his plate save a few crumbs, he bowed his head and said. "Let this food, this unexpected blessing be nourishing to our hungry hearts."

Bannerman looked at her and she at him.

She didn't understand this gaze, nor did she want to and demurred, turning toward her pie. She piled bits of the flaky crust upon her tongue. It was good, but nothing nourished her soul more than the hope that she was one step closer to avenging Papa and Agueda. By time the seeds arrived, perhaps she'd cobble together enough information about black powder to develop a recipe, one set to deliver a controlled explosion, one to kill Moldona.

Chapter Six: Restless Delights

For the old Hugh, a good meal was a necessary component to relax and get a full night's sleep. Then, he'd become ill. The research called for a bland diet of white foods to calm his system. That regimen stole his strength. Luckily, he had a great deal to spare. He rolled to his side, fluffed his pillow and thought about meat pies.

The wonderful taste of the chef's food stayed on his tongue. The lightness of the crust, the savory shredded beef, the tang of garlic and onions, yes, her medicinal onions were true delights. He could see why Hart would take her back despite her treachery.

If he were Hart, he would too. Maybe her food could be some continued ransom between him and his friend. Hugh closed his eyes. He tried finding a more comfortable spot on the mattress, breathing more deeply, counting seconds for imaginary detonations, even reading one of Henry's missionary tomes. ...Nothing. The excitement and questions about Kalaw seeds made his mind race. Had he been blessed enough to stumble on a cure, one coming from a part homicidal, part suicidal, part healer chef?

Well, if the healer part was the most dominant, then the Lord did work in mysterious ways as Henry claimed. Hugh sighed and stared at the ceiling. Who was Isadel Armijo truly? Could he fully trust her?

Armijo's father had gained favor with Wellesley. That was true. Mr. Armijo may have been a physician, but he may not have known how to cure leprosy. None of the physicians in London had. Why would Spain, a little place like Badajoz be different?

But a girl from Badajoz, one who felt the need to avenge deaths. Her claim that Moldona killed her family—that could not be correct. He was a lout, a womanizer, but not a murderer. Right?

If Hugh hadn't failed to turn in Moldona for leaving out the powder barrel, the one that caused the deadly explosion, he would never have been left in the military to cause havoc in Badajoz.

None of this would matter if Miss Armijo were mistaken. She sounded certain but errors happen, memories shift. Certainty. That was a luxury, one he desperately wanted right now. He'd hate to think Betsy was married to a monster or that he had indirectly caused another innocent death. "What am I going to do, Henry? I miss your council, your voice of wisdom."

The quiet of the room, his brother's old room, smothered. He pushed up, wanting the smell of Henry's cigars. Hugh couldn't stay here. The place he fled on nights like this, the tower room was occupied. The chef was there.

Somewhere else in Sandon had to have peace, a place to hide from his mounting guilt. He tossed on his robe and put his bare feet on the pristine planks of the floor. Henry's old room was the master quarters, complete with a Mrs. Bannerman or mistress chamber. Their father had made good use of it stowing Elizabeth there. She stayed in it until he and Henry were courting age as she put it. Elizabeth would hate how every other room of Sandon had been scarred by Hugh's temper.

Lumbering in the dark, he plodded to the window. The abrasions to his ankles had healed up nicely. One benefit to his poor diet. Losing a little weight made his clothes hang about him, stopping the chaffing that led to lesions.

He pulled at the curtains and let the moon shine bright upon the thick forest below. The trees had grown so thick he could see the crypt where generations of Bannerman's lay. Hugh didn't want to be put there. He wanted to be buried aside his brother in the fields. The guilt of Henry's passing, or the hundreds Hugh had killed doing his job, that's what Hugh thought would be the death of him, not leprosy.

His gut hungered but not for food. He wanted to stand and look at eternity from the tower. Did Miss Armijo enjoy the view? She couldn't feel the cold breeze anymore, not since he'd put a lock on the window. It felt wrong to deprive her, but so did awaking and finding her on that sill again.

Maybe something in his study could entertain him. Easing on his slippers, he started out of his room. In the dark, he managed his way, moving down the dark hall as if he were on a mission to retrieve documents. His fingertips touched dips and holes along what was once a wall dressed in beige colored paint and heavy white trim. Even though he couldn't see the destruction, only touching the holes through a leather glove, what he'd done hit him in the gut. As the leprosy progressed, he'd lose the ability to sense anything with his fingers and that frightened him more than the lesions.

Focusing his eyes, he picked up his pace and made it down the treads. As he spun toward the study, a glint of light caught his gaze. It came from the kitchen, a place that should be vacant given that Phipps and Armijo had retired already. Someone was in his house.

Fury fired inside and scorched up his innards. The Almeida Killer had come to him, invading his hiding place. If the killer expected an invalid to greet him, the fool had guessed wrong, dead wrong.

He balled his good fist and moved toward the light. Creeping to the kitchen proved daunting as the floorboards creaked beneath his shifting weight. He stopped and stole a quick breath. Who needed the element of surprise when you had power, unbelievable strength on your side? That hadn't been taken from Hugh, not yet.

He opened the door, pushed inside but found his face greeted by cold hard Wedgwood.

The dish smashed against his cheek. Shards dropped everywhere, but nothing could deter his momentum. He spun and caught a wrist, a tiny wrist.

It wasn't the Almeida Killer. Well, most likely not that killer, but a frightened chef.

Her small tanned faced had paled. She supported the fragments of the former dish in her palms.

He released her but stayed close, towering over the woman. "Miss Armijo?"

"I thought you were a robber. Vandals hold up in broken places like this."

He took a piece of porcelain from his robe's lapel.

"Well, I guess I should be pleased that you are trying to defend the place."

She moved from him, dropped to her knees, and scooped up the broken bits in a sheet that she'd spun about her waist like an apron. "Well, this is done for. I suppose effort doesn't make up for results."

The bits were shiny blue against the tar black floor.

He knelt too to help, but she closed her hand about his. "No. The pieces are too sharp. I don't want you to get another cut. I hurt you enough with the Wedgwood."

It startled him that she'd tell him no and that she'd touch him without fear. Her voice sounded stern as if he were a naughty lad. He caught her unsmiling gaze and heeded, but he didn't move and watched her collect the pieces. "You don't frighten easily."

"I frighten," she said, but kept her head down toward the scatter of the broken platter. "But, I haven't the luxury of fear. No one's coming to save me. I've learned to save myself."

Her words sliced him to his core. He knew that sentiment. Without Henry, he had to learn to save himself too. But as a man, it had to be different than what the chef meant. "You're bold enough to look me in the eye now. You didn't do too much of that during the rest of dinner."

"Thought we already discussed you having an eyeful and you offering me one."

Chuckling, Hugh pulled to his feet and glanced about the kitchen. It had transformed again from a sea of cleanliness to a bakeshop. A good dusting of flour snowed the dark table along with mounds of dough and cut out flat disks. "Biscuits, Miss

Armijo?"

She'd finished cleaning and began lowering the shards into a wastebasket. She didn't answer or wasn't paying attention to him as she moved to her wash water. After dunking her hands in the soapy bucket, she dried them then moved to the other side of the table.

"I asked if you are making biscuits?"

Her graceful fingers were pulling and pushing on the dough. "You can't live on meat pies alone."

"So many?"

"Your Phipps has a large appetite. You'd do better with more food, too."

"Very generous of you. You are very generous with food, not much with conversation. Were you this reticent at the abbey?"

Her hands stopped moving. She lifted her chin, maybe for the first time sense breaking the platter against his head. "I couldn't sleep. So, there will be plenty of biscuits."

Her eyes were large, swirls of honey and chestnuts and sadness. She lowered her chin and began to work again.

He was used to people telling him everything, even things he didn't want to hear — his stepmother's expectations, Betsy's inexplicable grief, or even Phipps saying none of these losses were Hugh's fault. The absence of complaints disoriented him. "I know I am large and some say given to tempers. Is that what keeps you from looking at me?"

Still refusing to look up, she punched at the dough.

"I asked a question, Miss Armijo."

She punched the dough very quickly, and it seemed to whimper. "Why does it matter? I'm a servant and a prisoner. Your only concern should be that the food is good."

Why did it matter? Male pride, perhaps. Her station hardly allowed for conversation. How many times had he been to Abbey Estate eating her food, not knowing she existed? He leaned over to take a hit to the dough but she blocked him. "If you help, you wash, then take the napkin and brush each biscuit with the beaten egg. It will help it brown, like me."

He did as she instructed and scrubbed the leather clean then returned. "That's what it takes to get a nice golden color? I like wonderfully healthy-colored biscuits."

The frown pressing her full lips rose to a line. Not quite a smile but far better than before. "You might want to use light airy, dancing gloves if you feel you must cover your hands. They can be laundered more frequently."

He wanted to say he did before he stopped caring. Instead, he began liberally wiping the biscuit tops with the bit of cloth she had used. "So why can't you sleep?"

The frown returned. "It only matters if you are going to help. Otherwise, it's just another sad tale. You don't need to hear it, if you can't sleep either."

"Isadel Armijo, who are you? I believe you are more than the angry pastry chef who stole a horse and wants to blow Moldona to bits. Is there no middle ground? If I don't know your story, how am I to decide if the man is guilty?"

She stopped attacking the dough and looked at him for a minute. He must look a sight with his burgundy robe dusted in flour.

"I can't help you with that." She turned to the stove and stirred a boiling pot. The heady scent of sugary apple and lemon filled the air. She stirred and hummed. The spoon moved in time with the notes.

At first, he thought she was being childish, ignoring him, but the count was too specific to the rhythm. Her music, it resonated in his soul. "What is that tune?"

She looked at him with a puzzled expression frowning her lips. "Something my mother used to sing. It helps with the whipping. I don't want the jam to overcook. You'll need something to go with the biscuits."

"Your mother was Negro?" It was an assumption on his part, but he wanted her to talk more, to trust him with a bit more of herself. It was a spy's job to build rapport. "Based on the name Armijo, I concluded your father to be Spanish."

"My father, he spent time abroad in the colony of Jamaica, helping with sugar plantations. One of the masters, who'd enslaved my mother, became ill with a disease. My mother's people came from Nigeria. The Kalaw tree is there. The oil of the nuts is cleansing. She told my father, and he got some of those seeds and healed the plantation owner right up."

"So how did you come into being?"

Her gaze seemed far away for a moment.

"The owner gave my mother to him as a present. They sailed back to Spain and he married her. Papa always said he loved a woman who could cook and one with a brain for herbs. He didn't realize his prescription was a recipe. Or did he?"

With a shake of her head, her frown returned, and she stirred the pot again.

"Did Moldona kill her too?"

"No. A fever. The fever did her in a couple of

years ago. She went quickly. I think that is preferred."

Her tone flattened and Hugh almost wished he hadn't asked and that she still hummed her tune. But it wasn't his way to leave things alone. He started wiping the egg mix again but there wasn't enough. "What's the recipe for this wash? Tell me, I'll make more."

"Three tablespoons of cow's milk for each egg yolk. Make three portions, if you can be precise or wait for me to do it."

"Precision is my forte." He took warm eggs from a basket, cracked them, and glopped the yolks and the yolks alone in a bowl. With the same precision he measured black powder, he measured three level tablespoons for each of the three eggs.

When he looked up, she nodded with something that seemed like approval lighting her eyes. Maybe she liked his precision. It was something he was good at. Her short smile made his chest feel full. Feeling as if he'd found his footing with her, he dared to break it and asked, "Tell me what Moldona did to your father?"

The spoon in her hand clanged the side of the pot. "The fiend killed my father and my sister, everyone I had left in this world."

"What did he do specifically?"

She took a long breath. "Slit their throats with his sword, but not before humbling my sister and passing her to his men."

"Why weren't you harmed?"

"I hid in the root cellar, like Papa said. But Agueda, she wouldn't. She couldn't stand being in tight places. She was such a free spirit, then she was noticed by the soldiers." Armijo dropped the spoon and it rattled like a broken top. "Why didn't she listen? Why did she have to be noticed? They make assumptions about girls like us as if we're formed of an illicit union not of a proper marriage. She was no harlot, no man's mistress. Just carefree, flirtatious."

Hugh came near, picked up the spoon. He forced it into her fingers and clasped his good hand about hers. "What was that tune you hummed? We've worked hard on these biscuits. I think I like your idea of a tasty jam to go with them."

She didn't withdraw, but she didn't sing either. "Do you know what it sounds like to hear the begging, the hurting, then nothing? I should've come out of the dark. Maybe I could've done something. I am so guilty."

"Miss Armijo, if you had you would've been killed. Your papa wouldn't have wanted that."

She pushed away and stood out of his reach. "How do you know what he wanted? You didn't even believe he existed."

"You come to me wanting to kill one of the men I grew up with, one who served with me in combat. He married my dearest friend."

Back at the table, she cut circles out of the remaining lump of dough. "I heard his name. I heard their clear banter, their glee at hurting Agueda. Moldona can be all those things you said, Bannerman, friend, husband, and Agueda's and Papa's murderer."

While he never thought much of Moldona, he never thought him to be so brutal, but he knew in his gut, that Miss Armijo did not lie. She truly believed him guilty. He wrenched at his neck. "You are working too hard. You've made enough biscuits for an army. You should go to bed."

With a shake of her head she pulled the jam pot off the flame, humming, half ignoring him as she walked to the table. Soon, she was elbow deep in dough and formed the last biscuits.

"Miss Armijo, you should retire. I insist. Phipps will think I am too hard on you."

"I'll tell him you are not too cruel. I don't sleep much. It's not your problem. Once you allow me to return to the Abbey, I will no longer be your concern."

"It does matters."

"Why?"

A good spy would've seen that question coming. Hugh wasn't a good spy any more. He twisted the belt in his robe. "You have a right to your anger and your want of revenge, but black powder doesn't discriminate. It will kill the innocent along with the guilty. The master, his servants, and his enslaved—all die the same death when the powder explodes. You must know that and respect it."

Those pretty eyes bloomed. "You will teach me how to control it? The seeds have not come. I haven't proven I can cure you."

"I'm going to teach you to respect it, for the rest we will see. Without respect, there is no moving forward. I will trust that you have told me the truth and you will have to trust that I understand the injury to your family. I am simply not convinced that your fiend is Moldona."

"Trust is very hard. Other than Phipps and Lord Hartland, do you trust?"

With slow steps, he wandered back to the other side of the table. "I let you put onions on me." He tapped the floured dusted surface. "Big men don't just let anyone do that. I'm trying to trust you more. What about you?"

"Well as you said, I guess we'll have to see, but thank you for the lock on my window. I loathed the breeze."

He couldn't help but chuckle. "You are witty, but I know how things were in that tower. You might've jumped. Then, I didn't want you to. Now, I know I don't want you to die."

"Isn't that the same thing?"

"No. One is a courtesy. The other is strong feeling for what is right."

She turned her face up to him. Her eyes weren't distant. They seemed to center on him, and he wished he wasn't on the other side of the table. He cleared his throat of the sugary lemony scent that could have easily been a perfume for Armijo, sweet and tart. "I need something from you, chef."

Her fingers flew to the revers of her jacket. "What? What do you want?"

"Saying Armijo, calling you like I would a man doesn't quite work."

"It's my name, a very proud name, my father's name."

"I'd like to call you Isadel, when it's just the two of us."

"This is your house. I am your prisoner. Call me what you like, Bannerman."

"I want your agreement, and when you say my name in return, I want it with your full accent, none of this pretending to sound English."

For a moment, she smiled and released the fabric she'd clutched. "You missed that biscuit. You must coat it well, Bann-er-man. Or it won't set up right."

It was music as he imagined it would be, very much like her humming. And he wanted her to say his name again.

For the next couple of minutes, Isadel kneaded and cut out more biscuits. Maybe it was sleep deprivation, but nothing seemed more interesting than watching her work the dough. Her fingers moved to her special rhythm. The tune would haunt him until he knew it.

She piled the latest biscuits into a stone container and covered it. With a shove, she pushed it into the hearth then pivoted and pulled a jar from a pot of water. "Ouch. This is still a little warm. I made you some cream, a little balm of lavender. Use this on your dry skin. This is not the seeds, but it will make you feel better."

The giddy hope made him reach over the table like a child in want of a present. He lowered his palms. It had to be the biscuits and the sweet fragrant food making him giddy.

Setting the jar on the table's edge, she slid it to him. "I created this to keep my skin from drying out. My work in the kitchen can be very taxing as much as I wash my hands."

It surely was a present. "Thank you, Isadel."

Her lashes, long dark wisps fluttered as she looked down. "So, what is your tale? Why have you put yourself in exile?"

Honesty could be a terrible thing, for one confession typically led to another. Weighing the should he's versus the should nots, he couldn't decide and defaulted to the truth. "Well, that temper I possess made it dangerous for others to be around me. My condition ensures that I am a danger or a disappointment to those I hold dear. I'd wish this on no one. Leprosy is lethal."

"What you have is not lethal. It can be treated. You can be saved."

"Says you, Physician Isadel. I've tried arsenic paste, corn pomades, and none have helped."

"None of those foolish things. Papa would tell you so." She sniffed and pivoted to her biscuits and pulled them from the hearth. They were deeply brown, not quite walnut. "You distracted me. This next batch will have to be perfect."

"I'm distracting? I have your full attention?"

Rolling her eyes, she put the next stack on the stone covered dish into the hearth. Then poked a few of the darkest ones. "I'll need to rotate the Dutch oven midway."

Wiping her hands on her makeshift apron, she gazed up at him. "Exile does not explain this. The ruined house, the thick ruddy beard. At the Abbey, you were neat as a pin, handsome and well groomed."

"Wait. You thought I was handsome?"

She lowered her head and seemed to smack the last bit of dough harder. "Oh, you know what I mean. Go to bed before you get hit again."

He finished mopping the last bit of rounds with egg mixture. "Not being able to change things. It can put you on a path of isolation. I think you know that road. If I could end it, stop the lesions, be whole again, then maybe I'd want things to be different."

With her small thin fingers, she pulled the tray to her side of the massive walnut table. "We'll give you a fresh bandage in the morning." She poked at the biscuits he'd slathered. "Good job."

"Week's end, you'll have your first lesson on black powder."

She lifted her face to him. The sight he beheld, a full broad smile, not half, a whole one, big and toothy, warmed him through. Then, she seemed to wince and it stole his joy. "But the seeds won't be here yet."

"They will in due time." He reached over to the almost burnt biscuits and scooped one and pressed it to his lips. "Hmm. It's a little tough on the outside, but it's also textured and buttery." He licked at the crumbs from his fingertips, "Yet, so tender and sweet on the inside. I wonder if the baker is like her art."

Her bronzed cheeks became darker. A blush? He hadn't made a girl do that in a while. "You're sleep deprived to think ruined biscuits fine. And no one has ever called me sweet."

"I don't think you've given anyone a chance to know. I like being your chef's assistant, Isadel. Don't stay up too late."

"Good night, Bann-er-man."

He dipped his chin to the woman and pushed through the door. With her jar of cream weighing in his robe pocket, all concern that she might be in league with the Almeida Killer left. Isadel wasn't trying to kill him, unless buttery biscuits and a balm were some new form of torture.

Isadel wasn't trying to ingratiate herself upon him. She was being herself, her slightly murderous, slightly caring self. He marched up the stairs intending to go back to bed, but stopped at the tower room. With his gloved palm, he crushed the lock, opening the metal loop and leaving it dangling for Isadel to find. A breeze was his gift to her for giving him peace this evening.

Still sampling buttery crumbs, he wondered if biscuits and black powder tasted as well together. He'd figure it out soon enough and then he'd have to figure out a way to convince Isadel to give up her vengeance. In his gut, he knew that would be as difficult as finding out the identity of the Almeida Killer.

*Chapter Seven: Raising of Sandon
Manor*

Isadel dressed quickly as she had all week.
Arising before the men gave her a head start on the
day and made her feel as if she had control of the
kitchen. That was something. Bannerman had yet
to say what her final punishment would be.

When she tossed on her jacket and buttoned it,
allowing the fabric to swallow her whole, the glint
of the broken lock caught her gaze. She moved to
the large window and unhooked it. She pressed on
the pane and it opened.

The air rushed in, followed by the call of a gull
perhaps heading to the sea, to freedom. The
haunting call of the clouds stirred inside her, but
not as much as it had before. She guessed surprise
did that. The cold metal of the lock felt good, almost
as good as the breeze.

When had this been done?

Had she gone day after day like a caged animal,
not knowing she could simply press on the glass
and be free? Bannerman must have done it when

she wasn't in the room. Why would he do this? Was it a sign of something? Clasping her fingers about the brokenness of what had been the lock, she took another deep breath of the fresh air.

He'd noticed her and now was being nice to her. Did that mean something? How would being noticed by an Englishman change her world?

Too much fiddling and second-guessing. Figuring out men was terrible—there was no recipe for them.

She stuffed the lock in her pocket and turned toward the door. Breakfast needed to be started. That was an easy thing to think upon.

When she stepped out of the tower room, a scent she hadn't smelled except in her kitchen greeted her. Pine soap. It made her nose twitch. She took a second and then a third breath of the clean air, but then her eyes popped wide as she saw grooms, hordes of men she hadn't seen before were working in the halls. Her mouth surely hung open gaping enough for flies. Sandon couldn't be invaded. Vandals didn't make repairs.

Pushing on her jaw to close her shocked mouth, she made her way down the stairs and then to the long hall to the kitchen. Water was heating over the hearth.

An older woman stood near it dressed in a wide apron and lacy mobcap. "Miss Armijo, ma'am. Good morning."

The lady seemed nervous half-grinning, half-rocking back on her heels.

A feeling of being replaced whipped up in Isadel's gut, stinging. She stared at the woman, the fixed doors, the polished knobs, then the floor. "Are you the new cook?"

"No, ma'am. I'm your scullery maid. Mr. Bannerman hired me to help you." She handed

Isadel a snow-white apron.

Someone to assist her? Lifting her head, Isadel took the beautiful thing and wrapped it about her waist. A sense of pride swept over her.

Then fear washed over her, too. Was Bannerman planning on sending her back to the Abbey before the seeds arrived or had he decided to keep her for a longer course?

"Ma'am, how do we begin?"

The woman looked very scared and Isadel wondered what the big man had told the new maid. She nodded. "Let's get the eggs cooked. There is left over chicken in the larder. We'll cook that up too. What is your name?"

"Nelson, ma'am. The widow Nelson."

"I run an efficient kitchen, Mrs. Nelson."

"That's what I've been told. I'll work hard. I've mouths to feed."

Isadel smiled at the woman. She had soft blue eyes and graying blonde hair. Maybe she was kind and here to help. "Well, Mrs. Nelson, with all the workers here, there seem to be hungry mouths, too. When we're done, let's make preparation for some cinnamon apple tarts."

"Yes, Miss Armijo."

Her domain was still intact for the moment but Sandon had begun a transformation. What did it mean? She sighed. That was other folks' business, Bannerman's business.

Soon she and Mrs. Nelson had the kitchen smelling of onions and garlic and mutton. The cooked eggs with chicken shredded and tomatoes diced up would be an excellent addition to go with her biscuits. The larder was full of vegetables and cured meats. What was Bannerman planning?

When everything was just about ready, Phipps

like clockwork appeared at ten sharp. Instead of sitting at her table, he scooped up a platter and forked on a good portion of the mutton, before balancing a smaller bowl of the eggs.

"What are you doing, Mr. Phipps? The workers can come get their due in here. You don't need to move anything."

"They can, but that's not what Bannerman wants. Gather a few plates and come with me, Miss Armijo. Mrs. Nelson can handle here. Right, Mrs. Nelson?"

Though the widow seemed amiable and capable, Isadel didn't like abandoning the kitchen particularly for games. "Why is this necessary?"

Phipps continued his work of piling and balancing. "Today, Bannerman wants to dine in the dining room."

"The man wants to eat in filth. I'm not sure what is to be done with either of you."

Mrs. Nelson started to grin but turned her head toward the hearth. Phipps's smile seemed bigger and Isadel was sure it was not for her benefit but the widow's.

With both hands full of food, the man-of-all-work toddled to the door. "Biscuits, Miss Armijo. Then follow me."

She picked up some plates put a healthy amount of biscuits on them then caught up with the butler.

Again, the smell of pine soap and freshness overwhelmed. The scent could make one giddy, well one not so jaded. What could be afoot with workman patching the floors?

They trudged to a room with the threshold freshly painted and a new shiny knob. Clearing the way for her, Phipps used his foot to hold open the door.

Inside, she paced. The room was clean, well lit with big whitewashed patches of fist-sized holes, Bannerman fist-sized holes. A wide window with a few broken panes let in a flood of light. With his back to her, Bannerman stood near the mantle with two gleaming swords hanging above his head. Where those the dirty one's from his study? Had that room undergone a cleanup too?

Phipps put the plates on the table and seated himself. "This is going to be delightful, delightful as always, Miss Armijo."

When Bannerman turned around, her breath caught. His hair was combed. His face was shaved. The baby hair about the sides of his face was trimmed and even. His half smile returned as he sat at the table. "Does this..." He waved his arms. "Does this meet with your approval?"

A lump formed in her throat. Was he merely talking about the paint and plaster? "You're not a lion any more. You decided to clean up...Sandon?"

"But, I'm still big like a lion. And yes, I heard I'd let Sandon get away from me."

Phipps slathered his plate in eggs. "I'd like to say that a good meal has restored your hearing."

The wink passed between them made her cheeks feel heated. A little seeing of skin, an accidental acknowledgment of her thinking him handsome— had it made him notice her more? She wasn't waiting to find out. Setting the biscuits on the table whose right leg was supported by a book, she pivoted then pitched toward the door.

"Miss Armijo, where are you going?" Bannerman's voice sounded annoyed.

"To the kitchen."

"You said we couldn't eat in the dining room because it was not clean. It is now clean. Or have I not met your standards?"

"Yes, you and Phipps can now leave the kitchen for your meals."

Bannerman stood up and marched toward her in a deep blue jacket and white gloves on his hands, evening gloves like she had recommended. "You shall join us."

"No." She tried to make her tone softer, but from the growing frown on his face, she hadn't succeeded. "The help and your prisoner shall be in the kitchen."

"Phipps, go retrieve the coffee while I convince our chef to eat with us."

The butler shoved a biscuit into his mouth then arose and left the room. "My pleasure, sir."

Sitting on the table's edge, he folded his arms. "Why must you be so contrary?"

"And why are you changing the rules? You're being flirtatious, with a prisoner none the less."

He frowned. "I am being kind to you, Isadel. I don't have to be an ogre." He smoothed his bare chin. "Or look like one. I think you did say you preferred me clean shaven."

"For what matter? What purpose? I am not a thing. Or a possession. And just because I said I thought you handsome, it means nothing."

"Miss Armijo, the balm you made has softened my hands. My skin feels alive. Forgive me if I've decided to follow more of your suggestions."

Perhaps he was just being kind. It just felt different and wrong for him to be considerate. There was always a cost, an ask or demand associated with kindness. Her stomach soured and she wiped at her eyes. "Sorry. This isn't easy for me."

"Isadel, you don't make it easy. That is what I like

about you."

"I can't afford to be carefree."

"Not like Agueda?" he asked, his tone becoming low and sharp. It pierced her gut.

Oh, she wanted to kick herself for saying too much. "All I know is the minute I become comfortable is the minute it all changes, and then no good happens."

"You will eat with us, Isadel. That's an order. Remember, part of your punishment is to eat with Phipps and myself."

"Yes," Phipps said as he entered carrying a tray with three steaming mugs. "And with his beard shaved, you might see his overbite. That is a punishment. His manners are subpar."

Bannerman's frown changed to a thinner short line and all of Phipps's chuckles stopped. "You forgot the cream, Phipps. I like cream in my coffee."

"I'll go get the cream, Bannerman."

"Phipps can go. Everything is a choice, Miss Armijo. Except for you, Phipps. The cream."

Biscuit in hand, the older man went running.

She didn't know what to say. All she could think was that her jitteriness may have cost her a lesson with the black powder. "The workers. They will need dinner. I will go make preparations for dinner, enough for all the workers in Sandon."

Sighing like a teapot, he nodded. "Just make sure you are ready to go to the park at noon. I'm sure our new hire, Mrs. Nelson, can make sure what ever wonder you create can survive an absence of a couple of hours."

Her eyes started to sting from popping so wide. She hadn't upset him. He said he'd keep his word. "Yes, sir." Before he could say anything else that that might make her cry, she rushed out the door.

She lay against the threshold. Her pulse beat a crazy rhythm and she laid her head back against the cleaned door. The scent of polish evaded her nose as shame swept her heart. At least this feeling was something stronger than hate.

Shaking herself, she marched into the kitchen. At noon, Bannerman would show her the ingredients of the recipe she sought. Vengeance stayed in her soul, no matter how nice Bannerman decided to be, Isadel would not be deterred.

Hugh watched Isadel retreat and the soldier in him wanted to chase and vanquish the resistance. She was too stubborn, too set in her ways. Why would a woman who broke rules to come to him want to adhere to them now?

Maybe this was Spanish or Jamaican resistance, something an Englishman wouldn't understand.

But that quelled his wanting to know.

Phipps returned with a metal pitcher of cream. He looked in Hugh's direction and grinned like a greedy mouse. "Miss Armijo almost ran past me. Is everything alright?"

"You think if I shake her, Phipps, I could make her less—"

"Resistant to your charms, sir?" Phipps set the cream down on the table he and four other men had rejoined from two halves. Hugh had split the table a month ago upon learning of Parks' death, a slit throat, an almost illegible 'A' written in blood on his shirt. That was the trademark of the Almeida Killer. Parks was a good man, terrific officer. He didn't deserve such a death.

His man slurped his coffee loud and long. "Are you resistant to the chef's charms?"

"What, that stubborn hellcat? I go to the trouble of raising Sandon and all she wants is to be back in the kitchen. What type of charm is that?"

"Her winsome manner is stuck your head. She's gone and you're still staring at the door as if that will bring her back."

Rubbing his clean chin, his unblemished face, Hugh sighed. "It wasn't her. Just frustrated with how far I let Sandon degrade and you told me about Parks in this room. I punched through the table you're feasting upon."

"A feast by our Miss Armijo. Mrs. Nelson can't cook like this."

It wasn't the first time Phipps had mentioned the widow to Hugh. He'd raise a brow and tweak his man's nose over it if he weren't still fuming over Isadel.

"What type of reaction were you expecting from our disciplined baker and recent caregiver to a brooding Bannerman? She is gone from the dining room and you sulk?"

The woman was all those things to Hugh and annoying. Her reaction to his efforts made that spot on the back of his neck tingle with hot rage. He took a deep cleansing breath. "I don't know, maybe a little enthusiasm. I definitely didn't think she'd retreat."

After refilling his mug, Phipps slid a piping hot one to Hugh. "Miss Armijo is a very hard worker." He pulled a piece of biscuit onto his plate. "Seems her influence around here is pretty good, but she's no soldier, not of the war we are still fighting or the one stuck in your head."

"What are you talking about? You've been after

me to clean up the past six months."

The man's cheeky smile widened, as he scooped up more eggs. It was the kind of expression one would see on a gambler who'd just picked up his second ace. "I could say you are doing this to impress her, but that's too shallow of a reason. Miss Armijo is life. She came to these doors and reminded you that you are still breathing and that life still has meaning even when you're ill or at the end of your hope."

After a long pour of cream, Hugh picked up the steaming mug and put it to his lips. It was made like he loved hot, sweet, nutty on his tongue, but that did not make swallowing any easier. "This was the first time in months I don't have to fight my beard to enjoy coffee."

He sat down at the head of the mahogany table. Soon it would have its leg fixed, heavy wax would be applied and the rich dark would shine. "Maybe she needs to see it completed to enjoy it more. She doesn't know what Sandon was like." He took a biscuit and wondered if more of the jam they made earlier in the week remained, but he couldn't go fetch some from the kitchen. Phipps would never stop laughing. "Miss Armijo's food is delicious, her ways are intriguing and irritating."

"Her ways are baking us sweet apple tarts for dessert this evening. She had Mrs. Nelson chopping up apples when I went to retrieve your cream. Whatever the chef's influence, I'd like it to continue. Sandon has not look so good in years. You even look yourself."

Hugh had let things go too far, but Sandon reflected himself, without hope, dying. Phipps was right. The intriguing Isadel's balm made his wound less tender. It was healing nicely and his skin felt human again, not like delicate paper. So much so he'd risked shaving and was surprised to find no patches or lesions like the last physician told him to expect. "The chef seems to like everything well kept."

Phipps's greedy smile scrunched up. "You've given me a great deal of freedom to speak my mind." He tapped his fork's tines on his almost empty plate, and then looked up. "You haven't plans for the lass other than the kitchen?"

"She seems happiest in there, so I see no need to put her on another task."

"There's a look in your eye. Like the week we caroused in London after you found out Miss Betsy had eloped with Moldona."

In a drunken rage, he had kissed good-bye his heartache with every woman that could be procured. "Not exactly proud of my prowess, but I was quite angry and inebriated. I'm not sotted now."

"You're drunk on the life that lass has brought to this place, but she's not that kind of girl. Not a street walker or a brothel worker, just a good honest chef."

Hugh didn't like being lectured to, but with no Henry, Phipps had become a cross between friend, faithful counselor and occasional partner in folly. Hugh knew exactly what kind of girl Phipps alluded to and Isadel Armijo was no harlot, no man's mistress. Hugh finished his mug then set it down with a crash. "I have no designs on Miss Armijo, but I know she likes me and Sandon clean. I liked being thought of like my days weren't numbered. She is safe from me, even if she thinks I am handsome and well built."

"Did she say all that?"

"No. But she implied a smidgeon of it, and sometimes that is enough."

Phipps shook his head. "Bannerman, don't upset the cook or you'll be back to my food or poor Mrs. Nelson, neither are a good comparison." He stood and gathered up the empty dishes, then stopped. "I know what your fellow officers thought of girls like her when we fought in Almeida."

"Like her?"

"Mulattoes. Some thought very little of them because of their mixed blood, but Miss Armijo, she's not to be trifled with."

Hugh closed his eyes and remembered the off-colored jokes, the ones equating pretty girls like Isadel as half-breeds, mutts, playthings to roll around in the muck with. He might've even offered a laugh at one of his peers' raunchy jokes, but not now. Not when the little biscuit-making wonder had treated him more humanely than he'd treated himself. Hugh adjusted his glove, stretching the clean white glove to fit more securely about the fresh bandage she'd put on last night. "As I've said, I have no designs upon her. I admire her work ethic, but how have you discovered her character? A few biscuits and she's won you over."

"Perhaps, but she's done what I've fought for these past months. Don't ruin it."

"I'm taking her to the woods to show her the power of explosives and why they should be avoided. There won't be a chaperone. Are you telling me the chef can't come out and play?"

"Bannerman, you are the master of the manor and her prison warden according to Lord Hartland. You might know best, but I see in her the rage that gripped a young man that only the gravity of war seemed to tame. Young women can't go to war.

Maybe kindness can help her harness her fire before she's burnt clean through."

That had to be the kinship Hugh felt for Isadel. They were similar with their rage, except she didn't break things. She ran and hid. "There's no hiding for the guilty, Phipps. Sins will find you out. Our dear chef believes Moldona slaughtered her family. I don't see him doing that, but the intensity of the battle made our side commit atrocities. Wellesley has commented on it, but no one was held accountable for the deaths in Badajoz."

"Moldona? That can't be true."

Hugh started to pace. "If I had told the high command that Moldona and St. Claire left the powder barrel out, the one the French hit and set off the explosion that killed so many in Almeida, Moldona would have been drawn and quartered. He wouldn't have been able to be in Badajoz, let alone lead a regiment there."

"And he wouldn't have married Betsy St. Claire, your childhood love. Is that your true concern?"

It had been a year since the two eloped. How many holes had Sandon taken as Hugh tried to sort things out? How could he have mistaken that Betsy had finally become partial to him, not Moldona? Not wanting to answer Phipps or punch through the repaired table, Hugh turned to the window. "Some things are not meant to be."

He pulled at the curtain and viewed the thick lawn, the place he'd show Isadel a few tricks with explosives, like he'd shown Betsy the day his brother died. "If Moldona did slay Miss Armijo's family, what part of our dear chef's anger will I bear? I created him by not admitting his culpability at Almeida."

Phipps headed to the door. "You chose to forgive

a childhood friend and Miss Betsy's brother. Their names would be in ruin. You deserve no guilt because Moldona may have taken your chance at life and run amuck months later. Every man has a choice, to sin or not sin, to live or die. You are only responsible for your choices, Bannerman, no one else's." Phipps's head turned toward the door as the sound of lumber dropping reverberated.

Like a reflex, Hugh was at the mantle retrieving his battle sword, swinging it, preparing for the attack.

"Whoa, Bannerman. It's just the workmen. The carnage at Badajoz is not your fault. May not even be Moldona's. Things get mixed up in the heat of battle. Hopefully, the Almeida Killer won't get to him or you before the truth is known."

"The Almeida Killer needs to be stopped. Wellesley is endangered. We won't win the war without him, but Hartland or the others will find the killer. I've retired from this business, remember?"

"So you say. I'll go see how the workmen are doing. Maybe they will be up to a good coat of paint by tomorrow. Take care with our chef on your walk in the woods."

"Why, you think I'll endanger her like I did Henry? Don't fret. My skill with explosives is much better than before."

"Bannerman, I think we are all safer when you are not denying your gifts. Ms. Armijo is in for a treat, but I wonder if you'll be able to quit when things are done."

"I am not going back into service. A few powder blasts won't change that."

"I meant not quitting at playing or living. That's one thing I want for you." He nodded. "Have a good time," Phipps said as he left.

So Isadel had softened his man, just has the bold woman had done to Hugh. Boldness and brains weren't the same, but given the right circumstance either might get you killed.

Hugh put back the sword then he bent and slung his sack of black powder over his shoulder and powered his way past the workers out to Sandon's park. There were a few surprises he needed to set before taking the chef for a demonstration. Perhaps a good scare was what she needed to shake her brainbox from wanting revenge by explosives. Isadel thought she could endure killing a person. Unlike Hugh, the girl didn't know the meaning of taking a life.

Chapter Eight: Truth Dare and Explosives

Isadel followed behind Bannerman, his broad shoulders towered high above blocking the little sun managing to seep betwixt the leaves of the canopy of trees. His greatcoat, a large endless weave of blue flapped in the wind like a sail. "A little further, Isadel." He said her name and it carried in the breeze.

She shivered but wasn't cold. The anticipation of the moment was worse than waiting for a soufflé to rise.

Her stomach swirled, whirling with excitement. It was purely Papa's comportment that had kept her voice level and clear, very English, as she instructed Mrs. Nelson on preparing the apple tarts for dinner's dessert.

She still hadn't recovered from the shock of the changes. Until Bannerman walked through the door of the kitchen to retrieve her, part of her didn't believe him.

"Keep up, chef," he said with that half-grin.

His face was so smooth without a hint of fur. She decided she liked it much better than she did with the bushy reddish gold mane. A great deal more.

He kept his word and that made her like the man even more. "What will we do first? I uh...uh... I've seen the black powder used in Lord Hartland's guns. Papa never kept any in the house. He said he didn't like the damage they caused."

Bannerman cupped his eyes and gazed up high. "You do run on when you're nervous."

"I'm not—"

"It's best you are." He'd turned to her fully, stopping her advance. She almost rammed him.

"Black powder can be very dangerous, Isadel. A bout of nerves about explosives is healthy."

How was it possible for him to seem even larger? Was it the uneven grounds that made it seem as if he was a giant, one that could touch the sky? She blinked at the sun streaming around him as if he were one of those Grecian gods, one built for war.

"Welcome to my laboratory." Bannerman jumped onto a stump. "This grove is where I did my earliest experiments."

"You mean you tweaked things as in a recipe?"

He leapt back down and waggled a finger at her. "Don't get any ideas, chef. A tweak can kill."

Her cheeks burned a little, partly from him guessing her thoughts, and for remembering Bannerman as Ares, the god of war or Zeus, the god of thunder or sky. "I'll keep that in mind."

Bannerman stuck out his hand.

She took it without thinking.

He pulled her close, lifted her high like the night he'd tossed her in the closet, but this time he spun her until her head fell back dizzy.

"What are you doing?

"I figured a little sprite like you might enjoy a top side view."

She did and held onto his shoulders, nestling between his back and neck.

"A little different. Aye, Isadel?" He eased her boots to the ground. "We've walked far enough away from the house to not rattle windows. Of course, no one can hear you or I scream if things go awry. Does that make you nervous being alone with me?"

As if he searched for an answer, his eyes seemed fixed upon her. Did he notice how hard it was for her to breathe? The anticipation of Bannerman showing her detonations, a way to right her wrongs, it surely made her bubbly like a bucket of soapy water. "I've worked harder on that trust idea you talked to me about in the scullery."

"I guess it helps that I no longer look like a scary lion, but I still have a lion's temper."

"What makes you change?"

"Dishonesty. Deceit. That can make me very angry."

"Then I won't make you mad, not because of that."

He chuckled. "It's the other things you do that make me a little concerned. He leaned down and sniffed her hand. "Don't take this the wrong way, but you smell delicious. Cinnamon."

"Dessert. I forgot to wash my hands. I was too excited, not thinking."

"Here's to anticipation."

"I want to see your work. I'm anxious for it. I've overheard the stories."

"Don't believe everything." His smile shortened. "And take care at what you ask for. There may be unintended consequences."

Part of her knew he wasn't talking about black powder. If she were Agueda, she'd bat her lashes and say something witty, but Isadel wasn't her sister. At this moment, she had to be worse, a chef enamored by the most powerful man of her acquaintance, one about to show her how to craft horrible things that she could use to make Moldona explode. "I'll take care."

He nodded and moved past her, releasing the sack he'd had on his shoulder. It fell to the ground, and Bannerman dug inside and pulled out a small burlap pouch.

"Black powder is quite benign, powerless really without flame." He tore off the knotted strap and let the grains, the deep ebony sands pour into his palm. "When this is mixed with fire, that is when the danger comes."

"May I touch it?"

His brow rose, but he paced to her. When she held out her hand, he took it and towed her to him. "You've been practicing trust."

She went willingly but kept her gaze on the pouch and her dreams of harnessing its power.

He slipped his palm beneath hers; it was an odd and warm grasp. The thin gloves he wore rubbed her knuckles. He dumped a teaspoon, then a little more until she held a tablespoon of the powder.

It possessed more grit than she'd imagined. The texture felt coarse like milled corn, very different from flour but still these grains meant magic.

"You can exhale, Isadel. Your breath won't set off an explosion, well not one from the black powder."

He bent his head closer and she could see a tiny reflection of herself in his eyes.

"Bannerman, why are you looking at me like that?"

"Like what?"

"Like I'm going to do something rash and run off with these explosives."

"I haven't seen you smile so much. It's alluring, Isadel, and frightening at the same time."

Dimpling, she felt her smile grow. "So now what do you do, Bann-er-man?"

His lips curled as he drew the powder from her. "It's too dangerous to be so alluring. I have your undivided attention. A woman's full attention can be quite daunting on a man. Good thing I'm not easily swayed. I can be unpredictable." He struck a match and tossed it over his shoulder.

The flame caught on a cord or something. It blazed and hissed with sparks. The wild dance of the fire moved to a pile of rocks.

Bannerman charged toward her, but she kept her vision split between him, the big hulking man and the spitting flame.

Her head spun as he seized her in his melon-size arms thrusting her high. The air rushed out of her as her stomach hit his shoulder. But who could breathe with the powder about to make the world disappear?

In a blink, she felt him jump. She scrambled to latch onto him more tightly as they became one, airborne on destruction's wings.

His low tone in her ear voiced his counting, and it continued teasing her lobe until they crashed into a ditch. She lifted her head to catch another glimpse of the spark and he snatched her and pulled her deep into his arms. Then the world blew away with a bang. Loud and proud, the explosion's roar filled the air. Rocks landed around her, but nothing struck her. She was too secure in his big arms. A cloud of choking dust fell on them, but this time she didn't look up to see what was left of the world above. Staying in Bannerman's strong embrace, stronger than Papa's meant more than seeing the carnage.

His heart beat hard against her cheek. A lifetime of thuds lulled and then slowed before she opened her eyes. "Is it safe?"

He lifted her chin and held her gaze prisoner. "This is your first lesson. Never let your guard down when working with black powder."

But it was too late for such a warning. The fortress, the hardened shell she'd put around her heart had crumbled. For the first time in a long time, she wanted to be Agueda. Her sister would know what to do with these feelings, and she'd know how to encourage this man to take notice of her.

Hugh couldn't keep his eyes off Isadel. The mild mannered facade he'd become accustomed to had melted away. She smiled and brimmed with joy like a light in his dark world.

"What's next, Bann-er-man?" Her tone was soft and airy. "What's next?"

That question was worthy of a hundred guineas. That part of him that didn't want to think about danger or consequences wanted to taste Isadel to see if the cinnamon went all the way to her kiss, like a sticky bun. Instead, he just held her tighter. "I think you see the power of the powder. A little more than flour, aye?"

"It was fabulous. The air rush. The boom. Wonderful."

It should disturb him to see her so enthralled about an explosion, but it reminded him of how much he enjoyed them too. With his gloves, he brushed dust from one of her glorious curls that had come down. "I didn't think you could be incorrigible about anything other a clean kitchen."

Her stare never wavered, and she did not shrink from his touch. Was she merely enraptured by the black powder, the overpowering sulfur scent of destruction, or did she feel the tension, the same tightening in his chest as he did? Could a dying man dare to capture something so vibrant and lively, even for a moment?

"Bannerman, it was so fast. I am amazed at the speed."

"My demonstration went off without a hitch. Like me at my first detonation, you are mesmerized. Your lesson is done. Let's return to Sandon."

"No." She clutched his lapel. "Do it again. Let me watch the preparation this time. I wasn't ready. I must know every step."

Still bundled in his arms, her breathing was so fast it scorched his neck. Even in the frumpy, baggy jacket, her bouncing made him aware of those curves he'd seen a tease of in the tower.

"Again, Bannerman. Do it for me."

"As a gentleman, it's hard to deny a request from a lady."

Sitting back a lonely inch. "I'm in my father's jacket. I'm in breeches. I'm no lady."

He wanted to correct her, wanted to tell her that the clothes did nothing to hide her beauty when she smiled, but she gasped as a branch fell behind him. His attention became captive to her lips again.

"Bann-er-man," she said again and it sounded like a purr. "Make another explosion."

Well, now he knew it was the danger. The euphoria of the detonation wore off and he tried to blink away his slow burning attraction to the chef. "Enough demonstrations today."

"Again, Bann-er-man. I must know."

There was something he wanted to know about, the taste of her, but that would ruin things, destroy the trust that had been hard-fought to gain. He gripped her wrists and shook her. "You are mesmerized. I was too."

She nodded, released his revers and stood. "So that was the lesson? Nothing more?"

He bounced to his feet. "Perhaps one more. Stay put in this ditch." He climbed out and put very necessary and much needed air between them. Perspiring, he took off his jacket and dropped it on her head. "Hold this please."

With a nod, she pulled his jacket to her bosom and Hugh was jealous of his old coat.

Resigned, he turned and pulled a packet he'd measured hours before from his sack. Trudging to the base of a dead tree he'd tested during his preparation, Hugh put the pouch inside. Taking great care, he unfurled the wool cord attached to the packet and stretched it about twelve feet. With one strike of the match head upon his boot, he lit it and turned around in dramatic fashion as he had before.

Isadel now stood in the ditch. Her hair had unraveled from her jumping, and he could imagine her biting down on the corner of mouth as she had when the ground shook.

His glove nearly caught fire, but he remembered himself and blew it out. He had to stop focusing on the lift of her tresses by the breeze. If only he were whole, he'd wrap a lock about his finger, not his gloves.

With a blink, he regained his senses. This was hours of study to make sure he knew there were no weak trees; that no harm would come to his bouncing chef. He sighed, releasing a longing and unspoken prayer, then lit a new match, started the detonation cord and trudged to Isadel.

At her side by the count of ten, he turned and watched the explosion. This one was more powerful. The tree shattered. Its stump rose in the air, and then fell in the spot he calculated.

"Wonderful, Bannerman. Again, Bann-er-man. Again."

"If only I had always been so precise."

"Nonsense, it was perfect."

The rush of air, the scent of ash swirled about them like it was good and perfect. "What do you think, Isadel, other than me being perfect?"

She dimpled even more. "The explosion was magnificent."

"It is powerful. But, can't you also see that it won't support your plans?"

"What?"

"Look how close I had to be to set the cord. You can't do that from the kitchen. Isn't the Abbey's kitchen much further from the dining room than Sandon's arrangement? You are not a server, Isadel. Would you trust a footman or the butler to light your explosive? Think of the carnage that can be accidentally unleashed if he stopped or served the wrong person."

She folded her arms about her. "I didn't think about that, but what of the stories I overheard? You've made localized explosions."

"Men talk a great deal about the past. We even tell the truth, sometimes."

Her face scrunched. "It has to work, a controlled detonation."

"Isadel, it was a good plan. But, do you really think you could light the explosive cake and watch him die? I don't think you can. You're not a killer. You are a healer like your father."

Her smile drained away as she lifted her palm, one filled with the powder pouch he'd showed her earlier. Before he could stop her, she'd drawn out a match.

"Isadel, don't light this. You can get yourself killed. And why did you take my powder?"

"I borrowed it."

"Like Hart's horse?"

Her frown swallowed her chin. "It was the only way to get to you. And this pouch is the only way to show you I can do it. I am not afraid."

He reached for her but missed. "It's not that simple."

"Yes, it is." She'd lit the cord holding the pouch close.

Batting away the explosives, he grabbed her and forced her to duck. The burning bag hit a tree as it went off. Branches started to fall and he batted them away. When he saw an adjacent tree falling, crashing toward them, Hugh grabbed her and dove deeper into the ditch.

Branches and chunks of massive trunk covered them, making everything pitch black. The creaking noises were the worse, reminding him of Henry's death, the image of the maple's thick trunk impaling Henry, smashing him to the ground had never left Hugh's mind. It was constant like his guilt.

Then everything quieted but the sound of his heart and Isadel's rapid breath.

He fisted his hand and punched through branches. Light slipped in as he adjusted to a sitting position in the small rut. As calmly as he could, he drew Isadel's face to his. "Do you have any idea what you could've done?"

"I showed you I could do it."

He gripped her by the shoulders. If he shook her this time, he knew he might break something. Trying to remove his hands from her made his gloves tangle in her locks that were everywhere. Now, he was heated for two entirely different reasons. "What do you have to say for yourself, Isadel Armijo?"

Isadel only laughed. "You didn't think I had it in me, Bannerman. I showed you and don't use that tone. You're not my father."

Oh, he couldn't think of being her father right now no matter how much a good paddling over the knee might do. He took a long breath and smothered his rage in pine and cinnamon. "You are a grown foolhardy woman and you showed me you can't be trusted."

"But I've watched you, how carefully you measure. In the kitchen, you were so precise. I knew the amount was less than the others. If you hadn't overreacted, I would have tossed it out to where your explosions were set. We could be laughing like before."

He punched another hole in the ceiling. "This is my fault? This is a problem. And what do you know about my precision? Accidents happen, things you can't control. If the trees around your explosion have more rot or weak roots they could fall too, but you don't know where. Henry died because I was reckless. I lost the best brother, my best friend because I hadn't considered the consequences."

She caught his fist before he could knock more of the debris from over top of them. "I'm sorry. I know what it means to lose someone you love."

"My brother and I packed the roots with powder and lit a detonation cord. The first explosion was fabulous."

"Ours was fabulous."

"But the second killed him. From this ditch, Isadel, my brother Henry and I watched the workman clear stumps. They left only the solid healthy ones. We sat here. He'd split my sides with his puns. The man was a biblical scholar and loved to twist up King James verses. Salt will never look the same for me."

"How does bad jokes about things one shouldn't joke about lead to his death?"

He balled his hand about hers. "We should've made more jokes. I should've heard more, should've laughed more but I had to exhibit. We set up another powder demonstration, then went back to Sandon to await our neighbors, the St. Claires and Moldonas."

Her eyes went wide, but she had to hear him. "Moldona?"

"Forget him, Isadel. I am trying to make a point. I didn't see the risks. Just the magic of the flames, the colors in the sparks. You have to see the danger not just the magic."

She touched his cheek and gave it a rub with her pinkie. "You're dusty."

He stilled her hand, pulling it to his chest. "Dirt comes with detonations. Another reason for you to avoid them."

"Maybe the workmen returned and put more powder. I don't think you measured incorrectly. Yes, accidents happen, but you, putting too much powder in the detonation — I doubt it."

How many nights had he replayed the events of that day in his head? Isadel was right in how careful he'd been in measuring the powder. "Who can predict with a hundred percent accuracy what will happen with explosives? The tree fell and knocked into another one. That one crushed Henry." Hugh shook his head. "It's my fault and though I should blame you for this. It's mine for not anticipating what you would do. Precision for a spy is his best asset but predicting behavior, that's a luxury. We are lucky to be unhurt."

"I watched you, Bannerman. You are as meticulous in measuring as I am with my cakes. I doubt you put too much powder in the tree. You never intended to harm your brother. I say some cook went behind you and added too much vanilla."

"This isn't cooking, Isadel."

The roof creaked and dirt and pinecone rained.

The girl threw herself atop of him as if the small crazy thing could keep him safe. "I didn't mean to kill us. Just wanted to prove a point."

Her face laid on his and his cheek felt the softness of her hair. She smelled like cinnamon and pine. The world above stopped shifting. He could easily push her to the side and break them free, but why move and send her from him. "You're crazy, Isadel."

Though her breathing didn't slow her limbs slacked against him. "The explosions were wild and amazing. I'm not sorry for it."

He wasn't sorry about her lying against him and couldn't stop from fastening his arms about her waist. She was tiny but well curved, just like the glimpse in the tower had revealed. He pushed his face deeper into her tresses. "You are crazy, chef."

She raised her head. Her eyes had grown larger than guineas. "Does this mean no more lessons?"

The innocence in her irises foretold of many things that he could teach her, but a man needed to know he was going to live before dreaming those dreams. "Perhaps. Good thing I like crazy."

Her smile warmed him even as their makeshift shelter shifted and groaned. Just another moment, another curl to finger, another second wondering what a kiss on those lips would feel like. Wincing at Phipps being right, that Hugh fancied Isadel more than he had anyone in a long time, he closed his eyes. He saw nothing, for he couldn't picture a future except a grave marker next to Henry.

"Good. I like you too."

If he ripped off a glove and touched her face, would the memory last? Holding her would lead to wanting more of her, so he put his fists to his side. "At least you now see your plan will fail. Black powder is too dangerous, but even if you could get revenge, what will you want next?"

She lifted her countenance to him. Her lips pressed into a line, maybe even biting the plump lower one. "I don't know how to think of a day without revenge."

He knew her struggle. The same hate and loathing had been in him, but Isadel was young, young and beautiful, and could make wonderful things with her hands. "My talented chef, you need to rise above it. Anger and wanting revenge can be as dangerous as explosives. It will ruin your insides, even give room for disease to root."

Tears ran from her eyes. It was so different from the joy that had filled them when she saw the flash of the powder.

It wasn't vapors as his stepmother was given too.

He could even sense its difference from Betsy upon hearing of the loss of her brother. These tears had to be from that moment when you give up, when one admitted to themselves all was lost. But it wasn't, not with another day to live and breathe. For the first time, he understood the new mercies Henry spoke of.

Hugh flicked a droplet from her eyes with his thumb and traced her cheek, stopping short of a mouth in want of a breath of hope. "Let the anger go. Don't let it have you."

"I must take revenge for Papa and Agueda. You're an expert at explosives. With your knowledge, I could have everything."

"What is everything, Isadel? Is it killing an enemy or finding a way to live past the pain?"

"Is there a difference, Bannerman?"

Her small face wrinkled along the temples, the confusion of what he meant surely marring her sun-kissed complexion. He leaned closer and stroked a fretful line smooth then stilled. His fingers lingered on her jaw longer than they should. Hugh had never been an envious person, not even when Moldona won Betsy. But right now, he stewed, hungering to be the kidskin leather of his gloves. He wanted to touch Isadel and know the joy of it. "Yes, there is a difference. If I had sought another path, I might be different."

She clasped his arm so tightly; it was as if she needed him to hold to her reason and humanity.

Deeper into his chest, she went. Her arms fastened about his neck as she cried on his shoulder. "I've failed them again. I should've died with them that night. Then this plague of guilt would be no more. I have no hope."

"You're brave, Isadel. Don't be the third victim of

your family's killer. Live past him and live well. Honor your father's hopes for you."

"There is no way to do this."

With both hands, he took her face. "Yes. Yes, there is."

There was no question in his mind about kissing her. He did so, savoring and schooling those pert lips. Inhaling cinnamon had made him hunger for her and admit to himself the need of her. When Isadel kissed him back, he was glad he hadn't hesitated. Even a dying man needed a moment to live.

Her small fist shifted against his rib and he released her.

"Does this mean you will help me? You will kill my enemy? You could be in the room to set the cord. My plan could work with your aid."

The remnants of a temper he'd slain reemerged and he jerked his hands from her. "I'm greedy, Isadel. I'll not be satisfied with a mere piece of you, especially when your lips only know revenge."

"Bannerman!!!"

The shout came from above. It sounded like Phipps, but the urgency in tone, made Hugh's racing pulse beat faster.

"Time to rejoin the world. Let's forget this."

She gripped his lapels. "Forget what? The explosives or that you kissed me?"

"Both. I'm a dying man. I'm not entering the heavens with another death on my hands or the incredible frustrations that you women can work."

With her delectable lips pressed into a full pout, she said. "You're not dying. My seeds will cure you, but do as you say and forget everything."

Moving as far as she could from him in the tight space, she put her back to him and began righting her bun. "Send me back to the Abbey and we can pretend that nothing has happened at all.

The huff in her voice sounded to his ears as if she'd have more difficulty in doing so. "You haven't completed your final punishment."

"I think so. Forgetting I kissed you is enough."

There was hurt in her words. For a man who lived by calculations, this was unexpected.

"Bannerman!!! Are you down there?"

"Yes. Stand back, Phipps." Hugh beat through the branches and trunks until a good three-foot hole formed.

Before she could protest, he picked her up by the waist and shoved her through. "Move thirty paces back and tell Phipps to do so as well."

She nodded and started running. When it sounded as if she'd gotten clear, he used his full strength to blow the hole wider. Pine and bark flew everywhere as he powered through. When he climbed out of the wide hole, Phipps ran to him. Isadel did too but at a slower pace.

His man wiped his brow. It brimmed with sweat. "You are alive."

"Of course."

"You don't understand. They're all dead. The Almeida Killer has gotten to Junot."

"What are you talking about?"

"He's dead. Lord Hartland sent intelligence from the Pearson spy. Junot's dead. The killer's reach goes into France."

"What did Hart say of it?"

"He's investigating, but the fiend will not stop. He'll go after Wellesley. The war efforts will be in jeopardy. We are vulnerable here, especially with you playing with explosives."

Being a sitting duck or waiting to be killed by an

assassin, that was worse than waiting for leprosy to do him in. No more. Hugh pumped his hand driving one fist into his palm. "It's time to draw out the killer. No more living in the shadows."

Phipps brushed leaves from Hugh's coat. "What do you mean?"

"Send word to my stepmother. She will know how to put a final sparkle on Sandon. Double the workers to finish the repairs as soon as possible. Then we will invite Moldona and all the rest of the commanders here. That will draw the killer to me."

"Moldona," Isadel said. "Here? Oh, now you'll send me back to the Abbey?"

In mid stroke, Phipps stopped, and then hit him a little harder as he brushed at his coat. "You're not sending her back to the Abbey. I was hoping she'd stay a little longer."

"Miss Armijo is not returning yet."

She lowered her head. "So, I will serve my father's killer under your roof?"

"No, Isadel. You will not be serving him." Hugh waved his hand stopping his man from attacking his great coat further. "She's not going anywhere. On the contrary, Miss Armijo will dine with us. As my mistress, she will have full run of the house. She will be free to eavesdrop or skulk anywhere in Sandon."

Isadel stepped to him and clutched the lapels of his coat. "No. Just because, I let... No."

"I think it an adequate final punishment, and as my mistress you can get as close as you desire to Moldona. You can even try to kill him."

Isadel whispered something under her breath before turning away. He almost wished she still possessed the freedom to speak her thoughts to his face.

Shaking his head like it had suddenly come loose, Phipps started pacing in circles. "You want me to invite Moldona here? He'll bring Miss Betsy St. Claire, your old—"

"Phipps, it's Mrs. Moldona. They've been married about a year now. Moldona may have done many things that warrant death. He may be the Almeida Killer. If that is so, no one will kill him. He will be turned over to the crown for punishment." He plodded in front of Isadel and kept his gloved hands to his side. She wasn't the only person who now felt constrained. He brushed at his dusty breeches. "Miss Armijo, I'll need your assistance to pull off this charade."

"I don't. We are not." She tugged at her father's jacket. "How will I fool anyone into thinking I am nothing more than a common harlot?"

"Yes." Phipps said. "A gentleman's mistress is a fancy one."

In lieu of pounding Phipps, Hugh pounded his own skull. "You are not helping. Miss Armijo, dearest, my stepmother will take care of that. She's quite acquainted with the role of a gentleman's mistress. She'll make you into the part."

It was hard to determine whose mouth had dropped open farther, his man or his pretend woman. He wiggled his finger at them. "Come along, you two, we've work to do."

It was almost comical the situation Hugh had constructed. With his stepmother arriving, Moldona bringing Betsy, and Hugh's enraged chef, there would be three women in Sandon who held him in disregard. Yet, the latest addition to his collection, Isadel Armijo, was the only one whose opinion concerned him, that and her ability to slice up things with her knife. There were daggers in the chestnut colored eyes right now and he dared not turn his back on her, literally and figuratively.

Staying a step ahead of her anger might prove as daunting as waiting out the Almeida assassin.

Chapter Nine: Mistress of Punishment

Humiliated and furious, Isadel stomped back to Sandon. She didn't wait for Phipps or Bannerman, the smuggest man in the world. How egotistical could he be that he'd use her position in his household to make her into a mistress? Even if it was pretend, he shouldn't have the right to do it as some extracted punishment.

Why did she have to kiss him back? Wasn't that consent? When Agueda waved at the redcoats, wasn't that consent, too?

Upon setting foot in the house, Isadel felt lost and unsure. Sandon had been further raised. The smell of fresh paint swept through the halls, but it wouldn't take away the scent of him—bergamot, pine and aloe, a medicinal clean smell. It was on her hands, probably on her coat from being so close to him.

She shook her head, hoping to make some sense of things and to forget the feeling of him kissing her and how his arms tightened about her when she kissed him back. "The kitchen. That's where I'll go."

"You mean hide." Bannerman was leaning at the

threshold, grinning.

Phipps pushed from behind him. His gaze seemed to cut between them. "I'll go ready the correspondences, but Bannerman, Miss Armijo don't let this affect dinner. Remember, pies?"

His man turned into the study.

"I have to go prepare dinner."

The euphoria of watching black powder causing sweet destruction fizzled the minute he said Moldona and mistress. Rethinking it continued to drain hope from Isadel with each step upon the newly repaired hardwoods. A sense of numbness replaced everything, except anger, closing off her insides from the comfort that Mama's song had tried to fill, especially the space behind her ribs.

"Miss Armijo, I must speak with you."

Bannerman's voice cut through her like an axe to the back. She wasn't a hen set to be slaughtered, so she kept moving.

"Chef, we have a menu of sorts to plan."

She pivoted and saw hulking Bannerman a few paces behind and gaining. "I have duties," she flung open the door to the kitchen.

He caught it and barreled inside. "This is a wretched beginning. If **my chef** can't stand a little heat, how will this ever work out?" He chuckled and the noise echoed as if he was at her ear.

Did he want her witless again and open to his charms? She swiped at her brow. "Mrs. Nelson, are we ready to start dinner?"

The widow bounced up from a seat at the hearth. "Miss Armijo, the stew pot of vegetables is almost done. What will you have me do next?"

Would scorching everything black be an option? No, Isadel would never have anyone waste food or ruin a clean. "When it is ready to serve the workmen, let's do so. Then prepare two bowls of it for Mr. Bannerman and Mr. Phipps. Place it in the dining room for them."

"You mean three bowls? Mr. Bannerman was insistent that you would eat with them, Miss Armijo. That's what he said when he hired me."

"Yes, ma'am." Bannerman said, with a smile that was less prideful. "Those plans haven't changed."

Mrs. Nelson drew back toward the stove. "I need this job very much. Just tell me what to do."

The way the widow said it, kind of fearful and with her gaze lowered made Isadel very concerned. "What other conditions did he advise?"

Bannerman shrugged as the widow fiddled with her apron strings. "To be nice... to respect you as heading his kitchen."

For a moment, the concern he had warmed her, as did his present of the crisp apron. But why was he concerned about such, when he reduced Isadel to a bit of fluff with his next command?

Bannerman opened the door to the scullery. "Miss Armijo, I need to speak with you alone. Mrs. Nelson, do you mind me borrowing our chef for a moment?"

Isadel couldn't be alone with him, not now with his kiss branded on her lips. She grabbed ahold of the table. "I mind very much. We've work to do before we serve the workmen."

"We have time. The potatoes are just about to soften in the boiled water." Mrs. Nelson stirred the stew pot. "Go on. No fretting about me, ma'am."

Isadel needed to wash her hands and slip on the pretty apron, both of which were in scullery where Bannerman wanted to meet. But she couldn't move, not with him gloating with his lopsided smile.

He slipped to her side and clasped her elbow.

"Come with me, my dear—"

"It's, Miss Armijo. I'm not your mistress yet."

Mrs. Nelson stumbled then caught herself on the table. Her face filled with a knowing grin, and Isadel's heart crumbled. She was Agueda to the widow. There was something Isadel craved more than revenge, respect.

Bannerman's eyes widened with crinkles. "I don't think it fair that we discuss our domestic situation in front of Mrs. Nelson."

"There is no situation. I'm a chef to you and that is all. I don't want to play your games."

"Oh, please do not force me to declare myself in front of the good widow and tell her how you stole your way—"

Isadel swiped a ladle from the table and clapped it over his lips. The smack was hard, probably enough to leave a ring. She did care that she hadn't hurt him, but she couldn't have him spreading more half-truths and lies.

He took the ladle. "Well now, this must be cleaned in the scullery. Right, Miss Armijo? He prodded her shoulder with the silver handle. "Shall we continue in private?"

Insides about to boil over, she threw up her hands and headed into the scullery.

Bannerman remained a few safe paces behind her, his laugh growing with each step. He closed the door. His chuckles had grown to a full body shake that made his wide chest puff bigger. "It would bode better for you if you listened. That might need to be your first lesson in this mistress business."

"You need to send me back to the Abbey now. We've played enough at this."

"And miss your big chance at revenge. Fine. The one thing I thought you were was brave, but I guess there is a coward buried in that burly jacket. Go to the stable down the hill, tell the new groom I told you to take the fastest horse."

She moved past him, but he caught the hem of her jacket.

"Before you flee, help me with my hand. Seems I might have re-injured it with our little outing."

Her anger softened. She pushed him to sit on a stool. "You should've told me you hurt yourself."

"You were a little too busy running."

She stomped backed into the kitchen, avoiding Mrs. Nelson's strange looks as she grabbed her sharp knife and a bucket of hot water. Lugging the heavy bucket of steaming water to him, she dropped it near Bannerman's boots. "Hand me your palm."

He did so with eyes that were no longer laughing, and suddenly it was hard to breathe. Like she skinned cod, she peeled the layers of leather. The dinner glove was stuck to a tiny break in the skin. "Sand or debris made its way inside from the punching."

"Isadel, I have a killer coming for me. Other men, good ones may die and the war could be lost if the Almeida Killer is not stopped."

"You mean the war effort that killed my family?"

Pulling his hand taut within hers, she waved her sharp knife then like she did chicken skin, thinly sliced away the last pieces of the silk glove.

He didn't flinch or move. "I trust you, Isadel, even though you nearly killed us in the park. What about trusting me?"

She pulled at the soft material. The old gash had been healing well, but the new injury happened because of her recklessness. "It's very hard to do, but I never said I didn't care. Hold your palm wide.

Let it get air."

"I only smell cinnamon. Your cinnamon, Isadel."

She clasped his hand and with fingers entwined, she dunked them both into the water.

"You're not afraid of what I have?"

"No. You will be cured."

His hands tightened about hers in the shared bucket. "How will I if you run back to Hartland now?"

She washed his wound with a clean rag, gently scrubbing the bits of dirt and bark that had worked into his glove. "Men have tried to make me a whore. They left with their lives and a few cuts they'll not want to talk about. At the Abbey, Lord Hartland made sure I was left alone."

"Yes, he left you to stew in your hatred and guilt for living. I've been stewing too over my brother Henry, until you came here delivering a message. You brought me good news, that someone still cared if I lived or died. You've shaken my bonds from me. I need to do the same for you."

"How? Why?"

"Isadel, you saw today how close you need to be to set off the explosives and to ensure it hits the intended victim. You can't do that from the kitchen. As my mistress, you will have free rein to get close to Moldona and get your revenge. What is wrong with my plan if it gets what you want?"

"And what do you want? You could have Moldona here, and I could serve food that wouldn't poison everyone without the pretense of being your mistress."

"The roles change the minute Sandon has guests. I don't want you hidden away in the servants' quarters. Part of this is selfish. I still want you attending me, making me balms. Gather your intelligence out of the shadows. It also affords you protection. Moldona has roaming eyes and hands. He'll know not to touch you, unless you permit it."

She dried his wound, sliced up an onion and layered it upon the wound to cleanse it. "But what of your hands?"

"Isadel. Spies must be covert about many things, but in this thing, I won't. I will say it plain. I am very much attracted to you. It's not every day a woman almost kills me or gets the same heady pleasures from gunpowder that I do. You are a rarity. I enjoy your humor, your modesty, and your kiss. But this mistress arrangement is pretend, even if a part of me might want it to be true."

His candor was her undoing, for her cheeks felt hot and that feeling of wanting to be in his arms, the one that overtook her senses when they landed in that ditch, returned. She couldn't say anything to that. She wasn't Agueda. She would lose no more respect from Bannerman. Stewing, she wrapped his wound, nice and tight and never uttered a word.

"What is it going to be, Isadel? Will you stay and pretend to be my mistress? Will you help me catch a killer or do I send you back to Hartland?"

"What about my problems? Your plan does not kill Moldona and it does not restore the respect Mrs. Nelson had for me."

"Isadel, you are not a killer, but as my mistress you have free rein. If you corner him alone and you convince yourself again of his guilt, do what you must. I will not stand in your way nor will I help. Will you pretend to be my mistress?"

Isadel dumped the water out of her bucket, and then scrubbed it clean. "If I do this, you will not mind if I kill one of your guests?"

Bannerman came beside her at the cistern and

put his bandaged hand on her shoulder. "Moldona is my friend Betsy's husband. He is rotten to her. So, killing him would be no lost to me, but do it only if he is guilty. The battlefield is chaotic. You have to be sure who the enemy is. But Isadel, you are a healer. There is a rhythm of hope about you. I've seen you move to it. It's not one of death or killing or even revenge."

"Moldona is the one. He is the slaughterer."

"Then you need the opportunity to get him to admit it. You'll not have that chance lurking in the background at the Abbey."

She pulled at her clothes. "I am a sorry excuse for a mistress. They will look upon you with pity."

"You will need some evening gowns, but my stepmother will see to it. It will be nice having someone else as her project." Standing, he took her hand and spun her around. "You will do nicely, Isadel. I will be proud to claim you."

She felt on fire as her anger turned to something else as he twirled her.

He put both hands about her waist and lifted her as he'd done out in Sandon's park. "You'll have to get used to my hands and my size hovering about you. I tend to tower over someone so small."

"I haven't agreed."

He set her back down. "But you will. You can't resist the challenge of it, Isadel. We are so alike. Which means you can be stubborn like a mule too. What have you? Mistress or stubborn mule back to the Abbey?"

With his palms still on her like they were dancing one of those jigs she'd seen at the Abbey, it was hard to reason, but there was no flaw to his logic especially for someone like her. "The soldiers mistook Agueda for a prostitute. I suppose a mistress is an elevation for a mulatto or blackamoor or whatever term you English have for girls like me."

"What is it you want, Isadel?" His tone sounded low and calm as if he cared.

The pound of a set of footsteps from behind made her turn. Bannerman hadn't taken his hands from her even as his man stood at the threshold. The lord of the manor had claimed his brown bit o'muslin.

Phipps cleared his throat. "Bannerman, I sent notes with the new footman. I requested your stepmother come right away and the Moldonas at month's end. Three weeks from now. Will you two be ready? This scheme will be dangerous if Moldona is the Almeida Killer or if this gathering draws the killer to Sandon. We can't be divided in this."

"I'm prepared, but I'm not sure about our chef." He folded his arms and thumbed his chin as if he were in deep thought, then said, "Phipps, hire more people. The place will need to be painted before my stepmother arrives. And some grounds men are needed. It seems my dove has damaged the landscape with an unexpected explosion. Naughty girl. And have a horse ready in the stable. Miss Armijo can borrow it anytime she feels the need to run."

She couldn't look at Bannerman anymore and focused on Phipps. "Your employer is having fun. I'm not sure I should play along. I don't want anyone to get the wrong idea."

"Yes, of course. Sir, Miss Armijo. I'll go see about more workers." He pedaled out of the room as if it were on fire.

Bannerman bubbled into more laughter.

"Phipps has left. You should follow. Mrs. Nelson

and I have to ready dinner."

"Yes, and one last thing." He picked her up and planted a kiss on her lips.

Startled, she swung back and slapped him as hard as she could.

He put her back down. "Yes, we'll have to practice this. My stepmother, the Lady Rhodes, and Betsy St. Claire Moldona are very astute. They can detect a sham."

She wiped at her mouth. "Then let them know this business between us is fake."

"The less who know the truth, the better. And unlike you, I don't trust them with my secrets. I need this portrayal to seem true enough to draw a killer and enough to potentially absolve my friend's husband of your family's murder."

"I thought you did not care for Moldona."

"Moldona, no, but his wife is an old friend. She has suffered a great deal. I'd like to spare her more anguish."

"Bannerman, what will you do if Moldona shows he's guilty?"

He shrugged. "There is no punishment for that crime in England. I will let you exact justice, but I must stop the Almeida Killer. There is much at stake, but believe me your feelings matter to me. And you can't keep calling me Bannerman. We need to be more personal. Call me Hugh."

"H-ugh." She shook her head. "Bann-er-man sounds better."

"It's all perspective, but my name does sound good on your tongue. See you at dinner, my sweet."

With the door swinging shut, Isadel was left with questions. What would she have to do to be convincing as a mistress, and what did she truly want other than Moldona's head on a platter? She sank onto her stool overwhelmed with the scent of Hugh Bannerman on her hands.

Hugh wanted to chuckle, wanted to delight in teasing Isadel. She deserved censure for going against his wishes and igniting the powder bag. She could've killed them. Yet, punishment was the last thing on his mind when he kissed her in the ditch or now in the scullery.

He slugged into his study. His desk had been cleaned. The fresh pine soap smell hit him, but he'd wished it was cinnamon, Isadel's cinnamon. Why was she so unsettled? Was it that she wanted Hugh to kill Moldona so badly nothing else mattered? Some women merely asked for pearls.

Pressing forward, he stared at the neatness of his study. The mounds of books he'd collected and scoured for a cure had been put away. With a fresh coat of buttermilk colored paint, this room wouldn't reflect his desperation, as if things were so easy to erase—like the aftermath of an explosion on the enemy or hapless innocents like Henry. What would he say to Hugh over forcing Isadel to play this game of baiting a killer?

Hugh sat in his favorite chair, which had been cleaned and polished. He tapped the fretwork of the stiles, circled a tattoo scribed into the armrest, measuring his actions and thinking of his favorite chef. From this seat, he'd searched in desperation for a cure, something to let him live. Today, he found something better than a reason to live a long life, a moment with Isadel smiling. But that was no more and the guise they were about to do felt more wrong.

Phipps walked inside and closed the door tight behind him.

"Bannerman. My father was steward over this place. It is in my family's line to serve the Bannermans. I followed you to war as your batman. I've seen you do a lot of strange things but drawing Isadel Armijo into this, well that's pretty low."

"Remember, she came to me to find out how to make explosives. She wanted to serve a cake that would make Moldona disappear."

Wiping his mouth, Phipps posted at the desk's edge. "Perhaps, but you can dissuade her of such."

"No. Isadel Armijo is reckless. She almost got us killed today, and I loved it."

Phipps leaned forward. "What are you saying?"

What was Hugh trying to say? Should he just admit to his loyal friend that he was right, that Hugh fancied Isadel. No, that was too much truth to say aloud. Spies don't divulge such secrets, not without torture. He drummed his finger along the desk. "Miss Armijo has the same anger that a certain young man had until his batman, his-man-of-all-work set him on a better path. Armijo has no batman. The guide she had was a father killed by one of ours and a song from a mother long past. She's alone. I want to help her, but I am a soldier too. I have to catch the Almeida Killer. Maybe that will right all the wrongs I've done."

"Your killing was for the English cause and the guilt you bear over Master Henry is ill-placed."

"Phipps, you don't know my dreams. The faces of those who died."

His man slammed a fist on the desk. "Accidents happen and your actions were in service to the king. No one could ask more of you. But what does that have to do with our chef?"

"She thinks she could have saved her family from the British soldiers who ravaged Badajoz after the siege. She believes that Moldona personally did this. She must know he is guilty with no doubts before she strikes. That is the only way to live with the consequences."

"Then you are helping her? Here I thought this was just an elaborate scheme to have her end up in your bed."

Hugh sat back in his chair and thought about putting his dusty boots on the surface but stopped. "If that is what I wanted, I'd be more direct."

Phipps's glance never wavered. "I suppose, but you are out of practice."

"Some things aren't so easy to forget, but she has me thinking. The day Henry died, how many people visited Sandon that day?"

"Betsy St. Claire, your stepmother, Moldona, and about five or six workmen. Why do you ask?"

"I've always been precise when measuring powder. How is it that the charge was enough to blow the stump and that healthy tree onto Henry? It's been a long time, but that explosion seemed a great deal bigger than the amount of powder I set."

"Bannerman, you're chasing ghosts when there is a chef who is crying in the scullery. I had to calm down Mrs. Nelson in the larder and convince her you are no martyr plying on foreigners.

Hugh scratched his non-existent beard. "Armijo was crying in scullery while you were begging in the larder? There is a joke in there somewhere. I'm sure of it.

With a shrug, Phipps pivoted and marched to the door. "Make jokes of it as you want, but don't ruin something that could be special. All of our kitchen staff is special."

"Just make sure Armijo has not escaped out the back door or gone near my black powder stash. It's been a long day."

"Well, prepare for a longer month. You know how it is when Elizabeth Bannerman comes."

"You mean Elizabeth Smythe, the countess of Rhodes. She found another old man to marry her, but he's still reasonably healthy. I think we sent her spoons."

Phipps shook his head, probably a perpetual happenstance as they prepare for this visit. "You need anything?"

"Just a hope and prayer that Moldona isn't more of a killer than me. If he is the Almeida Killer, he's walking in here a dead man. Wellesley will ensure it. Too many good men have died. If he is the Armijo family assassin, I don't know. Perhaps, he's still a dead man."

"You won't spare him for Miss St. Claire, I mean Mrs. Moldona's sake? I remember you caring for her a great deal."

Hugh had loved Betsy once, but the time was never right for them. He was in deep mourning over Henry. Then, she was in mourning for her brother. When it seemed as if their fates would mesh with her letters alluding to her possibly loving Hugh, she eloped with Moldona. With a sigh, Hugh decided to put his feet on the desk sans boots. They needed to be aired with all the tramping he and the chef did today.

"She will always be a friend. Check the weapons. Elizabeth's trappings will make enough noise to ensure the true killer shows. We'll need to be ready with enough power to stop the fiend. His life will be handed over to the crown. My vow to never kill again will remain intact."

"I hope you will be given the choice. War seldom works like that." Closing the door with a thud, Phipps left.

Everything hinged upon catching the Almeida Killer. Deep down, Hugh wished it would be Moldona. Then, he could turn him in to the crown. Enough men had died, so hanging was assured. Hugh would be able to keep his vow to never kill again and gain justice for Isadel.

Yet, things were never that simple or that clean. How was he to keep an angry woman from extracting revenge? He strummed his finger and had to admit he didn't know if he could stop her or even if he wanted to keep her from the one thing that would give her peace.

Chapter Ten: Stepmother Cometh

From the tower, Isadel watched a caravan of carriages approach. A few days had passed since Bannerman had committed her to this spying scheme. She'd have to pretend that she was his mistress. Every noodle in her internal pot of salted water hated that word, hated the accusations it thrust upon her. Plaything, hot little piece, prostitute, Isadel was none of those things. Tugging at the lapels of her father's coat, Isadel wanted to hide.

She'd absented herself from the kitchen. How could she be in her domain with everyone staring at her as if she had no morals, as if she were like poor Agueda who'd been labeled such for batting her eyes at men?

Upon seeing the carriage stop, she backed away from the window, then counted the minutes before she was summoned. How was she to get through this? And if she could, how would she be clever enough to get Moldona to confess or say enough so that Bannerman would know he was guilty and help her?

A series of hard knocks upon her door stole her breath. Her stomach lurched before twisting in knots. She was going to be ill. The last thing she needed was everyone to believe Bannerman's faux mistress was set to birth by-blows as the English called illegitimate babes.

"Isadel? Isadel? May I enter?"

Bannerman. Not wanting to be alone with him and his kissing lessons, she ran to the door. "I'm ready to go down."

She tried to brush past him, but he crowded her with his fresh smelling skin. Her eyes were drawn to his neat appearance with a freshly shorn face and newly trimmed brassy locks. Why did he have to look so well when she was tired, and perhaps like her sister, easily swayed by a handsome man? One with arms big enough to hold her, but didn't care enough to fight all her battles.

He took her hand and clasped it. "Follow my lead. A good spy stays as close to the truth as possible."

"Great. Does that mean we can tell the countess of this rouse? She's your stepmother. I don't her want thinking ill of me."

Playing with her fingers, rolling them within his gloved hand, he stopped mid-tread. "Why does it matter so much? You are a playing role, right?"

A man like him would never understand. She lowered her gaze to the attendants streaming through the doors. "I'm sure your stepmother will be well pleased with you openly flouting a mistress."

"She's one to judge. Lady Rhodes was my father's mistress. He only married her a couple of months before he died."

The edge in his voice coupled with the sordid

pronouncement, made her take a misstep and lose her balance.

Before she could fall, Bannerman scooped her up. "You are getting clumsy, my dear. No more flirting on the stairs with you."

She couldn't reply and lay wedged against his wide chest, his silky black waistcoat.

"Hugh? Put the girl down so I can get a look at you both."

Phipps, arms loaded with portmanteaus, shook his head as he passed. He led a line of servants up the stairs.

Bannerman set Isadel's boots onto the ground but kept her hand as if she'd run. "Lady Rhodes, this is Isadel Armijo. Shall we do our meet and greet in the study or the drawing room?"

The woman was elegant, trimmed in wine velvet and younger than Isadel expected. She seemed closer in age to be Bannerman's sister than someone who could be a mother to him. "Your father's study. I so miss its view of the grounds."

Lady Rhodes took the lead and wandered down the hall to Bannerman's study.

He swept ahead of them and opened the door. His gaze hadn't the humor it had before. The man seemed very annoyed and shut the door with a thud.

Marveling at how clean and light the room now appeared, Isadel ventured inside and stopped at the desk. It was fixed and finished to a shine, nothing like the wreck it had been the night she arrived.

Pattering to the window, Lady Rhodes spread the curtains wide. "Such beautiful grounds. Now, tell me the story you want me to believe."

Folding his arms and leaning against the threshold, Bannerman's face lost the remaining pretense of a smile. "What are you speaking of, Elizabeth?"

The lady removed her bonnet exposing ringlets and curls of her blonde hair. "The last I hear from you, you write to me telling me of an impending engagement. Then nothing. You've virtually disappeared for all of 1812. No one knows where you are or if you live. The Duke of Hartland won't tell me a thing. I know Sandon was abandoned and in great disrepair. Now everything is righted and you send for me."

Bannerman stood up straight. "Well, the engagement never came about. And as you can see, Sandon has been raised, but I apologize for causing you distress."

Isadel tried not to fidget, but it was obvious she was witnessing a strain between the two. Why would he not share with his stepmother his notion of dying? Isn't that when family is supposed to pull together? Maybe that wasn't an English way as it was for the Armijos.

Lady Rhodes came near swirling her bonnet betwixt her fingers. The white ostrich plume contrasted the deep red of the hat and the deep pink of her clinching fingers. She lifted Isadel's chin like she inspected a horse. "Spin around for me, and tell me of your connections. Who are your relations?"

Isadel looked at Bannerman who half-shrugged, half-nodded. So, she did as the woman asked like a prized pet.

"Her father was a physician killed in the war, but her people have roots in Jamaican sugar."

"Sugar money? Hmmm." Lady Rhodes then put her hands on the sides of Isadel face as if to block her view of everything else. "I want to hear it from her, Hugh. My dear, when his birthday, his favorite color, and how does he likes you to wait for him?"

Cheeks turning to flames, Isadel shook free. "Why do I need to say such private things? You are his stepmother, not mine."

The woman swiveled to Bannerman. "She's young and mouthy and very brown. How did she catch your eye, Hugh? You've only ever cared for one fair blonde, a respectful blonde as you use to laud over me."

He tweaked his perfectly done cravat as if it choked. "As you noted on more than one occasion, that type of woman doesn't love me back. Perhaps, I'd like more of a change and a woman that likes me back. You do like me, Isadel, don't you?"

He'd told her to stay as close to the truth as possible, so she would. "It's a moment to moment assessment."

Bannerman plodded toward her and took Isadel's palm. He bent and kissed it. "What about now?"

Why was he so determined to embarrass her? It would be wrong to swat him in front of the woman he was trying to convince that Isadel was his mistress. "Yes, I like you at this moment."

His light eyes lit and his frown transformed into a smile. "See, Elizabeth, she likes me at this moment. She keeps me on my toes. And when things are well between us, it doesn't matter that I'm pale or ashen. I know little of her except she is a wonder with knives, pastry-making and she likes explosions as much as I do."

The sneer on the Lady Rhodes's face disappeared. "He took you out to the clearing in the trees and showed you his powder experiments?"

Isadel nodded. "It was glorious."

The woman approached him and gazed up at him

with eyes that held tears. "You haven't done that at Sandon since Henry. God rest his soul. Betsy St. Claire was the last person you showed your tricks too. You truly do care for this girl, and you sent for me to prepare her for society."

His swallow was hard and loud. "Yes."

Lady Rhodes took one of his hands and held it. "Why are you in gloves, evening gloves?"

He jerked his fingers back and wrenched at his neck. "I am... I—"

Isadel moved to him and clasped his arm. "He injured his hands rescuing me, and I almost made it worse with the explosions. They're delicate, Hu-ugh." She took a breath and worked her tongue to say his name better, like she'd practiced. "Hugh, I don't want you risking injury again. They must heal."

That lopsided grin of his appeared. "Yes, for you, I'll do as you've commanded."

Lady Rhodes put her hands on Isadel's shoulder. "I never would have believed it if I hadn't seen it myself. Yes, Hugh, I will sculpt Miss Armijo. I'll change her—"

"Don't change her," he said. "Just enhance what's already wonderful."

The woman spun Isadel around and pushed her toward the door. "Hugh, thank you for entrusting her to me. I will not disappoint you."

Isadel lifted her head and marched through the threshold. Letting the fancy woman mold her into one of those English doxies, might prove useful. She might as well see Moldona again looking as much like Agueda as possible. Maybe he'd confess as if he'd seen a ghost. Then Bannerman would have to follow her command and use his healed powerful hands to strike the blackguard dead.

Hugh paced in his overdone study. The scent of turpentine wafted from the walls, which had been painted and repainted twice in the past few days. The perfect shade of peach had been what Elizabeth sought and he acquiesced hoping it would speed up the lessons or whatever she assigned to Isadel. Hugh hadn't seen his chef in over a week.

Pumping his hand looking for a place to punch but not leave a noticeable mark. The sheer silver curtain would expose him. Pummeling the desk would take too long to repair. Hugh was more agitated, more desperate to see his chef.

Back and forth, he moved across the burgundy tapestry spun by the best weavers of the east. It arrived this morning, another of Elizabeth's enhancement to Sandon, but what of Isadel? Would her fresh face be powered up leaving her looking ashen and tired? Would Elizabeth stain those cheeks with awful rouge?

Phipps knocked on the open door then powered inside. "I've done as you said. I made sure the villages know that Sandon will be hosting the regiment commanders. I put out a rumor that Wellesley may come. I spread your money around too. The Almeida Killer or killers will know where you are."

"Good. Has Moldona accepted the invitation?"

"Yes, his post came this morning. He will be bringing Mrs. Moldona. Are you prepared for that?"

"To see old friends, Phipps? Of course."

Laying a stack of papers, probably invoices on the desk, Phipps turned with arms folded. "Master

Henry's sheet music? His missionary things? You intend to do missionary work with all your fellow officers coming?"

Lord knows many needed it. Hugh shook his head. "Thinking of him, reading his papers on peace makes me less anxious."

Phipps flipped through some of the old parchment. "But, sheet music. You intend to exhibit during our big weekend?"

Not wanting to drone on about music or the absence of a tune, Isadel's tune, Hugh just shrugged. "One never knows. Our guests will love music, but Lady Rhodes will probably claim the piano. She had it tuned this week."

"The last time the former Miss St. Claire was here, she was trying to convince you to turn down your commission."

"Yes, she had some vague notion that her own brother wouldn't serve if I didn't. She didn't understand that it is a second son's role to do so. Charles St. Claire would have served with or without me."

"What will she try to convince you of this time? She had a habit of leading you by the nose."

"Well, she has Moldona to confuse."

"Do you think he ever told his wife that he and her brother left out the barrel of powder that exploded killing so many?"

"Not if he were smart. But, Betsy is a generous soul. She might forgive him."

"Had she known her brother's death was partly Moldona's fault, you could've won her. Doesn't that weigh on you?"

It did more times than Hugh wanted to admit until he became sick. Then he was glad. Betsy didn't need more disappointment. "That time in my life has passed. Is there a point to this?"

"I hope you know what you are doing, and I hope Miss Armijo is unharmed in this business. She's not Miss Pearson, not bread to spy work and Mrs. Moldona and some of the other wives of the officers coming to Sandon may not be receptive to her. It's not as if you can give them all a talking too like you did Mrs. Nelson."

"You don't think I know that, Phipps? But, she's part of this. She's searching for truth just like us. My hope is that the Almeida Killer is the killer she's looking for too. Then, she will have justice."

Phipps's frown deepened. "It's hard to know what one is looking for. Master Henry, he was assured in what he wanted and he didn't hunt for much. His soul had peace."

"Yes. Do you think he still has peace where he is? I think of that more. Dying, I mean."

"Your brother wasn't materialistic. He had no wanderlust. He might have turned up missing and started missionary work abroad. I think he always had peace, eternal peace because he knew he was loved and that he was worthy of love."

Hugh put a hand to his brow. "I killed a saint. I know."

"It was an accident."

Moving to the window, Hugh released a sigh. "Was it? I measured the powder exactly—always very much to the last dram. It should not have been enough to blow the two trees, just the one farther away from him. Isadel, Miss Armijo reminded me of how careful I've always been when handling explosives. What if it were tampered with?"

"What if's will drown you in despair. Concentrate on this gathering, staying well, and our live chef. I don't want her hurt."

"You really care about Miss Armijo, Phipps?"

"Don't you?"

"You know I do. I wonder what horror she now faces with my stepmother. She is missed. You know none of the fancy dishes Elizabeth's cook has forced upon Mrs. Nelson have been horrid, though nothing compared to Miss Armijo's cooking." Who knew one could miss meat pies and biscuits so much? He rubbed his fingers, reveling in the balm Isadel left at his bedchamber door. It was his only sign that she hadn't fled and would go through with the charade. "Things are heading to a climax to catch a killer, but my days are still numbered."

Phipps sighed and moved slowly to the door. "Everyone of mine are and the chef's too. But live knowing we are full like Master Henry, filled with peace then they count more. Those seeds she wanted. Our connections have located them. We'll have them soon."

"Another thing to waste my hopes upon."

"It's convenient to think you are dying. Maybe you need to figure out what happens if you live. If I were you, I'd go see what Miss Armijo is up to and if she has the heart to pretend through each day of this visit. Wellesley's spies are good at pretending." Phipps eyed him with that suspicious grin. "Maybe you aren't that good at pretending anymore. I think you've lost that spy tenet. Go seek her out. Claim love or peace, no matter how many days it might last."

As soon as Phipps left the study, Hugh took three more pacing laps, surely enough time for his man to be well onto his next task. Hugh didn't want Phipps to tweak his nose at how fast Hugh planted his boots outside of Elizabeth's suite. Her wing, on the far side of Sandon, would prove an excellent distance. Long enough to school his face so none of his impatience or longing showed.

He reached for the knob and stopped. This unease hadn't been with him in a long time. Must be a side effect Isadel's balm.

Before he'd fully committed to knocking, the door opened. A set of giggling maids left with linens in their hands.

As they descended, one said to the other in low tones. "The barbarian actually looks like a lady."

"You mean like an exotic courtesan."

Their laughter almost sent Hugh's fist through the wall. What had Elizabeth done? Before he broke the door from its hinges, he pushed it open with his thumb and barged inside. Isadel yanked on her baggy jacket. The glimpse he caught of her long neck and bare shoulders swathed in blue maybe deep purple was breathtaking but her face had been rouged and powdered. Her chestnut skin looked pale, sickly. Hugh missed the richness and freshness of her healthy chestnut complexion.

He stepped closer and saw great sadness in Isadel's brown eyes. That stabbed him deeper in his gut. He touched her cheek. The powder reddened his white gloves. "Is this Lady Rhodes' doing?"

Not smiling, perhaps smoldering in anger, Isadel tugged on his sleeve, lowering his arm. "It's what you wanted."

Elizabeth came from a side room. "Isadel don't fidget. Let Hugh admire you. Take off that frumpy thing. Hugh, burn the jacket."

"I'm not a stupid man, Elizabeth. The garment was her late father's. I think she should keep it." He tried to make his voice sound happy, maybe it would cut through the tension he felt drawing him to Isadel. "But don't fret, Isadel. I'd love to admire you."

She stared straight ahead. With a long breath sucked in between her soft lips, she dropped the jacket to the floor.

Humming her tune, the one with the lulling notes, she moved to the fireplace and then back. Isadel's curls had been brushed almost straight and swooped into a severe bun. It would be appropriate if he ventured to take the girl to the theater, but it wasn't his chef's simple style he'd come to know.

"Turn around for us again, Isadel."

The chef did so, spinning slowly. What a beautiful chef.

No one could take away from Elizabeth's taste when it came to clothes. The deep indigo gown made the small sprite's curves more pronounced, more delicious. Hugh bit his lip. He didn't realize he was hungry. "Except for the rouge, you look lovely."

Elizabeth caught Isadel's arm. "I couldn't get her any lighter, but she has a fine figure."

Hugh grimaced at the now ashy complexion of his chef. "I know what is the rage of the ton. If that was what I wanted, I would have applied for your help sooner. You've made Miss Armijo's rich skin look sickly. I don't want anyone as vibrant as she to look diminished. He moved to a sideboard, dunk a cloth in the pitcher of water and then handed it to Isadel. "Please fix your face."

She turned to the hearth.

Elizabeth's frown became more pronounced swallowing up the joy she had in showing off her latest project. "Why are you interrupting? It took forever to get this young woman to listen."

"You've had my mistress for a week. I should have some time with her."

A sparkle returned to Elizabeth's blue eyes. "Before you take Miss Armijo, I need you to look over this. She opened a box on the table and pulled out a long parchment and handed it to him. "A few things to settle upon."

He took the paper and scanned two or three legal sounding lines. "What is this?"

"A contract. You might think you can just get a girl from Timbuktu, but she needs to be protected."

Isadel pushed at her brow. "I tried to tell her this was not necessary."

"It is necessary. Exotics never understand that a man's fancy can change even quicker. Too many are dumped in the streets, used up with no means to return to."

"I want nothing from Bannerman. I will return to being a chef."

"You think you'll be hired once word circulates that you've been a mistress? No. It won't happen. That is why you must be protected. No married woman would have such a tender morsel underfoot."

Hugh scanned the pages again. The details of jewelry requirements and a monetary settlement made his head and conscience spin. Yet, in a completely twisted way, this would make things easier for Isadel if the Almeida Killer caught him unprepared. "I'll sign this. I want Isadel to know her future is protected."

"And make good on the jewelry. I know the first Mrs. Bannerman had things I was never able to have. Your mistress will look well in diamonds or sapphires."

The old girl knew how to squeeze out pence from crumbs. Hugh didn't consider himself ungenerous but without any jewelry, he must look like an ogre instead of a benefactor. "I'll correct this."

"It should be pearls." Isadel's voice was low, distant, a hundred miles away. "My sister, Agueda, had a pearl one. The soldiers took it from her."

"Good, this is settled." Elizabeth said as she straightened the chef's shoulders. "Isadel, would you like a moment alone with our darling Hugh?"

Still not looking at him, she nodded. "Yes."

"The balcony is convenient. I remember Hugh's father loved to talk on the balcony. Usually it was a correction or two. Then sometimes it wasn't. Good luck to you."

Isadel turned and led Hugh to the balcony doors. Her feet made no sound, so she wasn't in her boots, but he wasn't sure if she were barefoot.

Stuffing the paper in his pocket, he followed her out then closed the door behind him.

He took a moment to savor the sight of her in the sun. So beautiful and so sad.

"Isadel, I'm sorry Lady Rhodes is putting you through so much."

"Yes."

He nudged closer to Isadel. "But, I should sign the papers. In case things go badly and the Almeida Killer strikes—"

"Stop."

"I didn't think about how this charade would affect you. I said the next messenger Hart sent would lose their life. I didn't think it would affect their livelihood, but I suppose with no life you can't..." He was running on like a numbskull, and she glared at him like the witless fool he was. "Sorry, Isadel."

"Fine." Her tone sounded clipped and abrupt.

He felt more like a heel than a masterful spy. He'd try again. "The balm you made, I feel it has healing properties. Should be a good start for the seeds when they arrive."

She rolled the damp cloth between her palms. Her gaze lowered, exposing long lashes. "Good."

Her one word answers, proper without a hint of an accent grated. "You look beautifully appointed. I don't approve of all she's done, but she has dressed you well in preparation for our visitors."

"Your visitors."

At least that was two words. He sighed, a short noisy gasp steeped in frustration. "At least that was more words. Should I feel blessed? Not taking too much of Elizabeth's chats on mistress small talk."

Isadel's blank expression sharpened. Thunderbolts were in her eyes and he loved it.

"What do you want me to say, Bannerman? That I am happy doing English dress up. That I look forward to dining with Moldona, a man who should have his throat slit, the one with the pearl necklace. Or do you think me already a flirt like Agueda? She would take pleasure at a compliment coming from her killer or her prison guard."

"You know I have not treated you like a prisoner since that first day. You've had the run of Sandon. This is our truce. I don't want you serving poison from the kitchen. You might miss and get me."

"So, I will dine with my enemy, while you make eyes at your first love. Maybe you'll pass words in low tones thinking my exotic ears cannot hear."

"You know it's a man's prerogative to hear what he wishes. Do I detect jealousy in your words?"

She bit her lip as if that would take back things already said.

He couldn't help but grin. "So Elizabeth has warned you of Betsy and that angers you? You are a mixed up bag of kindling wood. I'm glad you still like me. This spy business can be trying."

"Oooh, you, Bannerman." She turned from him and pounded the stone railing. "Do you think I look forward to having Mrs. Moldona denigrate me as an unsuitable companion when her murderous husband is the one who is unsuitable? You're, as you English say, touched in the upper room, having a party hoping all the killers will come."

"Well, Henry would say a lot of good things come gathering in an upper room."

"But there's always a Judas in the gathering."

"Your wit is to be preferred. You must be a burgeoning Protestant. Isadel, I told you, I don't want you serving Moldona. You need to be close enough to confirm that it was him who did your family the injustice. Maybe you'll see the wretch and forgive him."

Her head spun around like it would detach and roll off the balcony's edge. "Forgiveness for killing the people I care most of? I heard his name clear as this wretched white powder. "

"I wasn't at Badajoz, but battles get chaotic. Maybe he was the one or maybe he wasn't. You have to be sure when you kill, if you want me to enable it."

"Don't joke of such things. You're not going to let me shed his foul blood any more than you would teach me how to control the powder. I don't go back on vows. I said I would go through with this. I will. I will be attired properly. I will wear your English gowns and sound English. I will not embarrass your English hide."

He took the cloth from her balled fist and gently wiped her cheeks and forehead free of the ashen powder, the hideous rouge. "Yes, do so, but with the face I know. The one I like a lot. I've been enough colors with my sickness, even green. I want you looking healthy and brilliant."

She took the cloth from him and finished the task until her complexion was pristine, chestnut silk. "Lady Rhodes was quite insistent that this is what you'd want. She's given me quite a great deal of instruction, even how to sit on your bed like a good little harlot."

"No, I'll tell you what to do there." He laughed hoping she'd smile at his offered joke but even her frown disappeared.

He sobered. "Moldona and his wife will be here tomorrow. The house will be filled with officers and attendants."

"Yes, your Mrs. Moldona. Will you be taking another mistress so soon?"

"Isadel?"

"So now it is your turn for a one word answer."

"Isadel. I'm a man if you hadn't noticed. I've loved, lost and lost some more. Betsy St. Claire, now Moldona is an old friend, one who cared more for my older brother than me. If there was anything ever between us it was because of Henry. He was my twin."

"You lost your twin? The loss of a sibling is horrible, but a twin? That seems closer."

"You and Agueda, were you not close?"

"Not always. I was the serious sister. She was light and filled with giggles. She couldn't help but attract men, poor silly girl. That's what got her killed, but she wasn't wanton."

He took Isadel by the shoulders. "You seem to hate a compliment and like to blend into the background. Is it because you don't want to be like her? You think her easy manner earned her death?"

"She was supposed to stay out of the window. We

were waiting for rescue." Isadel turned from him and stared off into the greenery of Sandon. They weren't high enough to see the waters, but he had that feeling like he had in the tower that she was close to an edge, a choice of what to do next.

He couldn't stand for her to feel so alone and wrapped an arm about her waist drawing her into his chest. "Agueda didn't deserve villainy because she was pretty or even if she flirted. What happened wasn't her fault, no more than it was your fault for not preventing it."

"I'm dressing up like her. I've seen the way everyone is looking. I'm a harlot to them, even Mrs. Nelson. Now she knows why you were so strict, because I'm a jade, a harlot."

"Agueda was no harlot for smiling. You're not one either. This is spy work. It's pretend."

"Bannerman, I might never have a position as a chef again. I worked so hard. My reputation, I was the good daughter." Her voice clouded in tears. "You said death to the next messenger who disturbed you. You are so right. Death to my reputation, my sense of right and wrong. I'm a hypocrite showing off my shoulders to you, for enjoying your compliments. Even twisting up your name hoping you'd do my bidding."

He lifted his hand and stroked her neck. He slid off his glove and let his finger feel the silk, the beating of blood pulsed the vein beneath so fast, so like his own. "Don't bury yourself in guilt. Don't hide your loveliness. Your sister didn't cause her death or your father's. Evil men are to blame. And you are not evil because you lived."

A tear rolled onto his wrist. He held Isadel closer as she cried in his arms. Flicking a few pins away, he unraveled her bun and rested his chin on her freed curls. They smelled of violets, not cinnamon. Other than that, this moment was perfect.

"Must be the powder, the white face powder is making me weepy, Bann-er-man." She pried away from the embrace he wanted to last a little longer. "Sorry."

"Lady Rhodes is helping you to be in the forefront where I want you to be. This will be your first spy mission, so indulge her in everything but powders and rouge. I want you robust looking." He clasped her hand and spun her to him. "I told you I like you as you are. When are you going to believe me?"

"Hugh Bann-er-man, you don't mind that your mistress is moody and very brown, barbarian brown?"

"I love your accent. Nothing is as tempting as my name on your lips. I think you are very fine, brown, round and beautiful."

"And will I make a good assassin?"

"Isadel, it's not in you. You're a healer and a bread maker. You are not a killer."

Her eyes squinted to mere slits. "There is no other way to make this right for Agueda. I've been blaming her for putting Papa and me in a position where we couldn't save her. So sorry, Agueda. If you can hear me, know I'm sorry."

Against his new waistcoat, Isadel cried old tears. Maybe releasing some of the trapped guilt that should have left her soul a year ago. She cried a little harder, a little longer, and his heart broke a little more for her. "You talk of your father and your sister, but what of your mother?"

"I told you she died a long time ago."

He lifted her chin so she wouldn't miss the concern pressing him. "She's alive in the song you hum. You think she'd approve of holding on to this guilt over Agueda or of you seeking to kill another human being?"

"Are you trying to shame me into giving up revenge? It's my right. And it's the only way to make things right for Agueda."

In frustration, Hugh shook his head because it would be wrong to shake Isadel. "The girl I've come to admire is not a killer. Don't let guilt make you into one. Moldona is skilled. He'll kill you and be justified, saying you attacked him."

She took his hand within hers and pulled it to her bosom. "If you admire me, then do it for me."

Her breathing sounded stuttered and harsh, and part of him wanted to give her everything, but he couldn't kill again. "I cannot. Ask anything else. I would give you my life, Isadel. I have been scraping for a chance to live whole, free of disease. I'd give it all up for you. I'll die for you. I just can't kill again."

She put her arms about his waist and hugged him. "What do we do now?"

"We go on with charade. Isadel, I need you. I can't do this without you."

"I suppose there is no chance you will make Moldona explode, but what about giving me his head on a silver platter? Like Herodias, the Judean princess' enemy."

Ah, Biblical puns. His twin loved them so. Isadel's wit had returned and it filled his lungs with much needed air. "Moldona's no John the Baptist. He is a skunk and a womanizer for sure, but murderer? I served with him. We've had our differences, but I'm not convinced he would do such evil."

She patted her eyes, and then gazed up at him with a bit of smile showing. "His head on a platter would be nice."

"Does this mean you'll dance for me to entice me and convince me to do it? That might have the power to sway me. You warm my heart. My brother, Henry, loved absurd Biblical puns. He'd be proud of yours. He'd also like to see how you'd sway to a violin set. We had similar tastes."

Behind him, the glass pane rattled. He wanted to ignore it, but knew the annoyance would not flee. "Great, Elizabeth is looking in upon us. Would you mind? I don't want her to think we quarrel..."

It would take too long to explain, so he reached down to kiss Isadel, but she turned her cheek to him. It felt awkward to not taste her lips, but he still gave her a long peck across her jaw. "Though we differ on Moldona, we are in this charade too far to abandon it. Are you still with me?"

She nodded and slipped from his arm. "Yes."

"You were far more amorous when there were explosives. I'd hate to have to resort to such to make you at ease. The house is starting to look nice."

"Don't worry, Bannerman, your barbarian is ready for every nasty innuendo your guests will offer. We'll catch your killer, though no one cares about mine."

"Isadel, it's not like that."

She rolled her shoulder away from his outstretched hand, the first time she'd shunned him. "Lady Rhodes has trained your courtesan well about when to offer favors and when to withhold them."

Frowning so big, her pretty face looking disappointed, Isadel traipsed back into the bedroom chamber leaving Hugh alone on the balcony.

How could he get her to understand? It stung his

pride to know she felt small and low and believed her pain didn't matter. He'd made things worse by placing the proud woman in an undignified guise as his mistress. Other spies had played such roles, but Isadel wasn't a spy. She was a woman in want of justice. The one thing he couldn't give her, the one thing that mattered.

Until she received it, she'd never be free. Today, she'd pushed him away, something she hadn't done when they were alone in the kitchen or even when they'd met and she talked to him on the other side of the closet door.

Angry at the circumstances he had made, he stomped back into the room. "Our guests will be arriving tomorrow. Miss Armijo, Lady Rhodes, I will expect you two to be ready to greet them."

Elizabeth came alongside Isadel. "We will be ready, and she will be returning to the adjacent suite next to yours tomorrow. It's quite a nice room from what I remember."

Isadel's frown became more pronounced. "I like the tower room."

Brushing Isadel's cleaned cheek. "Don't be silly, dear. Your place is at his side. And you need to be close to him, at his beck and call."

The sound of Elizabeth's prescription for Isadel held as much charm as it did anguish. His pretend mistress cringed, wrinkling her delicate brow. His gut twisted in response. "I like her face fresh and her curls not so severe."

"If that is what you want, dear. I'll make sure that's what we do. Don't forget the contract."

Isadel moved away from them as if she was consenting to them talking about her like an object. She put on her father's coat and sat primly on the chaise. The fire had gone from her again.

Smiling wide and toothy, Elizabeth took his arm and walked him to the door. "She'll be ready as your hostess. You'll be proud, but sign the papers and give them to me."

Truthfully, the contract would be a way to protect Isadel's future, but it saddened him nonetheless. It wasn't the chef who had to prove that a mixed raced woman could excel as his hostess. It was Hugh who had to prove that he was a worthy friend who wouldn't compromise her any further.

Yet, they were in this too deep to quit now. They had a killer or killers to catch. "Elizabeth, you did all of this for my father? You turned yourself inside out to please him?"

"I made the most of my options, Hugh. My choices made me Mrs. Bannerman and then a countess. Trust me. I know what I am doing, with or without face powder."

"Thank you, Elizabeth. I think. Unable to catch Isadel's gaze, he pivoted and went to the door feeling as if he walked on soggy ground, as if his boots were sinking. His gut knotted twice, for his fake plan might've ruined something that had begun to feel true.

Isadel took a breath when Hugh slipped out the door. Part of her wished she hadn't become emotional in front of him. The other part still raged. She didn't come to Sandon to play dress up or to make nice to Moldona over dinner. Agueda would laugh at her and Papa would be so disappointed in her.

Lady Rhodes sat across from her. "This is your first time being a mistress?"

Twisting her fingers about themselves, Isadel nodded. "Yes. I don't think I am very good at it."

The woman laughed as if she'd made a joke, but who could jest at such things.

"I see it now, Isadel, how much you care for Hugh. I was beginning to think you two were lying about this. What better way to tweak my nose, knowing how he closed me out of his world? I know I am not his mother, but I loved his father very much. I've always wanted the best for him."

"Why didn't he like you? You don't seem horrid."

"Flattery is not one of your strong suits, dear. We need to work on that. He and Henry had their own sensibilities. I wasn't borne of wealth. They were loath to admit that I was what the elder Bannerman wanted. I wasn't much older than them."

Isadel stood and warmed her hands, staring at her image in the silvered mirror. "So how can you be confident that I am what he wants? Your maids are openly incredulous."

"Dear, you're a female that's breathing, one that has somehow made a man who chose to separate himself from everyone open up to you. You're exactly what he wants. Hugh has always been different. And I'm glad he is no longer in love with Betsy St. Claire. Her parents used to visit during the summers. They were close to his father and tried to encourage an attachment. Then Henry died and Hugh went to war. I thought they'd given up. I for one was relieved when she married that Mr. Moldona. Hugh needs to be free of the past with someone who could admire his good qualities."

He did have good qualities. And Isadel knew he understood her rage. "He has a great deal of patience."

"I bet you keep him sharp, on his toes. But, never bruise his ego. Build it. That's the difference in why I've been elevated twice. Most women don't get that."

A brow popped of its own volition. Curiosity was Isadel's undoing. She settled down beside Lady Rhodes. "You won his father over by fanning him with flattery? Is it so easy to lie?"

"No lies, just choosing what to focus upon, the good over the bad. The bad is always there. Let that be another's job to rub his nose in it. You are his treasure. His reward. The late Bannerman saw that and made an honest woman of me."

Isadel caught her gaze, shocked at how practical the advice sounded, something like her mother would say, just not in such a Cyprian sexually tinged manner. Hugh was right. Her mama would approve of none of this, not being a mistress and not hunting a killer.

"A woman doesn't have to stay a mistress, Isadel, not when your sweetheart is single like Hugh or widowed. He just needs prodding."

This Lady Rhodes was worse than the marriage makers back in Badajoz. Isadel folded her arms, snuggling deeper in Papa's jacket. "Marriage is not on my mind."

"It should be. There's no security without it, especially for an exotic girl like you. Oh, he'll sign the papers that will afford you a settlement upon a break, but that will only last until you have another arrangement. How many times do you want to find a new benefactor? You must think of that. Youth seems like an impatient stew. You want to stir here or there, sometimes at the same time. But the kettle will cool down, so you have to know what happens next."

The lady had sermonized mistress making as if it were a recipe. It sounded rational to Isadel. Oh, her brainbox must still be rattled by the hulk of man and his gigantic doubts about Moldona. "Lady Rhodes, your thoughts are kind, but this thing between Hugh and myself will not last."

"Please, tell me you are not already contemplating new arrangements. Don't break Hugh's heart. If you can't see how much he cares, then you're daft. Not seeing you for days had him rattled enough to come find you and spend time in my domain. He hated coming to me, and I know he hated asking for my help. Rest assured, he will sign your contract."

She wanted to correct her, to tell her that this was a ruse to catch a killer, and it had nothing to do with money or sentiment. But that was a lie too. Hugh said he desired her. That he liked her as she was and her stubborn heart beat like it had gone crazy when he held her on the balcony. "It's so hard to think of this."

"It's hard to admit to what you feel when your situation as a mistress is so tenuous. I didn't let myself admit to loving Hugh's father until I was sure he loved me. To not admit it, I thought, would keep me from being hurt if we broke apart. The problem was I lied to myself. I wasn't brave enough. If I had been honest, I would have won his love sooner."

Isadel shrugged and paced to the fireplace. "I hear honesty is overrated."

"So says a stubborn woman. Well, keep him satisfied and when you are more confident in his affections you'll see things as I do. He is happier with you than without you."

Isadel felt her jaw become slack and drop open a mile wide at the woman's bold talk, her naked honesty. When she recovered, she asked, "Please, tell me more about the guests. What is this

Moldona like?"

Lady Rhodes leaned over the tea service and poured herself a cup. "I should've had you practice pouring again. Moldona... He was a nice young man. I think he was jealous of Hugh and Henry. Hugh had the better military assignment for his father purchased a better commission. And then there is Betsy St. Claire."

Not wanting to sound anxious or annoyed at this woman who chose a murderer over Hugh, Isadel swallowed and prepared her tongue to sound unemotional. "You've told me that she was pretty."

"Very pretty and very doting on her younger brother. She was devastated when he died in the war. He served under Hugh. I knew when St. Claire died she'd never marry Hugh. He was the reason the boy joined the military."

Knowing Hugh as well as she did, Isadel knew he felt guilt over such death. Poor Hugh.

The door opened and the two chattering maids returned with a bulk of creamy satin and sheer lace.

Lady Rhodes bounced up, her face lighting as if Papa Noel had descended with presents. "It's here." She grabbed the fabric and floated the translucent edge of the material in the air. "It's time to discuss one-for-alls and your robes. Nightwear is important."

Isadel bowed her head. Guilt wouldn't kill her. Sheer embarrassment would do her in before she could ever lay hands on Moldona. Yet, she knew she'd come too far to abandon everything now. Maybe Hugh would surprise her and reward Isadel with Moldona's head. If he didn't, she'd find a way to avenge Agueda and Papa. With a quick restorative breath, she stood and rent her arms wide. "Ready, Lady Rhodes. Show me what I must know to do this well."

Sometime during this weekend, she'd face Moldona. Then she'd show Hugh what she could do. She'd avenge her family, especially Agueda. She had to kill Moldona for her sister's sake.

Chapter Eleven: A Visit With Friends And Enemies

Sandon buzzed. It hummed with conversations and servants, more than Hugh could ever imagine. The retired commanders of Almeida and the ones that could be spared from the fight save Wellesley had arrived at Hugh's door, ready to spend the weekend supping and drinking at his table. If the killer wanted revenge against them all, then Sandon was a ripe target. The angst of waiting for death would be over, well at least death by this fiend.

He tugged on his gloves. His hands felt more human. Hopefully, his sallow fingers were soft against Isadel's cheek. Goodness knows her skin felt soft and silky.

He blinked to clear his head of the girl who hadn't shown herself or dared to come down and help greet his guests. Clarity could mean the difference between catching a killer and watching the best men die.

Drawing back the sheer curtains, he peered out his study window. Teams of carriages lined his grated drive, so much for Sandon's obscurity. Yet, he felt assured one of these horse-drawn vehicles brought a killer to his door.

A quick knock made him pivot. He slouched against the wall as Elizabeth waltzed inside the room followed by a familiar pretty face. "Lady Rhodes... Mrs. Moldona."

Betsy came to him with hands outstretched.

He stood up straight, and almost wished to yank in place his turquoise silk waistcoat that hung over his buff breeches. "Welcome to Sandon again."

After accepting his kiss to her gloved hand, she whirled around. Her deep salmon carriage gown whipped at her short heels. "Sandon looks wonderful. The rumors are false. It looks the same as when you and Henry and I were here. You are wearing Henry's watch. I gave it to him for his last birthday."

He picked up the gold chain and swirled it. "Yes, Mrs. Moldona. He loved it and it reminds me of him and how short our time with him was, how short time is for everyone."

Her face blanked as she touched its etched cover.

The brief joy he took in seeing her became engulfed in the memories of a day not much like this one where a fool thought he could play with detonations to impress a girl. He released the watch and it dangled once again over his waistcoat. "I've made some new improvements, and under Lady Rhodes skillful...hands, Sandon stands tall, as fine as ever."

Elizabeth sank into a chair by his desk. Her complexion looked a little pink, a little tired. Ten couples and servants to boot is a great deal to manage.

Betsy took a spin about the room, touching

paintings, and poking books along the bookcase. "Lady Rhodes, if I'd known you needed help, I would have had Mr. Moldona bring us sooner. I feel a connection to this place. With Hugh and Henry."

Pulling out a silken fan, Elizabeth fluttered the air about her face. Ringlets bounced, but her mouth seemed poised to strike. "I have enough help with Hugh's—"

"No. Mrs. Moldona," He said, "we handled things the best we could, but thank you for the offer." He strolled to his desk and sat on the edge feeling a little awkward bringing up Isadel to Betsy like this. "No need to fret. Elizabeth, you have out done yourself. I am grateful."

Lowering her powdered brow, Elizabeth smiled. "Dearest Hugh, it is my pleasure, but I am sure your special friend will be able to handle things, once she is more familiar with Sandon."

Stopping as if she'd tripped into an invisible wall, Betsy turned from inspecting the bookcase. "Special friend?"

"Elizabeth, please. Not now."

"Yes, Hugh's new lady friend." Elizabeth cooed and smiled wide. "She is quite something."

"I'm very happy for you." Betsy said the words, but her tone was cold. "You deserve some happiness. Henry would have wanted that."

A chill swept over him the way she said his brother's name. Was she still stewing in anguish over Henry? Well, Hugh had been too, only escaping the guilt the past few weeks.

A knock set upon the door. Small and constant. In an instant, he knew it to be Isadel. She'd decided to come down now when she felt the crowds had cleared.

He plodded to the door and opened it, then

caught her hand. "Ah, Miss Armijo, you've decided to join us."

Though Elizabeth looked on smiling perhaps at the mulberry gown and pelisse adorning the chef, Betsy squinted. "Is this your special friend? Hugh, what is this? You brought a trinket back from your travels."

Isadel closed her eyes for a second. "I see you are busy, Mr. Bannerman. I can speak with you later."

He kept a hold of her hand. "Nonsense, I want you stay. My old friend should meet my new friend. Mrs.—"

"That's quite fine. I'll retire until dinner." Betsy said and pivoted toward the door.

It hit him. The clarity of the cut Isadel was about to receive. A wife of the ton didn't want to meet a mistress.

"That's fine, Mrs. Moldona. You can meet my fiancé later."

Betsy stopped and turned. Her face became pale and blank.

Isadel's hold on his arm slacked. She didn't quite look faint, but she didn't seem quite sturdy.

"She..." Betsy said looking like a lost child. "She is to be mistress here? Henry's Sandon."

Elizabeth sprung off the chaise as if the pronouncement had given her new life. "This is Hugh's estate and what a fine wife Miss Armijo will make."

A small hint of a smile whisked across Isadel's face. "I came to speak with you, alone for a moment, but it seems you are still entertaining guests."

"No, my dear. Let's take a walk. Excuse us, ladies. I'll have you back in half an hour, plenty of time to be ready for dinner." Since he hadn't stopped holding her hand, it was easy to keep her at his side and lead her out onto the patio and beyond.

She nodded with the same enthusiasm one would have facing a firing squad, but she held onto his arm and let him lead the way.

Through the groves, past his explosive demonstration area to a spot by the stream, they walked in silence, but somehow the simple quiet felt right—to be in Sandon's park with a woman who he liked very much. And Hugh had enough imagination to pretend she liked him too. Time was short. A killer could be here or on the way, and all Hugh could think upon was the true smile his faux elevation had brought to Isadel's lips.

The quiet of the park, less the call of a gull heading to sea felt peaceful to Isadel. It was the most at peace she felt since Hugh announced his scheme to draw out a killer and her enemy. Hugh led her past the spot where she nearly killed them.

A lump nested in her throat, like a bird that had found a home inside, she coughed. Then she hummed. Mama's tune of hope needed to steady the rhythm of her heart.

Hugh stopped and stretched. "Phipps has had this area turned quite nicely. Doesn't look like we've done much damage."

If he wasn't going to explain the new twist in their plan, she wasn't going to ask. She pulled away and searched for pockets in her short plum jacket but found none. "Definitely doesn't smell like black powder."

"My hand is feeling better. Even though you've

been busy with Elizabeth, thank you for remembering me."

"Just because you banished me to lady school far from the kitchen, I did not forget you. I sneak down when everyone's asleep. I guess I won't be doing that with a house full of people."

He planted in front of her like a big tree and blocked her vision of the setting sun. "I suppose you have questions about what I said in my study."

"You mean your latest guise? I didn't come here to wear lace, pretend to be engaged, or have my hand kissed by a killer."

He took her palm and lifted it to his mouth. "But I've killed too. Do you mind me?"

"I didn't come for that either."

"It's a side benefit, Isadel."

She folded her arms about her. "What do I have to remember about this scheme?"

He scratched his forehead. "Why are you angry?"

Bending, she picked up a pebble and sent it flying into a tree. "When am I not? You could have left me in the kitchen. I could've waited on you...and your guests."

Towing her, he took her closer to the trees. The scent of freshly cut pine filled the air.

"Isadel, I saw you smile when I said fiancé. Mrs. Moldona was going to cut you direct. I didn't want that."

"You watch me that closely?"

"I like having my eyes on you. Next best thing to gloves."

"More jokes, Bannerman. You're like the rest. No, you're better. Your Mrs. Moldona will now treat me with respect while you are around, but she'll show her true nature to me." She bent again and picked up a coral colored rock. If it were all the falsehoods, she'd throw it as far as she could. "I'm tired of this, Bannerman. Other men made their advances, left with a few choice cuts and let me be. But you, you are the worse."

He scooped her up and lifted her high. "Am I?"

She slammed her palms onto his iron shoulders and tried to press free. "What are you doing?"

"My neck was hurting, and I'd like to look you in the eye as you tell me about myself. Or maybe as I tell you about yourself, Isadel. I finally understand why you want to be in the shadows. It's safer for you. You get to hide and stew in your anger because you are afraid. You've run from the safety of the abbey to come to me. You have the run of Sandon, but you hide in the kitchen. I elevated you from sham mistress to faux future Mrs. Bannerman and you are scared. Why do I frighten you?"

Frustration and truth swirled inside as his hypnotic eyes bore into her. It was hard to breathe levitating in his hands. Her arm shook and she pulled closer to him to steady herself but the smell of his clean pine soap and the sweet aloe of the hand lotion filled her nostrils, guiding her to nestle closer. "I'm frightened because I can't pretend so well."

Her lips found his, and she couldn't stop wanting his kiss. It did mean something to her to not be thought of as low. It did mean everything that he would want to show her off as a wife and not an exotic mistress.

She clung to his neck and enjoyed how tight his arms went about her. She was safe in his embrace, the first time she felt so since Badajoz.

"Hugh, Miss Armijo?"

Isadel opened her eyes to see Mrs. Moldona standing near.

Bannerman lowered her to the ground but kept his hand linked to Isadel's. "Betsy, I mean Mrs. Moldona, what are you doing out here?"

"I did not mean to interrupt. And I should congratulate you. I came to see Henry. I haven't been to Sandon in a long time."

"I'll take you. I'll take you both to see." Hugh secured Isadel's hands onto his sleeve then offered his other to the woman. They walked a little farther and came to a marker that was close to a stream.

Hugh released them both. He took a cloth from his pocket and wiped the top of the stone.

It read Henry Bannerman. It was Hugh's brother who had been killed in the explosion.

Mrs. Moldona bent down and touched the stone. "I still remember that day." Her voice took on a weepy tone. "You were trying to impress me, but there was too much powder in the trunk. Poor Henry was felled by that tree."

"I wasn't strong like I am today. I wish I could've saved him."

Mrs. Moldona put her hand on his shoulder. "At least you know where your brother is buried. My brother is laid to rest in Spain, some unknown spot near Almeida.

She started to tear. Hugh rose and held out a handkerchief, but she stepped into his arms.

"I'm sorry to be so emotional. I guess I know how you suffer. I wish he never served."

His face clouded. "Charles St. Claire was a good officer, but I know he'd want you to live and be happy. I did suffer until recently, when I remembered this myself."

Mrs. Moldona smiled one of those polite English woman smiles, the one that said I'm too much of a lady to disagree.

He patted her arm and stepped away. "Well, I will escort you two back to the house and we can all prepare for dinner. Should be a fine evening. You and Miss Armijo will get to meet the men with whom St. Claire served."

"It is my pleasure to meet them." Mrs. Moldona fastened her hand to Hugh's arm.

Isadel let them navigate the path ahead of her, but didn't like Mrs. Moldona hovering over Hugh like bees protecting their honeycomb.

Maybe he was right to want Isadel out of the shadows. How aggressive would Mrs. Moldona be if she thought Hugh was free?

Hugh tied his cravat tighter as he stared into the mirror, his finger slipping on the raw silk. Isadel's balm made his fingers slippery, but he felt more human, more alive than he had in a long time. Their interrupted kiss stayed on his mind, his heart. That feeling settled on him, the one he didn't want to name—well that had been a long time too.

"I found it," Phipps said. Dressed in a garnet and cream livery with his hair curled and freshly powdered, his man came out of the closet holding a long tailcoat. "Not a casualty of the moths."

He walked over swinging and shaking the jacket. "A search of our guests' belongings has found nothing out of the ordinary—a few guns, a few knives and lots of female trappings in a sea of portmanteaus. Nev did have more flintlocks in his bags."

Nev, from what Hugh recalled, was a brash officer with big dreams to win the war on his shoulders alone. "He must be expecting trouble. No one ever said he was stupid. And, what do you expect when officers travel with their wives?" Hugh adjusted the knot of his cravat. Third time was the charm. "Now, a perfect tie. I guess being out of practice has consequences as there would be if you were caught elbow deep in petticoats."

"To be sure, Bannerman. Pity your practice comes from trying to catch a murderer. I don't think The Almeida Killer has arrived yet. But he could be working with someone here."

"Very much so. And now that word has spread that everyone even Wellesley might be at Sandon, the killer will be here. I feel it. Before the weekend is done, we will know the fiend's name." Adjusting the billowy material of his shirt beneath his onyx waistcoat, Hugh noted the way the fabrics draped, each hiding several sins, a smudge of gluttony, powder burns and a scar. Old battles, old sins. Sighing, he hung Henry's watch from his pocket. "Our guests have settled in. The Almeida Killer hasn't struck. Isadel hasn't killed Moldona. Good so far."

Straightening Hugh's collar, Phipps stood near him at the mirror. "I saw you return from a walk with Mrs. Moldona on your arm. Miss Armijo followed behind."

Sliding on the ebony evening coat with its fine silver threads on the buttons, Hugh shrugged. "Betsy Moldona is very much the same. Still lovely, still mourning Henry."

"Your brother was a good young man."

"Yes, yes he was. But he wouldn't want any of us mourning him like this. I realize it now. He'd want us to take his humor and zest for life and keep marching. He'd want us to see that even though things didn't go as we planned, there are still blessings."

A smile lit on Phipps's serious face all the way to his bag laden eyes. "Master Henry would enjoy the way you have Sandon looking. I dare say he'd approve of your mistress's influence."

"It's faux fiancé now."

Phipps's lips puckered to an o-shape as he marched back to the closet. "A little elevation for our chef? She deserves it."

In the looking glass, Hugh studied his reflection, one of strength, with a complexion that seemed healthy, even rosy. "I mashed together enough truth to hopefully satisfy Mrs. Moldona and any others who might not want her to attend our little gathering."

"By saying you're to be wed..." His man still rummaged in the deep closet, but his voice pierced. "This marriage to our chef feels more natural."

Not wanting to examine his own motives too closely, Hugh wrenched at his neck. "I suppose. I surely didn't work into our disguise that she was bequeathed to me like a ward. More or less. This wouldn't stop Mrs. Moldona or any of the other wives from feeling uncomfortable with Miss Armijo joining our little party. Why choose a lesser guise for her when we can shoot for lucky stars? If one would count pretending to be engaged to a sick man as being on the top."

Returning to his side, Phipps held out a wooden box. "This is just as you requested. Your mother's pearl necklace and the other **gift**. Are you sure you want to give it to Miss Armijo? She's still seeking revenge."

Clasping the smooth wood betwixt his palms, he pulled it close to his chest. "She deserves a chance to choose. Shall she choose life or death? It's her right."

"I suspect you think she'll choose correctly. Your brother would approve of Isadel Armijo because she took a dying man and helped him choose to live again."

Phipps moved to the door and stopped. "I saw Mrs. Moldona had you penned up on the patio."

She hadn't changed much since the last time Hugh saw her when he wished her well on her elopement. "We'd just seen Henry's grave."

"Many things can happen in two years, and to be honest, she's never been that attentive. Master Henry or Moldona always occupied her. Was it different, once you mentioned our chef?"

Memories were a dangerous thing. They should make things fuzzier not clearer, not when Hugh lost his brother trying to impress Betsy. "Maybe she needs someone to listen. Perhaps Moldona slipped up and she found out about his womanizing. It's a shame if he's broken her heart. She doesn't deserve that."

"Hugh Bannerman, Mrs. Moldona is married to your enemy. Your father struggled with his morals, but he never once took up with a married woman."

"Why would he with Elizabeth taking care of his every need?"

"You may not have approved but when two unattached adults find love, is it wrong? Is it wrong when the love does not come from a conventional situation?"

Phipps didn't seem to be talking about Elizabeth and Hugh's late father. "Timing is not my friend. We have a murderer to stop before he strikes again. Whether Betsy Moldona has finally figured out that her husband is unworthy is none of my concern. This weekend is to draw out a killer's hand."

Phipps nodded. "And beyond this weekend, what is your concern, your past or your fiancé?"

When the door closed, Hugh put down the box and pumped his fingers. The skin had healed with no open wounds, but there was still swelling. If his days numbered a year, was that enough for a woman full of life?

At any rate, his hands had enough strength to stop the killer. Of that Hugh had no doubts.

Chapter Twelve: Dinner and A Song

Isadel sat still as a watched pot as Lady Rhodes'
maid yanked and pulled at her tresses to form
another el bollo, a twisted bun. "This chignon looks
well on you, Miss Armijo. If you need anything,
ma'am, send for me."

Agreeing with the maid who'd called her a
barbarian, Isadel sighed inside. The news of her
false engagement spread fast. Even those who
mocked her now acted differential.

The maid left, and Isadel was sure she wouldn't
think of her as wanton but lucky. Well, maybe she
was in this pretend world.

She sighed again. This was Hugh's doing, that big
impulsive spy. Isadel knew in her heart she cared
for him deeply but playing pretend to catch a killer
of English soldiers did little to cheer her. Resting
her head on a palm, Isadel was a failure. She'd waltz
on Hugh's arm, speak politely to his friend, the man
who ruined Isadel's world. How was this to be
done? Even flirtatious Agueda would never do such.

A noise from the adjacent room, perhaps footfalls
and a closing door meant Hugh was alone. She was

alone but she couldn't move, couldn't even conceive of doing anything else but sitting in her chair and hoping the night would end quickly without her ever coming down and having to see Moldona.

A tap on the door made her bolt up. "Isadel, let me have a look at you."

After the way she slobbered all over him, she couldn't see him either. "I'm not ready."

"Even more incentive to look at you."

She heard his confident tones and could picture his lopsided grin as he said it.

He knocked on the door but didn't open it. "I was mostly joking. But I have a present for you before we go down to dinner."

"You go and check on your guests."

"Isadel, come to me and don't be afraid. I know you were pretending earlier. Perhaps to tweak my nose or you saw Mrs. Moldona coming. It's fine. All in a spy's work."

Call it ego, but to hear him belittle her mixed up emotions stung. She stood up and swept to the door. "You think my kiss was for show?"

"Yes." Thud. It sounded as if he sat or sank against the door. "And I'd love for you to show me again."

His laugh, full throated and bubbly, made the tension in her shoulders lessen. She opened the door to give him a few choice words, but he flopped onto her translucent silver slippers. "Are you ready to go down to dinner, my dear?"

"Did you hurt yourself, Bannerman?"

He loosened his cravat as he stared up at her. "I don't want our guests to come up here, so it is essential that we go down."

"Can't we say your mistre...fiancé is not well?"

"Tell me what this is, Isadel."

"I'm all dressed up in this fancy wear." Her voice sounded so pathetic and strained even worse than when she tried to sound English. It made her ears hurt. She started again trying to hide her desperation. "I want to wear my father's coat when I see his murderer again."

"Well, for one it's not appropriate for ladies to wear menswear to dinner." He put an arm behind his neck as a deeper smile crossed his lips.

"What, Bannerman?"

"I suddenly know why I like cream in my coffee. Or is it coffee in my cream."

Her cheeks grew hot against her will. "You should go down. I'll come later. Maybe when dessert is served."

He tapped the crystal beads that floated about the hem of her snowy gown. "You are quite striking. Elizabeth knows how to pair the perfect cap sleeves with such toned arms. Every girl should take up kneading bread."

She sidestepped him and let his head bang to the floor. "Will you stop?"

He righted himself and leaned against the threshold very much as he'd done at the closet in the tower. "If we go down, we'll go down together, Isadel. Or we can wait here until the Almeida Killer strikes."

"You'll need to be downstairs so you can see him coming."

"Not without my bold chef. Can you send her along?"

She spun to him with arms folded. "You shouldn't be on the floor. Up with you."

"There she is, but am I to admire her from afar?"

Regretting what would happen if she came close enough to see the gold flecks in his hazel eyes, she neared with caution and lowered her palm to him. "Up."

Stretching, he fished in his pocket. "Let me put my gloves on first."

Not wanting to delay him any further, she bent and tugged on his arm.

His gaze wrestled with hers. She felt it sneak past and settle on the beading edging her scalloped neckline. The hairs on her neck to the upsweep of her bolle chignon raised in anticipation of a kiss.

"You are a wondrous beauty, Isadel Armijo." He stood up and towered over her, commanding her full attention.

"With your hair up in curly ringlets, tendrils swinging down to your shoulders, I want to play in them, loop them about my fingers and draw you close."

"No one's stopping you."

She took his bare hands and put his fingers on her cheek. "I know the seeds will cure you. I'm not afraid of you."

"But you are afraid of going downstairs? I want my kitchen goddess by my side."

"Just for a dinner? You can make do."

"Not only for one dinner or one night."

She kissed his fingertips like she wanted to kiss him, full forced. "You should go before one of us says something we both will regret."

"I don't regret anything with you, but I know you can't say the same, Isadel. You didn't come here for me. You didn't choose to live because of me. Everything you want is downstairs."

Surprised at his words, she squinted up at him. "I came for revenge, to be taught how to kill."

"Is that still what you want? I want what is left of my life to be yours."

Still holding his gaze, she pulled his hand to her heart. "I want two things. I want you well, living a long life, but I still wanted Moldona dead. How can I be happy when Agueda can never be happy?"

"She wouldn't want you to suffer any more than Henry would want me to suffer. That song you hum, your mother's tune. I found something similar in Henry's papers. He wanted his world tour to include missionary work. He was influenced by George Liele, the man who wrote your song. The words: Life is the hour which God has given to escape from hell and fly to heaven. You and I, it's time to escape the prisons of guilt we've built."

She wanted to break free, but couldn't grasp his outstretched hand. "I've journeyed to this moment. I must try. I sat and listened in fear. Papa's last admonition was to stay put. I did and they died. He's gone and this is my one chance to right this wrong."

Hugh bent and picked up a wooden box and handed it to her. "Then this might help. Open it."

She took it then gave it a shake. The dull stiff tone gave nothing away.

His lopsided grin showed for a moment then settled into a serious line. "It's not black powder. Something more your style."

The hinge of the box squeaked as she pried the lid open. She looked up at him and saw his smile. The reflection of a small pearl necklace shone in his eyes.

A pearl bigger than Agueda's. Her throat closed. She couldn't speak.

Hugh lifted the pearls to her neck and fastened them. He took full advantage of touching her skin, making her shiver with each stroke of his fingertips. "This will serve you well but maybe not as well as what else is in the box."

She poked inside and touched a gold metal stick. "What is this?"

He took the object from her and pushed the small button on the handle. A sharp knife about four inches in length flipped out of it. "Voila." He hit the button again and the blade retracted. "This is my little gift to you. My very first spy knife."

"You used it on one of your missions?"

He shrugged. "An unlucky footpad in London. But you will be the first to kill with it. If you are going to take revenge, it needs to be with a weapon you are very comfortable with. No onion has a chance around you, and neither will Moldona."

"I don't like your jokes." She pushed the knife away. "Put this away."

He took her hand and shoved it close to his chest. "When you kill with a knife you shove it between the ribs, between the second and the third is the most effective, just like I told you."

"I don't want to kill you, Bannerman."

"Why not? I was an English soldier. One who fought and killed thousands in Spain. Might've killed a cousin to you. War isn't fair. There is no time to ask questions. Like Almeida, the fighting was horrific, death was everywhere and when one side wins they can be as ugly in victory."

"Are you excusing Moldona, the man who slaughtered my family?"

"No, not at all. If you are sure he is guilty, you do what you must. You have to choose and be confident in your choice.

She slacked her hold on the knife and dropped it. "How do I do that? The repercussion will fall on you."

He stuck the knife in her silky reticule. "Don't fret

about me. I'm a big boy who can take care of myself. You came to me, not for dinner, not to have found a special spot in mine and Phipps's hearts. You are here to kill. There's a horse with a pouch of money saddled with supplies in the last stall in the stable. Do what you came to do. Don't hesitate. Then leave in the confusion."

The weight of the knife made her satiny reticule spin then droop about her wrist. "You will let me do this? I thought you said I wasn't capable of killing."

"Every man has a breaking point. I suppose it's the same for a woman. It's not what I want for you, and I've vowed to never kill again, so I won't do this for you. You must do it and live with the consequences. I had a choice long ago, to turn in a man to my commanders for causing a deadly explosion that would have been death to him. It would have ended his career. I chose to forgive."

"I can't forgive Moldona."

"Then Isadel, you can't forgive me. I didn't report him at Almeida. That's why he took a command at Badajoz. Moldona may or may not be your killer, but he was there because of me."

It couldn't be true. Her lips trembled. "Bannerman?"

He tucked her hand about his arm then pulled on his gloves. "Those seeds when they arrive. Do I chew them or make a paste?"

"Make a weak tea from some. A paste with the rest, then apply it directly to any wound or lesion." She swallowed her tears, her stomach shrinking from his admission. She couldn't let him see her confusion, so she focused on the steps in front of her.

"I don't know why I asked about the seeds. With you gone, it won't...I won't do it right." He tugged one of his slipping gloves up, making the taut fabric snap. "Doesn't matter. You have exactly what you want, just don't hate me, Isadel. I bear a lot of guilt. The weight of failing you would be too much."

Towing her from his room, he stopped at the top of the stairs. The music and conversations below touched her almost at the same time as his gloved hand flicked a curl behind her ear. "Maybe the Almeida Killer will take his revenge before the weekend is done. Then no one will be left to prosecute you. I will have peace knowing you have peace."

Was he hoping for the killer to win? Her heart squeezed tight. Air could barely siphon between her faltering lips.

They headed down the treads, and he plastered a smile that she knew to be fake across his face.

He'd given Isadel everything she needed to exact revenge, but now everything she thought she wanted dwarfed to the haunting notion of her giant Bannerman seeking death.

Gold plates, blue Wedgwood dishes, shiny silver forks, and crystal goblets — the dining room hadn't look so well in years. Yet, how was Hugh to stomach the jellied dessert molded into a heart after consuming the dry pheasant? He should take joy in Sandon looking so well, that the commanders, his colleagues, had taken the time to come, and that all talk of the Almeida Killer wouldn't happen until they were dismissed from the ladies.

But he couldn't.

The meal paled after enjoying Isadel's wonderful

creations, and it didn't help his digestion watching his chef make small talk with someone she believed killed her father. Why Elizabeth had set the Moldona's to Isadel's left was beyond his imagination?

Yet, the chef sat at his side, chin raised, looking resplendent, but to know her was to know her rage. Her long neck looked very well, very nibble worthy draped in pearls. The high neckline of her gown should imply modesty, but did nothing to soften the scream of her curves. Her waist was small but more than enough for a big man to hold onto, but Hugh's rare temper flared when he saw Moldona admiring the same.

Gulping his goblet of water, he turned to the other side of the table. Mrs. Nev and Elizabeth were steeped in conversation. Elizabeth looked well arrayed in a peach colored gown. Her soft blue eyes drifted to the door ever so often. Was she waiting on his father or Henry? They both were here the last time she threw a big party in Sandon.

Hugh made his voice a low whisper. "Well done, Lady Rhodes. Thank you."

She dimpled and gazed at him and perhaps Isadel too, smiling like a worldly godmother or a bawd owner. "My pleasure, dear Hugh, my pleasure. Miss Armijo is a treasure."

"Well, Bannerman," Major Handle raised his glass. "I must be the first to compliment you. Rumor had it you'd lost your mind and become reclusive. Nothing could be further from the truth, unless loss of reason can be equated to falling in love. Let us all raise our cups to Bannerman and Miss Armijo."

The man had always had a backward way of dealing in compliments. Handle like half of the men in the room wore cranberry colored regimental. They were still active in the fight. All had futures... Hugh's gaze swayed toward Isadel again. She had a future, but which path would she choose? Always on the run or one enslaved to guilt?

Mrs. Nev, who made gossip her past time, looked over her quizzing glass in Isadel's direction. "I hear Miss Armijo used to be your chef. My, that's convenient. That's why I'm an advocate for an older chef."

Hugh put down his goblet. "I don't know. I think Miss Armijo is the right age."

The snickering that followed satisfied his funny bone, but he could see Mrs. Nev readying for the kill.

"Miss Armijo, do you think it will be a great transition for you managing Sandon like a normal lady...of the ton?"

"Why normal?" Isadel asked with a voice that sounded clear and sweet. "I think Mr. Bannerman appreciates differences. Why else would he be unattached until now? And you know what they say? The way to a man's heart is through his stomach. At that, I am uniquely gifted, not normal at all."

Mrs. Nev's cheeks reddened even as her husband nodded.

Lieutenant Nev directed Phipps to refill his crystal goblet. Same old Nev, a lover of fine wines. He plucked the glass. "Bannerman, when are we going to discuss the reason we are here? Almeida."

"Gentlemen, we'll do that in the morning in my study. No need to bore the ladies."

A round of nods and a few here here's sounded. They were the same. Entertainment first, and then serious business in the morn.

With bags under his blue-grey eyes and more grey in his dark hair, Moldona looked older than the year or so, since Hugh had last seen him. His hands possessed a little shake as he dragged his knife across the plate. "Miss Armijo, in what part of Spain did you live?" His lisp sounded stronger than Hugh remembered.

Her forehead creased as she said, "Badajoz."

Betsy gasped. "My husband has told me of the savage fighting that took place there. It mirrored Almeida."

The table seemed to quiet at the mention of the city.

Isadel patted her mouth with a napkin. "The battle was horrid."

"How did you get out of there?" Betsy picked up her fan. Her tone changed from light to almost accusatory. "Did Mr. Bannerman rescue you? Is that when you two met?"

Isadel's face, which had remained somewhat unreadable, became focused and a smile bloomed. "No, Lord Wellesley remembered the good work of my father and saw to our rescue."

If Hugh didn't know better, he could attest to a bit of spite salted into her words. And Betsy seemed crestfallen. Had she tried to imply that Hugh had courted Isadel and her at the same time? Even if he had been so foul, being married at least a year, why did it matter to her?

Women and the games they play. He could not help but admire his little chef. He reached over, grasped her hand and pressed it to his mouth. "I think she found me. I am a lucky man, and one who is ready to dance."

He rose and escorted her through the sea of dinner guests to his drawing room. Couples filtered in behind them. Lady Rhodes had the floors chalked as always. Soon music overtook the room. He leaned down to his chef. "I'm proud of you, Isadel."

"Why, because I haven't killed your dinner guest?"

"Well, that too, but you never play games. You are very direct. I suppose I like that. I am sorry to have brought you into this spy business."

"Hugh, there is no luxuries in lies. I'm not one to fool myself."

A tap to his shoulder, made him stop. Upon seeing Moldona, he knew it was her time.

"May I cut in, old man?" Moldona stood there at his side, looking every bit a hungry scoundrel.

"You can have the dance if the lady is so inclined. Are you, Miss Armijo?"

The look in her brown eyes spoke of a battle being waged. She grasped Hugh's hand maybe for a final time. "Yes, I will dance with you, Mr. Moldona, when this set is done."

Hating the smirk on the braggart's face, Hugh whisked Isadel away. If this dance would be their first and their last, it should mean something.

Isadel wanted to be lost in Hugh's arms, wanted a second with him smiling at her to last a lifetime, but the moment she'd waited for was about to arrive.

"Well, my dear, you are the hit of Sandon's ball."

"Why do you say that?"

"You've caught more than one eye."

"Even a murderer's attention, Hugh?"

"You have others besides Moldona. I might have to fight them off with a stick."

"We both know you won't. Your new nonviolent

stance, remember?"

"I said I wouldn't kill, Isadel." He spun fast and turned and caught her for the next part of the jig. "But I can be quite effective with a stick."

"Sir, I should take a stick to you."

"Why?" His lopsided grin grew.

"Why didn't you tell me he had a lisp?"

"You never asked."

"You let me run on and on about it being Moldona, about hearing the clear tones and conversations."

"Isadel, I don't know if he is or isn't guilty. You and you alone must be sure. I've been angry and aggrieved just like you, but I've learned that you have to be willing to live with the consequences."

She moved out of step but quickly recovered. "You just don't think I can do it. Call me a coward."

He pulled her close in time with the music. "I'll call you strong. The woman I love."

The music ended and he had the nerve to leave her breathless. He put her hand on his arm and led her to the side. "The horse is in the last stall, Isadel Armijo. I will keep them off your trail as long as I can."

He bowed and left her. He walked over to Lady Rhodes and Mrs. Moldona.

Before she could fill her lungs, Moldona came to her with an outstretched hand.

As the violins started, she fingered the knife in her reticule before she took his arm.

"So, you are from Spain, Mrs. Armijo?" His words hissed on the S's. Why didn't she remember that?

"Yes."

Moldona moved her to slowed music and changed sides as the dance prescribed. If she timed it correctly she could have the knife to his chest in the next exchange.

"Have you been in England long?"

No longer eyeing the spot that would be the third or fourth rib, she lifted her head to him and watched his greedy eyes burn into her form. "Yes, from Badajoz, sir. I said that earlier."

He reared back. "Now don't get angry. I know your kind to be full of fire, Bannerman is a lucky man, but luck runs out."

Did he just threaten Hugh? She snatched her fingers free. "I think this dance is over after all."

"Now don't be that way." He grasped her palm again. "Badajoz was a disaster." His frown became very pronounced, as did his hiss of the s and j's. "I suppose you are glad that you are away from there. The siege took a mighty toll on both sides."

"Which sides? The horrid French or the horrid liberators? Funny, I could not tell which side was good."

"I suppose it looks that way. War does things. It changes people. Sometimes you forget what is good and decent."

Was that an excuse? Were a few polite words over dinner to change the things that took Agueda's life? She put her hand on her knife and folded her fingers about it so taut that she felt the blood of revenge pulsing in her veins. She pushed her hand to his side, with her finger resting on the switch. All she could think was, *Agueda, I love you sister. I will kill to make this right for you.* "Do you know what the siege did to the innocent, Mr. Moldona?"

He stopped dancing. "As much damage as it did to those who lived."

"No, my sister was killed, humbled by English soldiers. She was innocent just smiling at the men her papa said was in the right in the war. How is that damage worse when you live?"

Her reticule swung close to his side again. She should stab him then disappear. All she had to do was flick the switch.

"I am sorry, Miss Armijo," Moldona said. "No greater cost is the loss of a loved one. I'm sorry."

The hiss of S's sliced at her ear, cutting at her conscience. She lifted her reticule again, but she couldn't kill him. Not remembering hearing a lisp, Isadel wasn't sure anymore of Moldona's guilt. Hugh was right. She couldn't kill if she had doubt. She lowered her hand. "I'm tired. Thank you for this dance."

He clutched her wrist. "Meet me tonight, Miss Armijo."

"What?"

"In Bannerman's study. There is much to tell you."

"No." She pulled away.

"Please. As the daughter of the physician Armijo, you must know."

She froze in her steps. Lost in her thoughts, her doubts, she didn't know what to do, not until she heard the tune the violinist now played. The music found her, reached into that dark place she had enclosed her heart and showed her light. It did not matter that she couldn't kill Moldona. It mattered that she finally defended her sister, the girl who wore pearls and smiled as bright as the sun.

"I think this dance is mine." Hugh was again at her side. He claimed her palm in one hand and put another about her waist, then moved her into the hall. They were alone, all alone, except Mama's tune. It still played in Sandon and in Isadel's heart.

"Breathe, chef. Who can think of killing, when there is dancing to be done?"

"You knew. You knew I couldn't kill him. I spared him like you spared him."

"It doesn't matter. You're no killer, Isadel. That's what I've been trying to tell you."

"I've been telling you that you'll live, but you don't listen either." She pried away from him, but he caught her wrist, laced his fingers with hers. "If only for one dance, let's forget about anger or killing or the past." Against his chest, he held her. Warm and secure, he kept her and she relearned to breathe, taking in air with him, in and out, in and out, humming Mama's tune.

With her composure restored, she stepped away. "I must leave here. What I came for no longer exists."

"When are you going to stop running, Isadel? You had a change of heart. You offered mercy. That is not shameful."

"I need some air, Hugh." She left him in the hall and headed to the tower room. Before she could get to the stairs, she ran into Moldona again.

"Whoa, Miss Armijo. I can lend a sympathetic ear, but meet me later in Bannerman's study. I know him to be less than generous to his women. He's dangerous, Miss, and should be put in his place."

"Leave him alone."

"I will if you meet me in his study later tonight. What I have to say about your father is very important."

Her face surely riddled with confusion. The man had the nerve to make a play for her as if her affections would change so easily. And if he only knew the venom inside for him or the idea of him as a villain, he would never come near her. "There is more party for you, Mr. Moldona. Be grateful for that."

On shaky legs, she navigated up the stairs. She didn't head to the tower but to the room adjacent to Hugh's. She needed to watch out for him. She might not be able to prove Moldona killed her family, but she'd stop him from hurting Hugh if the man was the Almeida Killer.

Chapter Thirteen: Truth and Consequence

When Isadel fled upstairs, Hugh wanted to chase after her, but he couldn't. A house full of guests, the Almeida Killer on the loose—any of those could be an excuse to say his hands were full, but he needed her to stand on her own, to find a reason to stay.

Phipps passed him. The man looked as if he was looking for a surprise attack. "I see your fiancé has left."

"Her work here was done. She couldn't kill Moldona."

"You don't seem happy, Bannerman."

Not knowing how things would be betwixt Isadel and himself, Hugh rubbed at his brow. "I'm not. The grumblings of being targeted swept about the drawing room. The flames were mostly diminished by the second round of port which the servants happily dished."

"I have first watch," Phipps said. "Go on. Maybe you should console a pretty great chef."

"Release the musicians and make sure Lady

Rhodes retires safely." Knowing his man would handle everything, he trudged out of the drawing room. Maybe he should try to console Isadel or at least keep her safe. That feeling in his gut that something would happen grew.

Moldona leaned outside the room. He drank from a crystal goblet. "Nice gathering, Bannerman."

"Things are winding down. You should be off to bed."

The man shrugged and took another sip. "I'll be off in a few moments. I'm a little on edge. Don't want to keep Mrs. Moldona awake."

Hugh folded his arms behind his back. "It's good you are considering her."

"I am. I've been completely honest with her about everything."

"Everything?"

Moldona nodded. "Yes. I thought we'd found renewal, even took her to a private island near France. But as soon as we came to Sandon, she grew distant."

France. Junot was killed in France. Maybe guilty Moldona didn't know.

"Maybe you can speak with her, Bannerman. She was always a favorite of yours and Henry's."

It was difficult to balance his suspicions about Moldona, the desire to have him guilty of something for Isadel's sake, with the humbling tone coming from his rival. For once, the man sounded sympathetic.

Maybe the love of a good woman like Betsy changed Moldona. Hugh knew loving a good woman had changed him. "I'll leave it to you. I've my own woman to speak with. I'll see you at the briefing."

With a shrug and another slurp, Moldona

nodded. "Bannerman, I always thought you strange or maybe that was jealousy talking. You are lucky, and I hope you never grow tired of your spitfire."

He didn't respond at such a silly notion. How could one grow tired of an enigma wrapped in lace?

"Get some sleep." Hugh climbed the stairs. He thought about Isadel and headed to the tower. He opened the door and found the room vacant. Like the rest of Sandon, it was neat as a pen, very much the observatory it had always been before he let things degrade, before Isadel. He moved to the window and stood looking out to eternity, the edges of the tree line falling onto the sea.

Henry, his father, all the ghosts of his past—they'd been banished, but now he'd be alone.

How long he stood there gazing, he did not know. But there was peace in his soul. He could be alone, not that he wanted to be, but he felt whole. The disease of guilt wouldn't eat at him anymore.

The scent of cinnamon kissed his nose. He turned and Isadel stood behind him.

"When I first found you, Hugh, this tower guided me. I knew I could find the man who could help me."

Bundled in her father's jacket over the fancy cream gown, she never looked more beautiful. "Did you find him, Isadel, or just a placeholder?"

She folded her arms about her, but then eased them to her side. "Perhaps you can sway me again by playing my mother's song."

Wanting to take a step to her, he glued his feet to the floor. She had to stop running and come to him. "Emotional blackmail is another tool of a spy. I wanted you to make the right decision, but I am not above giving you a little help."

"I should strike him down now without the

benefit of violins. Goodnight." She walked away and his resolve crumbled. He followed her to his room but didn't catch her. She slipped into the adjacent room and slammed the door.

He put his head against the door. "It was wrong to manipulate you, but I wanted you to do what was right so we could have a future together." He threw off his jacket and undid the waistcoat that had become constricting. "Stubborn woman. Sometimes I might know better."

One sleep shirt tossed over his head, he fell into his bed. Then he heard her moving about. Famous Isadel pacing. He wanted to push the door open, but he'd done that before. The intrusion had done nothing but make her more withdrawn. She was much more attentive when she opened the door, when she decided she wanted him.

About to rip off his gloves, he stopped. Maybe she was waiting for him. He wrapped the door humming her tune. "Except for being beautiful, you are an absolutely horrible mistress."

The door cracked a little. "I didn't want to be a mistress, just a chef. And remember you elevated me. According to your customs, a gentleman cannot take it back."

Her voice sounded bright, too proper. She wanted to speak more. She wanted him even if it was to air her grievances. Grinning, he sank into Henry's reading chair by the window. "Why don't you come here so we can see what a gentleman will or will not do?"

She opened the door fully and marched inside. A simple chemise claimed her form, but her father's coat cinched her waist, that very seize-it-never letting-go waist. "What type of gentleman is your Moldona? He wanted to meet with me in your study. His wife is upstairs. I spared him. Isn't that enough?"

Hair swinging from side to side as she paced, she didn't seem humored or like a woman that was flattered. Isadel was no Betsy. A fact he appreciated more and more.

"Are you listening, Hugh? The bounder, that fool. Doesn't he know I want him dead, not to end up in his bed.

"His wife must be mortified."

Hands to her hips, Isadel stopped moving. "Is that all you are concerned about how his bored wife must feel?"

"What are you talking about?"

"Mrs. Moldona is desperate for your attention. You haven't noticed how she fawns over you, waits for you to see her? Only then does she pay attention to her horrid husband."

"You sound jealous, but surely you are just biding your time for your next strike at Moldona."

"Ohhh." She started pacing and mumbling to herself. A few of her choice words he caught, something to the effect of him being a burro, a donkey.

He tripped her on her second pass with his ankle and shoved her with enough momentum to launch her into his lap.

She tottered and clasped the strings of his nightshirt. "Bannerman. Not fair."

"Why don't you tell me, Isadel, what is fair? You didn't kill Moldona and you didn't take my horse and return to the Abbey. Why are you still here? Tell me. Don't be withdrawn, hidden like in a pastry shell."

"You can make jokes about cooking. I haven't been in the kitchen in a few weeks."

"A chef without a kitchen is almost as bad as a man engaged to a woman he is unsure of. I've admitted what I feel about you."

She drew the strings of his shirt about her fingers, her long slender hands. "I haven't cooked in a week. Wouldn't you suffer if you couldn't do what you wanted?"

He smoothed the hair tumbling on her face. "Yes, there are a great many things I want to do. "

He fingered her cheek and watched her eyes grow dark. "I want to feel the satin of your face."

"What's stopping you? Gloves?"

"I'm not well. I don't want to not be able to give you—"

"Tomorrow is not promised. You and I both know that."

He sat up straight and took off one glove. With his pinkie, he traced her jaw, stroking it to that hidden tune he'd seen her move to.

Her silky skin grew warm as he touched the fullness of her cheeks. He tickled the curve of her neck as he played with the lace encircling it.

"Is that all you want, Hugh?"

"Enough for now with a killer in the house or one or two on the way as word spreads of this gathering." He pulled her deeper into his arms. "As I think about it, there is never enough of you."

She lifted her head and took his lips. Not a short kiss. Not a play kiss. Not an ugly cousin kiss. She kissed him waiting for his mouth to accept her. She grasped his collar and yanked him closer.

There was nothing shy about her embrace.

Leaning back, he let air cool his still hungry lips. "I guess this means you like me at this moment."

"This moment."

"I'm going to go downstairs and retreat. I mean

get something to eat. That new chef is not what I've been used to."

"Then I will go too. Lady Rhodes told me it's my duty to keep you well satisfied. I suppose that still applies if I am now your fiancé."

Food may or may not have been what Elizabeth meant, but being away from the temptation of his chamber had to be better, especially when Isadel hadn't owned up to loving him. Donning his gloves, he led her to the stairs. In quiet, they moved in lock step. Having her at his side smiling felt right, lasting.

When they got to the kitchen, she pointed to a stool. "You sit, Hugh Bann-er-man."

There were traces of biscuit flour on the table. "I thought you hadn't been cooking in weeks. You've been in here tonight."

She shrugged. "I saw you didn't eat. I kneaded biscuits for your breakfast."

Back in the domain she seemed to love, Isadel appeared to be at peace. And he liked her like that. He liked himself, watching her filled with joy.

"But that is for breakfast," she said. "I'll see what I can fix for you now." She looked around, poking at the stove then moving into the scullery and back. "My knife is missing. I hope your kitchen staff has not dulled it. She took a dull knife and hacked through a thick barley loaf, cutting it into sections. She slathered them in butter and put them in a pan aside the hearth. "Nothing like crunchy toast to begin our meal."

"Are you fine with your choice of letting Moldona live?"

She clanged a spoon on the side of a cast iron pot. "I have to be. I have doubts and as you said, you can't have those and be able to live with the decision. I've taken on too much guilt already. I don't need blood too. Let's not talk of him."

Hugh knew the pain she felt, but the burden of taking the wrong life is something no one should bear.

In the cast iron pot, she put the remnants of the pheasant and before his eyes could grow heavy, he smelled the heady scent of gravy, the sizzling of garlic and onions.

"Now we eat like the best peasants." She smeared the gravy on the crusty bread with a little of the warmed through duck meat, then presented matching saucers. She slid one to him and began to nibble on the other. The taste of this food had heart and spice. It was Isadel.

Devouring the sandwich, he still found himself aching in hunger, hunger for love, and a life that he should not claim. "What do you want, Isadel?"

"The sandwich is enough."

"What if I want this sandwich every night?"

"I could make you one, but I could make other things, Hugh."

"Isadel, I feel healthy and powerful now. I'm not sure about next week. The contract I signed will give you some means."

"What are you talking about?"

He reached for her and swiped the butter from the crinkle corner of her lip. "Isadel, do you love me?"

She dimpled and opened her mouth to respond when a shaking Elizabeth ran into the kitchen.

"He's dead."

Hugh moved to his stepmother and held her up by the shoulders. "Elizabeth, calm yourself. Tell us what has happened."

"I saw a light in your study. I was going to

chastise you for working when your fiancé, who was a success—

Hugh led her to a stool as Isadel fanned her with a plate. "Elizabeth, please. Just tell us who is dead."

"Moldona. He's been stabbed in your study."

Hugh hugged Elizabeth then pushed her into Isadel's arms. "Stay in here. The Almeida Killer is here."

When he turned to leave, Isadel was behind him.

"No, sweetheart, stay here."

"Not letting you go alone and you can't stop me."

"Fine. Elizabeth, hide in the scullery."

There was no time to argue so he gripped her hand. They ran down the long hall until reaching the threshold.

He wanted to have her wait outside, but she'd witnessed a massacre before. How much worse could things be beyond the door? "Come on."

Inside, the window was wide open. The new curtains fluttered. A man was slumped at Hugh's desk.

They walked over and sure enough Moldona was face down.

Isadel shuttered and Hugh wrapped her arms about her. "Well, you wanted him dead."

"Yes, but I left him alive."

"You mean on the dance floor?"

"No. Here."

Lighting a candle from the sconce, he tried to sound normal, without panic or accusation. "Isadel, dear?"

"He said he had something to tell me about my father. I met him here."

He wanted to ask her again if she'd killed Moldona, but he knew her too well. She would have said so. "What did he want?"

"He thanked my father for aiding the regiment at Almeida and for trying to save his friend."

Holding out the candle, Hugh moved from her and studied the window. No broken panes. "The killer did not come from the window. They are inside Sandon. Did Moldona say anything else?"

"He made another inquiry about us. I slapped him and left. He was redder, the bounder, but alive."

Hugh went over to the desk again. Moldona had scrawled something in ink. *'Sandon, Explosion, St. C.'* What could that mean?

That feeling that something else was going to happen pounded in his chest. "This was a warning." He went to the window again and stilled the ghostly curtains. Caught on the sill was a wool cord. He flicked it. The stench of sulfur, the perfume of explosions, wafted. This was a detonation cord. Angling the light, he saw the wool leading to a barrel. If full of black powder, it would be enough to blow the face off Sandon. He cut the cord on it and cast the end far from the stash, a temporary fix. "It's a detonation, Isadel. The killer wants everyone dead."

She grabbed his arm. "Hugh, how do we get everyone to safety?"

"You suddenly care about the English? Aren't we getting our just desserts, chef?"

"They are your guests. I care about you, so I care about them."

"Well, I don't want to start a panic. I am going to take you back to Elizabeth."

"I'll not leave you. Someone needs to take care of your hands."

The look in her eyes, so filled of warmth and tenderness, Hugh knew for the first time what her nonsense statement meant. "You are stubborn. We'll need to fix that if we live."

Phipps bounded through the door. "You found one at this window, too?"

"What do you mean, too, old man?"

Taking a huge breath like he'd just run a marathon, Phipps pointed to the hall. "Outside the front entry. Is that Moldona?"

"Yes, Isadel and I found him dead."

His man wiped at his sweating brow as he came to the body. "A knife to the back? Bannerman, with more explosives outside, the Almeida Killer is here."

"Isadel, go to Lady Rhodes. Phipps, let's follow the detonation cord."

"No, Hugh. I want to stay with you."

"Please, Isadel. I can't do this and be concerned about your whereabouts. I need you to listen to me." She nodded and left the study.

Phipps and Hugh jumped out the window and ran into the black night. "My hope is we are ahead of the killer."

"You sure it's not Miss Armijo?"

"Yes, Phipps."

"That knife wound in Moldona was a very personal way to kill. And why stab him with all these bombs set to explode?"

Phipps made a good point, but nothing prepared Hugh for seeing the cords tied off at Henry's grave. "You are right. Moldona's killing was personal and the killer is still in Sandon."

"You mean killers?"

"No. The killer. It all makes sense."

They took off running again. When they got to the door, he cut open one of the oak barrels. The air filled with the scent of the battle, smoky black powder. He filled his pockets with it. "We're walking into a battle. I don't know what we'll face, but Phipps, save Elizabeth and Isadel. I don't want them hurt."

They opened the door and eased inside. A new line of cord lay on the floor of his study.

This was intentional. The fiend wanted Hugh to know and to agonize about the powder and the cords.

"No more games. Phipps, it's time we strike."

Chapter Fourteen: Who Do You Love

Isadel stared out the high window of the turret. So many emotions ran up and down her spine, twisting her to the breaking point, but the knife at Lady Rhodes' throat made Isadel think and rethink her actions for she didn't want the countess hurt. What would Hugh do at this moment? What spy tenet would he invoke? "Why are you doing this?"

The fiend, Betsy Moldona, made Lady Rhodes stumble forward then knocked her into Isadel. She unraveled the last of her long detonation cord. If she took a candle and lit the cord, everything would be lost.

"The Almeida commanders with their wrongheaded plan killed my brother, Charles. He was my baby brother. He didn't need to die and be left in some unmarked grave. It's all their fault."

Isadel focused on thinking through an escape, but she squinted at the sparkle of her soiled knife, her knife the evil woman held, that she'd killed Moldona with. "Because your brother was a war casualty, all must die? Why hurt Lady Rhodes or the other wives who have come with their husbands? They've done you no harm. And though Lady Rhodes can be a little irritating and wears too much rouge, she's a very nice person. Let her go."

Lady Rhodes patted Isadel's arm. "Thanks, dear, I think. Betsy, this is ridiculous. You let Isadel go. She's done nothing to you."

"She's the perfect foil. The crazy mulatto chef killed them all when Hugh let her play house at Sandon."

The countess shook her head. "That's not a reason."

"Does anyone need one to blame you, Miss Armijo? If Mrs. Nev. lives, she'll do all the dirty work of spreading the lies. Lies will become truth, like saying my brother left out a barrel of black powder and caused the death of six hundred men. That's a lie. Charles would never do that."

The woman was crazy. Her mourning of her brother had surely turned her crazy. "How do you know if it is true or not? You weren't there, Mrs. Moldona. You have no way to be certain."

"My husband was there. He's the one who quoted this garbage to me. He won't ever do that again."

If that wasn't a confession, Isadel didn't know what one was. She looked to the door, hoping in her heart that Hugh would come and save them, but he wasn't there. "If you set off the detonation cord, you are going to die with us. You can't set the charge and run clear of Sandon, Mrs. Moldona."

"Maybe, maybe not. It doesn't matter anymore. I wonder who Hugh will morn more, me the woman he's loved all his life or his mistress."

"She's his fiancé," Lady Rhodes said as she pointed to her chest. "I made that happen."

"You old harlot. You ruined a very good plan. I was going to torture him one last time with my marriage to Moldona, but then you made this strumpet happen. He didn't care a whit about me."

As if Lady Rhodes had forgotten that Mrs. Moldona wielded a knife, she stomped her foot. "I'm sorry for you, but things change. People change. Betsy, you can stop this now and make things right."

"What is right? My brother was a boy too young to decide to follow in Hugh's big footsteps. You don't know what it's like to lose someone you love, how it eats at you day and night."

Isadel did know. She knew better than anyone and it gutted her that she and the fiend had that in common. "I do. The war stole everything I cared for in this world. My family was slaughtered by your soldiers."

Wide eyed, she stuck her gloating face over Isadel. "Well, you're about to lose Hugh, too."

It wasn't wise or prudent and against all the rules Hugh had tried to teach her, but she slapped the snow off Mrs. Moldona's cheek, leaving it ruby red.

"You shrew." The woman reached out to strike, but Isadel ducked. The fiend tried again but wobbled as a large boom shook the room.

A fireball blazed outside. Isadel could see the oranges and reds through the rattled windowpanes. It had to be a huge blast, bigger than what Hugh had showed her. Her heart ripped open wide. Hugh couldn't be lost.

Dust hung in the air as the sound of men and women awaking, screaming, and running echoed all around them.

Betsy rubbed her jaw then began to chuckle. "He was rusty. Hugh must've caused one of my explosions to go off. "It had more powder than you thought!" The woman shouted like Hugh could hear her. "I knew the rumors of him slowing up had to have some truth. Like last time I was at Sandon, I put in too much powder and ended up killing Henry, not Hugh. This time it got him. He'll join Henry at last."

Whether it was the strain of the moment or regret for not telling Hugh she loved him, Isadel lifted her leaking face. "If you think this revenge will lead to peace, you are mistaken. You've dwelt and stewed in hate until you've boiled over. It has led you to madness. How will you face tomorrow, you unrepentant woman? It will crush you, what you've done."

Tying off the cord, Betsy made the explosive look how Hugh made his in the park. "I won today. I don't care about tomorrow."

Isadel brushed away the water basting her face. "The well of your soul is empty. It's not too late to turn from this."

Betsy clapped her hands. "Henry, my beloved Henry, could've given that speech. We'll meet him soon, but you stay away from him. He's mine."

"You killed Henry trying to hurt Hugh," Lady Rhodes crumbled to the floor. "Why hurt Hugh at all?"

"Moldona and Hugh and all the others up to Wellesley, they killed my brother. At Almeida, they kept up the brutal fight until Charles St. Claire was struck. He would not have been there if not for Hugh."

Dashing out of the tower might be an option, but the crazy woman could set the explosion and bring Sandon down on their heads. Isadel had to reason with her. That was her only chance to stop the fiend. All she had was the truth. Maybe it could set them free. "Your brother's death is his fault. He and

Moldona left the powder barrel out that exploded and killed so many."

"You lie, witch." Betsy walked back and forth, between the candle in the corner and the detonation cord. "You are a liar."

"Moldona told me tonight. He tried to thank me for all the hard work my late father did to save your brother and so many others."

Betsy paced faster. "Charles wouldn't have gone if not for Hugh. He idolized him and his military talk."

"He was a second son, you twit. He was supposed to go into the military." Lady Rhodes cried harder. "Your treachery took dear Henry. Now you've taken my Hugh. "

The crazed woman stopped and swung Isadel's knife life a meat cleaver at them. "Now, you and the liar will be dispatched. Then, I'll set off the final powder barrels. Sandon and all the bad memories will be no more. I regret that Wellesley is not here. For everyone else, time is up."

"Not yet. According to my chef there is more time." Hugh was at the door. He tossed a bucket of water, hot steaming water on Betsy and her detonation cord.

The fiend screamed and shook her wet arms and Isadel kicked her in the shin.

Hopping and shrieking, Betsy dropped the knife. As she scrambled for it, Isadel knocked it away and it slid to Hugh.

"You little she-devil." Betsy lunged at her.

Arms tangling, Isadel punched at the octopus. She could feel the woman dragging her. It was as if evil gave Betsy super human strength.

Hugh tugged on the mass of limbs. "I always wanted women fighting over me, but somehow I thought it would be more romantic."

Isadel could feel his hands on hers, bare and rough on her arm, but she didn't want him hurt. "Back up, Hugh. She's crazed."

Knocking the window fully open, Betsy tugged and had Isadel's head on the sill.

The world looked upside down and grey, so much like that night when she first arrived at Sandon, when she wanted to jump. But that was before Isadel found herself and her place at Hugh's side. It was before she truly forgave herself for all the guilt and blame she'd kept in her heart. She was worthy of a future, one steeped in hope, just like Hugh. She wasn't going to let Betsy or anyone else take it from her. She fought the arm that had fastened about her neck.

"Betsy, stop. I'll do anything. I'll give you something. Henry's watch." Hugh took it from his pocket and dangled the gold watch by the chain. "Take it and be gone. You'll have a head start."

"Henry's watch?" The woman stopped tugging.

The pressure on Isadel's arm eased. She pushed away and fell back along the wall.

Betsy clapped her hands. "Give it to me. Henry used to use it to time his steps to it."

Hugh's eyes looked like iron, grey and determined. His head nudged slightly to the side as if he were giving an unspoken command. "Yes. Henry loved this watch."

Lady Rhodes wiped at her eyes. "Hugh don't give her a thing. She's taken too much from you. Kill that cow."

All pretense of a sophisticated tone melted away from the countess's voice. It had a cockney sound like many of the kitchen help at the Abbey. "Let her rot before she does another thing."

Isadel loved Lady Rhodes more.

Hugh shook the watch. The piece spun and shone in the candlelight. "Take the watch. There's a horse in the stable saddled and ready for your retreat."

Betsy froze. Her gaze was firmly in Hugh's direction. "Now, I know you lie."

"No, it's true." Isadel said, "He did it for me. Hugh Bannerman wanted me to escape if I killed Moldona for murdering my family."

Coming closer, Betsy backhanded Isadel. "You little troll. Hugh does love you. He'd never let you kill anyone with no consequences if he didn't." She put her boot on Isadel's neck. "I'll snap her spine and let you watch her die, Hugh. That will mean more to me now."

"Catch." Hugh tossed the watch high.

Betsy jumped and the motion was enough to allow Isadel to roll from underneath her.

With her palm, Betsy caught the chain and then started to laugh again. "You thought I'd miss or maybe I'd be lucky and fall out the window. You never could do anything right. You couldn't even die right."

"Henry never cared for you, Betsy, any more than a friend. Maybe he saw your heart was full of darkness. Charles St. Claire was sloppy, but he fought with bravery worthy of the St. Claire name. You are charlatan, Betsy. A disgrace to womanhood. You deserve nothing of Henry's. Give me back the watch. Don't even open it. You're not worthy to see it.

"I am worthy, and I have it." She opened the watch and Hugh leapt forward covering Isadel and Lady Rhodes in his arm.

A new explosion, this fireball came from the watch. The world smelled of soot and sulfur.

Choking dust and rubble fell everywhere. A full minute passed before she could see. Half the turret was gone, along with Betsy.

Hugh stood up and Isadel clutched his side. Together they moved to the edge.

"Is she down there, Hugh? I've seen too much death."

"Yes. She's down there among the twisted limestone. The Almeida Killer is no more."

Phipps came running through the door, relief etched in his face. "Bannerman, you found them. And you're all well. The house was evacuated. None of the other commanders or their wives were hurt."

"Good, Phipps. This is over."

Isadel wound her arms around as much of his chest as she could get to. "I'm so sorry, Hugh."

He slid off a glove and put a hand in her hair. "Phipps, help Lady Rhodes back to her quarters and send for a doctor to make sure she is well. I'm so glad you are unharmed, Elizabeth."

Lady Rhodes got up and shook her cloak of debris. "I'm glad the harpy's dead, even more so that you and Isadel are alive. My work here is done, so I'll go at day break."

"Elizabeth Bannerman, I don't want you to go, not yet. Sandon is your home as much as you want, you can even bring your new husband for visits, but I'll need a chaperone until this little chef makes good on her promise to marry me. Will you stay?"

Isadel tried to raise her head to see what new joke he was sharing, but he held her fast. "What?"

"I'll leave you two to discuss things. See, I can be a good liberal chaperone," Lady Rhodes said. "I might even keep you two apart." She laughed and Isadel could feel her winking and tossing one of those sultry looks she had her practice, but Isadel didn't care. She wanted to be alone with Hugh.

When Phipps's heavy footfalls faded, she held onto Hugh tighter and with his help climbed the tree of a man, until she could see into his eyes. "I thought you died. I heard the explosion, saw the smoke."

"Well, I always had a death wish. I knew the explosion would buy time and clear Sandon in rapid order. Time is pretty precious."

"You are right, and I'm not wasting another moment. I am a stubborn woman, and I love you, Hugh Bann-er-man, with my whole stubborn heart." That was all she could say before smothering him in kisses. She held onto his neck as he sank to his knees.

"Isadel, I want to get this right." He took off his final glove. Palm to palm, he held her. "You made me want a future. If my days are numbered, I will live them fully in your love. Is that enough for you? Can I be greedy and have all of you, even if my time is short?"

"Yes. But, you are not dying. The seeds will cure you, Hugh."

"You have healed me, Isadel, just by making me want to live. By reminding me that I am worthy of life irrespective of my past or the guilt I bear. Marry me."

"Hugh Bann-er-man, you gave me something to feel other than rage. I don't know what I am going to do with this love I have, but I want to try. Yes, I'll marry you."

Taking her face in his hands, he kissed her gently. "I am so in love with you."

"I'm sorry you broke your vow. You had to kill."

He sighed. I made Henry's watch into an explosive. "When I saw that she wanted to destroy

Sandon from his grave, I knew she was obsessed. She made the choice to catch it, to open it as much as I made the choice that no one would take you from me."

"It took you nearly dying for me to... Wait. I thought you said you couldn't make a controlled explosion."

That lopsided grin appeared. "Never trust a spy to tell you the whole truth. I said you couldn't. I never said it was impossible."

She put a hand to her hip and pushed him back. He rolled to the floor laughing. "You better be telling the whole truth when you say you love me."

"I guess I'll just have to show you." He propped a hand underneath his head and smiled at her. He looked so happy, so at peace with the world that it stole her breath. "I intend to show you every day, even more so once you are Mrs. Bannerman."

Epilogue

Four weeks after his wedding, Sandon Manor still smelled of gardenias. Hugh stood in his study watching the sun go down drinking the bitter tea Isadel had made for him from the seeds. Unlike the earlier cures he'd tried, these foul-smelling pods had worked. The paste had cleared the lesions on his feet. His hands felt stronger.

Phipps plodded inside. "I found the lid of your watch. It is still so disconcerting about Betsy Moldona. She was the mastermind of it all. She killed four men, five if you count Moldona."

Hugh took the lid in his bare palm. It had a dent but the initials could be read. "Six, if you count my brother." He shook his head and came away from the window.

"I did. Hartland's latest correspondence said that Junot's death was a suicide. Mrs. Moldona didn't get to him."

"Maybe she did. The power of a woman scorned is intense."

Phipps nodded. "Almost as much as one on a mission. Yes, the new Mrs. Bannerman is doing quite good work on you. You are the picture of health. Mrs. Nelson has mentioned how much in love you look."

A grin was set to rise on Hugh's face, but he'd save that for Isadel. His man had fallen for a cook too. "I think you know what they say about the love of a good woman."

"I'm finding out." Phipps took his empty mug. "You have a good evening, Bannerman."

When Phipps opened the door, Elizabeth's piano playing filtered inside. It was a jaunty tune, one meant for dancing. Her husband, Lord Rhodes probably sat dutifully at her side.

"The love of good women." Hugh said to himself. He walked out of his study and headed to the stairs. He clasped a hold of the knurl post at the first tread. His bride wouldn't go to bed this early.

He pivoted and marched to her happy place, the kitchen.

Pressing on the door, he cleared his throat. Sneaking up on Isadel wasn't advised. His nose smarted a long time the last time he had entered unannounced. "Isadel."

Swinging the door wide, he saw his chef. In her father's jacket with its sleeves pushed up, she showcased strong forearms coated in flour. The simple gold band on her finger glistened with butter. She looked simply delicious. "You are working too hard, Mrs. Bannerman. You can leave this task for Mrs. Nelson. She'll return in the morning."

"No, you go on to bed. I mean to your chamber."

His brow raised of its own volition. A spy is not to announce what he's thinking. And Isadel seemed to become a better spy every day.

He plodded in front of the table and began to sit

upon it but stopped. His wife was agitated, and it didn't bode well to make her angrier. "I'm not a mind reader, Isadel. Why don't you tell me what has upset you?"

"Lady Rhodes made the menu for tomorrow."

"It's a suggestion. Elizabeth knows you are mistress at Sandon."

Looking down, Isadel punched the dough. "Some mistress I am."

"What are you talking about?"

"Look at the menu."

"Mussels with a pomegranate sauce. And for dessert, chocolate biscuits dipped in chocolate. Sounds very tasty. I don't see—"

Isadel wiped her hands on a towel, tossed the cloth onto the table, and tossed her pristine white apron. "She even made me put on this." She rent her jacket wide.

The lace nightgown left little to the imagination. And he was glad of that. He moved near and pulled her by the jacket. "I'm definitely not going to understand the problem, not with you dressed so well. You're going to need to be very plain. You've been happy since we wed. You seem pleased these last few weeks. At dinner, you were smiling. You kissed me in the study as you brought me tea. What has happened?"

She put her arms about her as if she were cold.

Impossible with the heat his gaze had to offer. "Tell me, Mrs. Bannerman. You can tell me anything."

Isadel shook her head. "Lady Rhodes says I am doing things wrong. That I should be ravished by now." She covered her mouth, for a moment, and then lowered her hand. "Just tell me this marriage was a mistake. That you don't desire me."

Holding her stare, afraid she would miss his meaning, he hauled her high so their eyes were level. Then he shook her senseless. "Woman, you drive me to distraction, don't you know that? I had to make sure your cure took hold. It is enough of a risk touching your face, your lovely face."

He set her back on her feet and grasped her countenance betwixt his palms. "Don't you know I love you more than me? You are young and healthy. I didn't want to risk any more of you, not until I am sure. Wanting to live is only one part. Knowing I will, that is a new world."

"Oh." She clasped his hands. "Don't you know you are worth the risk, but the medicine has taken hold? You see that."

"I see it now and the look in your eyes, Isadel, so full of love. I don't know how I could be so lucky."

Her head fell back as she took his kiss. Sweet. Perfect. His arms wound about her determined to prove how much he loved her.

She pressed on his shoulders and moved to the other side of the table pressing out biscuits. "Hugh, we are both lucky. Let me finish up here then I'll be up. Forget about Lady Rhode's mistress talk. As long as you love me, as long as that is true. It is enough. I had to know if you had regrets. I am so glad you do not."

Maybe it was pure male pride or the way her curves looked in lace that forced him to pound over to his chef and wipe her hands clean. "This will wait."

"What? No, a clean kitchen—"

He picked her up and tossed her over his shoulder. "It's not as important as graduating from Elizabeth's lessons. My wife must know that she is desired in every way, not just for her biscuits."

Hanging down his back, she tugged on his coat. "But let me leave a note for Mrs. Nelson."

"No, she'll understand and you'll need Elizabeth's special meal for strength. You may not see outside our chamber for a few days."

She spun in his arms and held tightly to his neck. "I love you, Bann-er-man."

"May we love a little Bannerman or two. God willing."

"You feel healthy enough for this, Hugh?"

"Oh, definitely, Mrs. Bannerman. Definitely. Or I'll die trying, like a good spy determined to complete his mission. So be gentle with me, my love."

Tucking her securely in his embrace. He headed up the stairs to their chamber listening to his wife hum her special tune, her well of hope and abiding love.

Author's Note

Dear Friend,

I enjoyed writing No Hiding for Guilty. It was a great deal of fun and a bit of a challenge to shape these characters burdened by guilt. I hope you enjoyed their journey to freedom and love.

My diverse stories will showcase a world of intrigue and romance, and offer a setting everyone can hopefully find interesting, and a character to identify with in the battle of love and life.

Stay in touch. Sign up at www.vanessariley.com for my newsletter. You'll be the first to know about upcoming releases, and maybe even win a sneak peek.

Thank so much for giving this book a read.

Vanessa Riley

* * *

Many of my readers are new to Regencies, so I always add notes and a glossary to make items readily available. If you know of a term that should be added to enhance my readers' knowledge, send them to me and I will acknowledge you in my next book.

Here are my notes:

The Siege of Almeida took place in 1810 during the Peninsular War. During the battle, a leaky powder barrel of black powder was ignited and killed over 600 soldiers.

The Siege of Badajoz occurred in 1812. It was a very violent battle with over 4,800 soldiers killed. In the aftermath of the bloody siege, English troops burnt and pillaged Badajoz raping and killing many of the inhabitants, killing over 4,000 Spanish civilians.

The Siege of Almeida

The Siege of Almeida took place in 1810 during the Peninsular War. During the battle, a leaky powder barrel of black powder was ignited and killed over 600 soldiers.

The Siege of Badajoz

The Siege of Badajoz occurred in 1812. It was a very violent battle with over 4,800 soldiers killed. In the aftermath of the bloody siege, English troops burnt and pillaged Badajoz raping and killing many of the inhabitants, killing over 4,000 Spanish civilians.

Free blacks in 1800's English Society

By Regency times, historians, Kirstin Olsen and Gretchen Holbrook Gerzina, estimate that Black London (the black neighborhood of London) had over 10,000 residents. While England led the world in granting rights to the enslaved and ending legal slavery thirty years before the American Civil War, it still had many citizens who were against change. Here is another image from an anti-abolitionist.

The New Union Club being a representation of what took place at a celebrated dinner given by a celebrated society – includes in picture abolitionists, Billy Waters, Zachariah Macauley, William Wilberforce. – published 19 July 1819. Source: Wiki Commons

The Heart of A Hero Series

The Heart of a Hero Series

What if your favorite superheroes had Regency-era doppelgängers? And what if a group of them were recruited by the Duke of Wellington to gather intelligence for him during the Napoleonic Wars while they protected their own parts of the realm?

You'd get The Heart of a Hero series.

Nine authors are bringing nine full-length novels to you this summer, each telling the story of a man or woman who is a hero in all senses of the word.

No Rest for the Wicked by Cora Lee (prequel novella)
Only A Hero Will Do by Alanna Lucas
Once Bitten by Aileen Fish
Lightning Strikes Twice by Jillian Chantal
No Hiding for the Guilty by Vanessa Riley
The Marquis of Thunder by Susan Gee Heino
The Good, The Bad, And The Scandalous by Cora

Lee
  The Archer's Paradox by Ally Broadfield
  The Missing Duke by Heather King
  The Mercenary Pirate by Katherine Bone

Book 6: The Marquis of Thunder

The Marquis of Thunder
by
Susan Gee Heino

Threatened by violence and storm...
Miss Seraphina Janesley has her hands full.
There's war on the continent and a Luddite uprising
in the village. The river has flooded, Papa is ailing,
and her roof has blown off. Now their landlord--the
scandalous Marquis of Thunder--plans to host an
orgy in their crumbling home! What on earth is she
going to do? She'll make a bargain with the
Marquis, of course. A bargain that might cost her
dearly.

What she needs is a Hero.
Lord Thorston--called the Marquis of Thunder by
those who know his reputation--is not simply here
for a wild party. He's come to unmask a spy. As part
of a secret organization, Thorston is working to

protect the crown from those who conspire against it. Is Miss Janesley one of these foes? He'll have to get close to her to find out. In the end, though, will he be able to betray her, or will the gathering storm in his heart prove too much even for him?

Chapter One
April, 1813
Nottinghamshire, England

THE SKIES WERE seething with dark clouds. Distant thunder rolled over the surrounding hillsides, ominous in its persistence. The storm would be raging soon; it would show no deference for Lord Thorston, the infamous Marquis of Thunder.

Indeed, Thorston was about to get wet. He felt it in his bones.

His horse felt it, too. The elegant black shuddered with nervous energy. Thorston patted him for reassurance.

"We'll be there soon, long before the first drops, my friend."

His mount flicked his ears and tossed his dark head. Indeed, it wasn't raindrops the sleek warmblood feared, it was his namesake. When Thorston had named the colt five years ago he'd thought he was simply paying homage to his own unfortunate epithet. At the time he'd had no idea he was being ironically prophetic. Thunder, unfortunately, was terrified of thunder.

Thorston knew he had better get them both safely to Northgate Hall before the storm hit. He barely held his worried animal under control as it was. If they were out here much longer, Thunder was likely to go into a panic. Thorston touched his sides and gently urged him into a trot.

Rounding a sharp curve in the road, he was forced to pull up to a stop. Thunder champed and snorted as a too-near flash of lightning cut through the clouds. The corresponding thunder answered a few short seconds later. Progress, however, was impossible.

The roadway ahead seemed to be blocked by a flock of jostling sheep. One very determined collie dog darted about, keeping the flock tightly together, perfectly in the way. Thunder shied backward and Thorston calmed him as best he could, searching the steep banks on each side of the road for a possible escape.

The ancient roadway had been worn deep into the landscape. The earth rose up on either side, with decaying rock walls lining the rim above that. Tufts of grass spilled over the edge. There was no chance of getting a horse up out of the roadway here.

He could not reach Northgate Hall as he'd hoped. At this point, he'd be lucky to reach the village that lay between them and the ancient estate. But to get even as far as Little Crossing he still had to get past these damnable sheep.

Apparently he would have to convince Thunder to backtrack. They'd have to ride toward the storm for half a mile or so before they might find a way up, out of the rut and over the wall. And then they'd have to negotiate the soggy fields. The road they traveled on ran roughly parallel to the River Trent. This storm was not the first to pass through here in recent days and the river was already breaching its banks. The road was treacherous enough. Sending Thunder through open grazing lands would not make for quick headway.

It seemed there was no other route, though. He was about to turn the animal to retrace their steps when his eye caught on something. A lone figure appeared, rising up from a stooped position in the midst of the sheep. Not one of the local farmers as Thorston might have expected, but a woman. Instantly he worried that she was in danger, trapped by the agitated animals and likely to be trampled.

To his surprise, though, she whistled at the dog who immediately came to her aid and directed the sheep away from her. Unflustered, she stooped down again. Thorston sat up higher in his saddle to see what might have her attention in such a tenuous situation. He could not tell, so he nudged Thunder to move closer.

The horse was unsure, but trusted Thorston's leading and took a few hesitant steps. The dog glanced their way, but seemed to care only for the sheep. They pushed and pressed against each other, their noisy feet and worried cries only slightly louder than the gathering wind and distant thunder.

The woman, Thorston could see now, was down low in gap through the bank at the right side of the road. Apparently this was an area that was used as a crossing. The rock wall that lined the roadway was obviously a barrier that usually kept the sheep out of the road. Now, as the river on one side was rising the sheep needed to be moved to pasture on the other side. Something was blocking their passage. A gate, from what Thorston could see. It should be open, but it was not.

Why this lone woman was out here trying to repair it by herself, he had no idea. He could see easily, though, that she could use some help.

Whatever obstacle she struggled with seemed to be more than she could handle.

Thorston slid off of Thunder and prayed the horse wouldn't spook and bolt away. There was no telling how far the terrified animal would run without Thorston's governance. It was risky to leave him in the road now, but the pitiful sight of the woman—a young one, at that—struggling at the rock wall in the midst of all those nervous sheep was not something he could turn his back on.

If Fate had granted him anything, it was strong arms and a broad back. His tailor often complained of his less-than-elegant musculature and his own father chastised him for participating in frequent strenuous exercise unbefitting a gentleman. Thorston ignored them both, of course. His physique and his experience made him perfectly qualified to render assistance in this moment, and by God he would do so.

He only hoped it would be in time to avoid the tempest that blustered and swirled in the wall of dark clouds that roiled steadily toward them. Despite his broad back and generous stature, Thorston had no great desire to be drenched today. The unpleasant nature of his visit to this area was more than enough to have put him in a sour mood. The sooner he could get the young woman and her sheep out of his way, the sooner he could get himself and his horse to safety, then get on with his business.

Seraphina steadied her foot on the large, moss-covered rock and steeled herself for another try. The wind carried the scent of rain and the current of urgency. Any moment now the heavens would open and unleash their downpour. She had to get this gate open and drive the sheep up to higher ground.

Unfortunately, the rocks had tumbled, trapping the heavy wooden timbers that ordinarily would have been removable to allow passage. Unless she could miraculously shift the rocks, the whole lot of them would be trapped in this narrow gully as the river raged higher and higher over its banks. She knew this area flooded often and it had not been her intent to leave the sheep in the low pastures at this time of year.

But secrets had to be kept, so here she was tackling the problem long after she should have and totally alone. Papa's health had required her extra attention these last days, and she'd been especially mindful of that more than anything. He did *not* need to learn about things that might upset him. Such as a flock of sheep that had not been listed among their assets when she and their man of business tabulated their rents.

Ordinarily Seraphina would be opposed to any sort of deception, but Papa was so fragile, and their man of business assured her that this was the only way to make ends meet. Papa needed to feel calm and secure, he needed his physician and medicines, and Seraphina needed to do whatever it took to see that he got those things.

Surely the duke would not suffer if the rents he received from them were slightly less than usual. They had heard nothing from the man in years. She wondered if he would even notice if they did not bother to send the rent money at all.

But of course that would be dangerous, and this was not the time to court danger. With all that was going on—the war on the Continent, the war in America, the violence and unrest here between workers and mill owners—it was hardly the time to do anything but try to survive.

And that was getting harder every day. Papa's last two hired men had now come up missing—gone with no word and no warning. The household staff was down to a bare minimum, and Papa's meager investments had failed. If they lost the flock to flash flooding, it would send them into ruin. She'd already sold the wool—even though it was still on the sheep—to one of the local hosiers. How could she ever pay him back if they did not have the wool to give him?

But because they did not officially have these sheep, she couldn't very well go around begging for help with them. She really had made a fine mess for herself and now here she was, surrounded by animals much heavier than she while a raging storm bore down on them all. She had no one to turn to, just her own strength and Tess, her tireless sheepdog who was doing her best to keep the sheep under control even as a bright flash of lightning sizzled the air all around them.

The sudden shriek of a horse accompanied the flash, just moments before a loud boom of thunder rattled the earth. Seraphina jumped. The dog darted across the road to keep the sheep from erupting into mindless frenzy, but as the thunder rolled over the landscape the frantic effort seemed pointless. The sheep would rush back over the other bank and be trapped in the lower meadow, easy prey for the gluttonous river. As soon as this next downpour was unleashed, flooding would be inevitable and swift.

It appeared the only thing keeping the sheep from breaking past Tess now was the huge black horse that seemed to appear out of nowhere. He stood in the narrow road just slightly above them, his rider completely composed despite the tenuous situation. Seraphina shoved her damp, disheveled hair out of her face so she could get a better look. Had someone come to help her? One of the men from their village, perhaps?

No, the man on the horse was no one she'd ever seen before. No one from Little Crossing had ever cut such a fine—and enormous—figure. The stranger sat tall and straight on his stately mount, apparently impervious to the weather. The horse danced nervously, but the man kept him expertly in check. Even his hat sat obediently atop his head in elegant perfection, defying the wind. The man's cloak was as black as the horse and the multiple capes flapped like foreboding wings behind him.

Seraphina could not make out his features, but one distinguishing element caught her eye. The man, although clad in black on the huge midnight steed, was not a dark figure. It surprised her to note that beneath his raven top hat, he was crowned with a shock of wild, waving hair that was every bit as yellow as hers. It was almost as if some golden archangel had donned human attire and dropped from the heavens, assuming gentlemanly form.

Unfortunately, at this moment she didn't need an archangel or a gentleman. She needed someone who knew something about dislodging big rocks and keeping sheep from drowning. In her limited experience, she'd never found angels nor gentlemen to be particularly useful in either of these.

Apparently he was willing to give it a go. The man dismounted, his horse becoming noticeably more nervous with his absence. Seraphina half expected the animal to charge off in the other direction when the man dropped the reins and took a step toward her. It didn't bolt, though, which she counted as a testament to the man's horsemanship, or perhaps his ability to install dread in anyone who might wish to disregard his will.

"Are you having some trouble there?" he called. His voice boomed over the gusting wind and bleating sheep.

"I need to get the sheep into higher pasture," she yelled, hoping her own voice might somehow carry. "But I can't move the bar that is blocking our way. It's wedged under these rocks."

He must have understood because he glanced toward the low-lying meadow that the sheep had been in and nodded. Her collie growled low as the man advanced toward them. Seraphina murmured an admonition.

"Easy, Tess. I'll let you know when it's time to bite the fellow."

Tess dropped low to the ground, ears back, her gaze flicking warily between the man and sheep under her command. Seraphina had no doubt in her faithful canine. One motion from her—the slightest whistle—and Tess would forget herding duty and become a formidable protector. But how effective could it be against such a man?

His clothes and his voice gave the appearance of social standing, but his broad shoulders and strong stride hinted at a more physical power. The man was huge, and built as a laborer. Surely if he were so inclined, he just might be able to do something constructive for them. If he were not so inclined, however, Seraphina could be in for some trouble.

She was not quite sure what his inclinations were right now.

"A sturdy hammer might be useful for this," he said, uncomfortably near.

"It would," she agreed, standing as tall as she could and keeping eye contact with Tess. "But my hammer got caught when those rocks tumbled, pinning it as well as the bar that I need to move."

He leaned in, so close to her she could smell the scent of his soap. His shoulders practically blocked the light and his very nearness took her breath away. Before she could react to defend herself, he was reaching, stooping so that his face was almost against hers. She choked on her surprise, but as quickly as his action terrified her she realized what he was doing.

He had his hand on the shank of the hammer where it stuck out from under the pile. If she'd been in control of her tongue she would have reminded him that it was pointless, that she'd already tried—and failed—to remove it. When the rocks in the wall had tumbled, they'd trapped it securely. His attempt would be fruitless.

But she couldn't tell him that. The words simply wouldn't form as her eyes caught on his, locked in an uncomfortable but unbreakable union. In the icy blue depths she saw defiance, impatience, assurance, and perhaps even a touch of mirth. Was he enjoying his needless display of supposed superiority? Yes. The hint of a smile at the corner of his lip gave him away. He stared at her with the most annoying overconfidence.

Soon it would be her turn to smile when he tried to retrieve the hammer and found that, indeed, it was stuck. She smiled her own hint of a smile to imagine such a proud gentleman humiliated by a simple workman's tool. He would not be so smug then, would he?

Her imagining was short lived, though. The hammer, it seemed, was even more intimidated by him than she was. It didn't so much as try to frustrate his arrogance. With one effortless tug, the hulking stranger pulled the traitorous implement free of the rocks.

The hammer was his and he held it up before her. Lightning flashed through the darkening clouds. The man's golden hair tossed in waves with the wind. Thunder rumbled with the same timbre as his voice.

He grinned when he spoke. "I'm good with hammers. Now, how can I help you, little shepherdess?"

Order *The Marquis of Thunder*

About Vanessa Riley

Vanessa Riley worked as an engineer before allowing her passion for historical romance to shine. A Regency era (early 1800s) and Jane Austen enthusiast, she brings the flavor of diverse peoples to her stories. Since she was seventeen, Vanessa has won awards for her writing and is currently working on two series. She lives in Atlanta with her military man hubby and precocious child. You can catch her writing from the comfort of her southern porch with a cup of Earl Grey tea.

Books by Vanessa Riley
Madeline's Protector
Swept Away, A Regency Fairy Tale
The Bargain, A Port Elizabeth Tale, Episodes I-IV
Unveiling Love, A London Suspense Tale
Unmasked Heart, A Regency Challenge of the Soul Series
No Hiding for the Guilty, Book 5, The Heart of a Hero Series
Sign up at VanessaRiley.com for contests, early

releases, and more.

You can find me at: www.VanessaRiley.com or www.facebook.com/VanessaRileyAuthor/

Sign up for her newsletter to get access to free stories, giveaways, and more at:

www.VanessaRiley.com

If you like these stories, please leave a review.

I love being able to write these books. I hope you love them too. As an author, I depend on you, the reader, to get the word out about my books. If you liked this book, please leave a review online and recommend it to a friend. The more you spread the word, the more books I can write and nothing would please me more than to create more of these stories for you.

Thank you.

Vanessa Riley